Christmas at Whispering Hills

A BERKSHIRE ROMANCE

E.A. BRADY

SANDGATE EAST PUBLISHING

Dedication

This is for everyone who has encouraged me to keep at this writing gig.

I see you.

I appreciate you.

I love you like crazy.

And, as always, these stories are for my very own Happily Ever After Hero...

I couldn't do any of this without you.

And I wouldn't want to anyway! xo

Carson

T ALK ABOUT FEELING ALONE in a crowded room. If she squint- ed her eyes and blurred her vision, Carson Everett could almost convince herself that the family gathered for their annual Christmas party was her own. The women in their fancy outfits were her sister and their cousins. The older people, their parents and aunts and un- cles.

Almost.

Discarded wine glasses and beer bottles littered the tables. Plastic soda cups and empty coffee mugs covered the haphazard sprinkling of silver and gold glitter that spilled from beneath each small evergreen wreath centerpiece. Various members of the hotel banquet staff crept around the room, some clearing away dirty dishes or pushing in un- used chairs, others topping off supplies at the coffee station.

Melody Hatch-Stevenson, as primary decision maker for the family party, had agreed to hiring a magician, or as he preferred to be called, an illusionist, as entertainment this year. His act had been superb. More than once, Carson found herself watching him as he made a rabbit disappear and reappear, or when he transformed a red ball into a bright white dove.

As Event Coordinator for Southern Dreams Event Planning, Carson had overseen the Hatch Family Gala for close to ten years and had gained a level of closeness with several of the family members.

"Carson, you have outdone yourself yet again," Melody said, approaching Carson once the final round of applause for Gregory the Great had died down. The DJ started the music and people began to leave their tables to get out to the dance floor. "Gregory the Great was... Well, he was great!" Melody said with a big, open laugh.

"He was great, wasn't he?" Carson said.

The women stood together and watched Melody's parents move in a gentle dance toward the side of the dance floor, while some of her nieces and nephews, aunts, uncles, and cousins had the main floor hopping, somehow all moving at different tempos to the same song.

A distinct loneliness settled behind Carson's ribs, wishing it was her own parents and cousins strutting their stuff all over the dance floor. "I might be a little bit jealous," she said. Had she and Melody not become friends over the past decade, she never would have admitted that out loud to a client.

Melody's eyes popped open. "Jealous? Of these weirdos?" she said, jerking a thumb in the direction of the mass of bodies that moved like disparate parts of one off-rhythm beast.

Watching the gaggle of children run from table to table stealing candy from the dishes in the middle of each centerpiece pulled a smile from Carson as she imagined her own niece and nephew doing the same. She shrugged. "Yeah," she said. "They might be weirdos, but they're you're weirdos."

Melody looked thoughtful. "That they are." She playfully bumped shoulders with Carson. "What about your weirdos? Where are they?"

"Mine? They're all up in Massachusetts freezing their butts off. My sister told me they had almost six inches of snow Thanksgiving night."

"Oh, no," Melody said. "No snow for me, thanks."

Carson was quiet for a moment. "Thank you for being so flexible and keeping an open mind right from the get-go this year," she said.

Melody turned and pulled her in for a hug. "Everything was amazing, Carson. I never doubted you for a minute."

Carson laughed. "You might be the only one who didn't."

Melody let out a gasp as she released her hug, then stared at Carson with wide eyes. "Are you for real right now?" she said. "I am not kidding when I tell you this was the best party we've ever had. You listened to me, then you took my vision and ran with it." She gave Carson's arms a gentle squeeze. "I am already starting to think about what I want for next year, assuming you'll be the one to organize it."

"I don't see why I wouldn't be," Carson said. "Unless Anderson finally gives me the boot."

"He'd be an idiot to do that, and it would be one hundred percent his loss," Melody said, scrunching her nose in distaste for Carson's boss. "But I was thinking more along the lines of you finally getting out of there and hanging out a shingle for your own agency."

Carson had perfected the art of not appearing shocked, no matter what a client said to her, but she couldn't hold back the laugh that escaped. "Me? Open my own agency? In this town?" She shook her head and sighed. "Not while Southern Dreams is still the only real player in Savannah."

Working for Anderson had certainly given her reason to entertain the idea of quitting, but she'd never been able to work up the courage to open her own business. She enjoyed what she did so much, she'd learned to put up with Anderson and his perfectionist crap rather than find a new line of work.

"Selfishly, I'm glad to hear it," Melody said. "I'm going to ask for you specifically in the spring and we'll work on doing this—" she cast her glance around the room "—all over again." Melody's sister waved from her seat, calling Melody over to where she sat. "If you'll you excuse me," she said with a smile. "I have to go see what the queen would like."

With a noticeable spring in her step, despite the late hour, Melody Hatch-Stevenson disappeared into the crowd, her words of encouragement tucked into Carson's heart for when she might need them again.

Seeing her boss out of the corner of her eye, Carson knew right away he was on his way to her. Slipping her hand into her pocket, she flipped the small plastic container open and shook out two of the chalky antacids she always had on hand and tossed them into her mouth.

"Anderson," she said to the impeccably dressed man as he approached from the back of the room. "Was this one for the books, or what?"

"Ten minutes, Carson. That's how long they had to wait for their after-dinner coffee station to be set up," Anderson said, flipping his wrist and staring at his Rolex, as if Carson was unaware of how the passage of time was measured.

The feel-good bubble of a job well done burst as she crunched through her antacid tablet. Technically, he was right, but she also knew that not one single guest noticed or cared.

Dessert took longer to be served than they originally anticipated but by the time everyone had received their bread pudding with bourbon sauce or chocolate mousse with Irish cream drizzle, the event staff had caught back up. They had the coffee urns set up and the table laid with cups and creamers, sugars and stirring sticks, and every other thing a coffee station required.

Melody hadn't even noticed the delay. Apparently, Anderson was the only one bothered by it, and as usual, he made sure Carson knew how bothered he was.

Event planning was a science but there was also an art to it and sometimes art refused to stick to a schedule. "Come on, Anderson. Nobody even noticed it." When he stood there, unmoved by her logic, she added, "You know that managing people means having to allow for the unforeseen."

"It's our job—or, more precisely, *your* job, to foresee the unforeseen, Carson."

The knot in her stomach twisted tighter, pulling on every muscle in her body until she felt like an elastic band about to snap. "I understand that Anderson, but there was no way to foresee the few extra minutes the staff took to get out all the desserts for a group this size." She tried to keep her voice light, her tone upbeat. "It just happened. There's really no need to get worked up about it."

What she wanted to say was closer to *Shit happens. Sometimes you've got to lighten up and go with it*. But needing a job was more important than feeding her own ego at that moment.

Anderson dipped his chin, stared at her over the rim of his designer glasses. "I'm not *worked up*, Carson. I just have high expectations." The rest of the message was implied by his pinched facial expression. *Obviously, you failed to meet those expectations. Again.*

The uncomfortable standoff between them carried on an additional few seconds before the buzz of Carson's phone in her back pocket stole her attention. Glancing at the screen, she saw her sister's name and immediately feared something was wrong. She and Nicole hardly ever talked on the phone, and never that late at night.

Walking away from Anderson, she flicked her eyes to his. "I have to take this." The way his eyes squinted a fraction was Anderson's *pissed off* tell. He was not happy to be relegated as less important than whoever was on the other end of Carson's phone line. In his mind, Anderson wasn't less important than anyone. So that little angry-squinty thing he did released a hit of dopamine directly to her brain.

Straightening her spine as she walked away, she held the phone to her ear and headed through the ballroom doors, through the kitchen, and into the comparatively quieter back hallway. "Colie, what's the matter?" she said, using the pet name she'd had for her sister since the day Nicole was born. "Is everything all right?"

Nicole's sniffling was the first sign that everything was, in fact, not all right.

"Nicole, tell me what's wrong. Why are you crying? Are the kids all right?" All manner of catastrophe bubbled to the surface of her mind. "Are you OK? Did something happen to Mom and Dad?"

Nicole heaved a heavy sigh. "Everybody's fine," she said, then choked out a sob. "Except me, Cari. I'm not fine," she said through her tears. "I don't know how to be a single mom on regular days, but I have no freaking idea what to do at Christmas. How am I supposed to work and spend time with my kids, and find some way of taking care of them while they're home over their vacation, and bring them to all the holiday events, and do all the things they want to do... and I how the hell am I going to do any of it?"

As her rambling words petered out, Nicole gulped down a breath and started crying all over again. "I don't know what to do," she whispered.

Carson had always taken her role as big sister to heart; she was the one who always had it together and knew the right thing to do. Nicole was the baby, the free spirit who came and went as she saw fit, never giving much thought to the serious things in life.

Once Nicole had gotten married, responsibility for her shifted from Carson to Nicole's husband, Ian. For a few years, things went well for them. Or at least it seemed that way from the outside. Until the rat-bastard cheated on her and left her with two kids. Of course things would be different for them once he left.

An overwhelming surge of guilt washed over Carson for letting her own life get in the way of her family, and not checking in on them more often.

"Take a deep breath," Carson said, half to her sister and half to herself. "Everything's going to be fine."

"Is it?" Nicole asked. "How am I supposed to do all of this, Cari? How am I supposed to do any of it?"

"Colie," Carson said. "You're not giving yourself enough credit. You've been doing it for almost a year already. How did you manage over the summer having the kids home while you worked?"

Nicole sniffed and blew her nose again. "They went to Mom and Dad's."

Carson had known that but forgot, just one more thing about her family that had slipped her mind.

"Since they're going to see Aunt Peggy, they won't be home to take care of the kids. Mom offered to stay but I told her to go." Unexpectedly, Nicole giggled, a soft sound through her tears. "I mean... Peggy is like two hundred years old; this might be the last Christmas they get to spend with her." She let out a soft sigh. "I told Mom I'd be fine."

"But you're not fine," Carson said gently.

"No," she whispered. "I'm not."

"Don't worry, Colie, everything really will be OK. I promise."

Once the call ended, Carson pulled up her calendar for the next two months.

Now that the Hatch Family's party was finished, the next big events on Carson's schedule wouldn't be happening until after the first of the year. She made a short list of things she had to be in town for, then gave a thought as to who might be willing to stand in for her for a couple of weeks. Obviously not Anderson, but her friend and coworker Vanessa might be willing if Carson asked nicely.

Everything else that needed to be done could be handled remotely. She fired off a quick text to Vanessa, who was somewhere inside the ballroom at the moment. Within a few seconds Vanessa texted her response:

> Family first, sis. I've got your back. Do what you need to do.

Grateful for Vanessa's support, she crunched through another antacid, the small plastic bottle almost empty. She marched through the kitchen, pulled the ballroom doors open, and went to find Anderson to tell him the "good" news.

Carson

I T HAD BEEN YEARS since she'd driven in the snow, and even though the roads had been plowed, it added a whole other level of stress to the otherwise beautiful drive.

If not for the bright white moon reflecting off the snow, she wouldn't have seen much beyond the reach of her rental car's headlights. Even with the added lunar help, she missed a couple of turns and had to find driveways in which to turn around.

By the time she reached Vineyard Hill Road, her knuckles were white on the steering wheel and her back was as tight as a drum. Her antacids had run out halfway through the hour-long drive from the airport in Albany to the small western Massachusetts town of Hazelton.

Relief washed over her as she followed the gradual incline of the gravel road to Nicole's house, just before the dead-end road stopped.

On the right side of the road was a small ranch-style house that her GPS said was her destination. Directly across the street sat a large wood-sided building that could have been a barn except for the large front porch and glass-bordered doors. Almost hidden in the dark hung a small sign: *Whispering Hills Winery*.

Just past the winery sat a beautiful log home, two stories high with a wraparound porch and a garage, and a truck in the driveway. The home was nothing short of stunning and she wondered if it looked like a ski chalet on the inside as well. The whole area overflowed with that rustic charm of which New England had been given more than its fair share.

The three buildings were surrounded by hilly fields of snow-covered plants. Considering one of the buildings was a winery, she assumed the plants to be grape vines. Independent wineries and craft breweries were also not in short supply in these parts, so maybe they were barley or hops?

Despite the charm of her surroundings, something still felt off. Technically, the holiday season had only started three days ago, but something about being in the hilly terrain full of evergreen trees blanketed in snow brought her seasonal cheer to the surface and she realized exactly how dark her surroundings were.

She had passed one small house at the bottom of the hill that had been decorated with a few strands of white Christmas lights. However, neither Nicole's house, the winery, nor the log home seemed to know it was the time for festive cheer.

Aside from the porch lamp and the sliver of light that escaped through the closed curtains on the large picture window, Nicole's house was dark. As were the winery and the log home.

Snow was a natural sound absorber and the silence that greeted her as she stepped out of the small SUV made the darkness a touch deeper all around her.

Lugging her suitcase out of the trunk and slinging her backpack over one shoulder, Carson determined her first course of action for the next morning; find their outdoor lights and help her little family get their Christmas on.

"Oh my gosh, I'm so glad you could come," Nicole said, as she pulled Carson into a huge bear hug as soon as she walked in the door. "Thank you, Cari."

A small undecorated Christmas tree stood in one corner of the room, next to a line toys, that included a plastic refrigerator and oven, as well as a small wooden tool bench. The home was cozy and welcoming.

From their place bundled up on the couch across the room, Carson's niece, Lucy, and nephew, Drew, stared at her with wide eyes. It was Lucy who jumped up first, as the eight-year-old followed her mother's lead then wrapped her arms around Carson's waist.

"Hi, Sweetheart," Carson said, running a hand over Lucy's ponytail. "I've missed you." She squatted down to give the little girl a proper hug. Drew came close but stayed behind Lucy. "Hi, Drew. You probably don't remember me. I haven't seen you in a couple years, but I'm your Aunt Carson." Not wanting to scare the kid, she smiled but didn't attempt a hug. He nodded then reached out to hold onto Lucy's pajama sleeve.

"He's shy," Lucy said, appearing perfectly comfortable having her brother tag along with her. "But don't worry, he's really nice. Oh," she added, "and his tooth is starting to get wiggly."

Drew bared his teeth, stuck his fingers in his mouth and started to push on one of the little teeth in the front of his bottom jaw. "Ith thith one," he said around a mouthful of fingers.

"It's still got a ways to go, I think," Carson said, staring hard but noting that the tooth didn't appear to move in the slightest as he pushed and pulled on it. She smiled at the two of them, as sweet as sweet could be, and felt a pang of protectiveness spike through her as she wondered how the hell Ian could have chosen his stupid girlfriend over his own children.

"All right, you two, let Auntie take off her coat and get warm," Nicole said, looking down on the little trio. She helped Carson stand, took her coat and her backpack, and said, "You're staying in the guest room. It's just down the hall here."

Wheeling her suitcase behind her, Carson followed Nicole toward her new digs. Lucy walked alongside her. "It's going to be my room soon," she said. "For my next birthday, Mama said we can paint the walls and move my bed into there."

From behind the little group, Drew piped up. "Then I'll have my own room, too." Carson smiled at the sandy haired six-year-old and hoped he would get that new room.

"Up until a month ago, I'd been using this space as a studio," Nicole said. "But now that I have my store up and running, I do a lot of my work down there." Her words were optimistic but the feeling behind them felt a bit unsure. Asking how the store was doing would have to wait until the kids weren't around, just in case it wasn't going well.

Nicole hustled the kids out of the bedroom, leaving Carson alone to unpack. The trundle mattress under the day bed had been pulled up to make a king-sized bed that took over a good portion of the small room. She unpacked her suitcase, refolding her clothes and placing most things into the bureau opposite the bed. She hung the few hangable things in the closet and set up her toiletries on the small bedside table.

Once Carson finished unpacking and changing into her comfiest, and warmest, sweats, she returned to the living room. Lucy and Drew were snuggled up on the couch, big sister reading a Christmas story to her younger brother, who sat in rapt attention at every word she read.

"They're really something, aren't they?" Nicole said as Carson approached the kitchen. The sisters stood together as they watched the lovely little scene. Beside her, Nicole sniffed and when Carson turned, tears were rolling down her sister's cheeks.

"Are you OK, Mama?" Lucy asked, as she closed the book and peered through the doorway.

Nicole quickly wiped her eyes. "Of course, sweetheart. I just love it when you two read together. It makes me really happy."

The children may not have understood the strain in their mother's voice, but Carson did. Despite Anderson's protests and borderline threats of termination, she had made the right decision to come back to Massachusetts.

"Who wants Aunt Cari to read bedtime stories tonight?" Carson asked.

Lucy said, "Will you read like Granddad?"

Unsure what that meant, Carson glanced at Nicole.

"He does all the different voices when he reads," Nicole whispered.

"Absolutely," Carson said to the kids, leaving the kitchen and working up her most enthusiastic voice. "I love doing the voices. I used to do all the voices when I'd babysit your mom and I would read to her before bed." The five-year age gap between them meant that Carson was often called on to babysit, and any babysitter worth their salt knew enough to do the voices.

Lucy's eyes lit up. "Mama let me babysit Drew once, too!"

"Yeah," Drew said, clearly wanting to back up his big sister, who only had two years on him. "And she always does the voices, too!"

"That's awesome," Carson said. "Why don't you go brush your teeth and I'll meet you in your room in like five minutes."

The kids bolted out of the room to get ready for bed. Nicole chuckled behind her. "I literally left them alone for about five minutes when I ran across the road to give my landlord the rent check. The way they tell it, I took a vacation to the Bahamas and left my eight-year-old in charge for the week."

Carson laughed. "Don't worry. I figured it was something like that." She took a step toward the hallway. "You know, it's amazing how much they look like you when you were little."

"You think so? I always thought they favored Ian more than me," Nicole said.

"Maybe a hint around the eyes but other than that, they are carbon copies of you. Even more than that, they are amazingly sweet and kind. And that's exactly how you were." She pulled Nicole in for a quick hug. "Still are."

"I HOPE IT'S ALL right," Carson said when she returned to the living room twenty minutes later. "I read them each a story they chose and then we read one more that we all wanted."

From her seat, cocooned in a blanket on the couch, Nicole laughed. "They may be just like me but you are just like Dad."

Carson thought about that for a few seconds. "I've definitely been told worse things about myself." Despite the heat in the house, Carson shivered because she still struggled to keep warm.

Already feeling at home, she grabbed the Afghan from the back of the overstuffed chair and threw it over her lap as she sat. Immediately she stood back up. "I think I need a cup of tea," she said, walking to the kitchen. "Can I get you one?"

"That sounds nice," Nicole said. "Cups are over the microwave and teabags are in a box on top of the fridge."

When both cups were ready, Carson handed one to Nicole.

"Thank you." She accepted the cup and perched it on her knees, staring at it like she was about to tell it something important. "Do you know how long it's been since anyone got me a cup of tea?" she said, still looking at the steaming mug.

"Since Ian left?" Carson asked, her voice just above a whisper.

Nicole shrugged, shook her head gently. "Nope," she said. "I don't actually know when the last time was." She looked up at Carson. "He never made me tea. Or did much of anything for me, actually."

Carson's mouth hung open before she remembered her manners, then took a small sip of tea as she sat down. She'd assumed they were madly in love with each other at the beginning and did things for each other the way their parents always had. "Really?"

Nicole huffed out a small, humorless laugh. "Aside from giving me those two amazing humans in the other room, he didn't add all that much to this marriage." She shifted her gaze from Carson to the mug of tea in her hands and sat silently for a few seconds. "How the hell am I supposed to do any of this by myself?"

Carson expected her to start crying but Nicole just sat, silently staring into the swirls of steam rising off her mug.

This was where Carson felt the most comfortable—being present and willing and able to lend a hand. Even if only for a few weeks. Christmas could be a hard enough season to get through, and if she could help Nicole get to the other side and see what an amazing mom and artist and sister and daughter she was, Carson would consider the risk to her job more than worth it.

And it's not like there was anyone at home waiting for her to get back.

"Do you hear from him at all?" Carson ventured to ask between sips of gingerbread vanilla tea.

With a deep sigh, Nicole shook her head again. "Not really," she said. "He calls the kids now and again. They FaceTime every once in a while. Nothing on the regular though."

Clearly the topic of Ian wasn't a good one. Carson's blood boiled at the lack of involvement of her former brother-in-law in the lives of his own children. Nicole didn't need Carson's thoughts on the situation because they wouldn't be very constructive anyhow, so she held her tongue. "How's the store going?"

Nicole had chosen to move to Hazelton because she was able to find an affordable storefront on the main street of town where she could move forward with her dream of owning her own store. Earlier in the year she had opened Happenstance, an eclectic mix of pieces created by local artists, including herself, that she sold through consignment.

"Ummm..." Nicole said. "It's doing OK. I wish it was doing a little better but I was warned when I signed the lease that October and November could be a little slow until ski season kicks in. Summer tourists are gone and the snow bunnies haven't gotten here yet. Although the leaf peepers were around and kept me busy for a couple weeks, so that was nice. And since it snowed early this year, maybe the ski season will start early too?"

"What about your online store?" Carson had tried to get her sister to open an online shop, either through an established selling site or just through her own website. It would increase the visibility of her little shop, opening it up to anyone, anywhere she was willing to ship.

Nicole's shoulders slumped. "I haven't given it much thought. I'm sorry. I know you were trying to help but... I just didn't have it in me to add another thing to my plate."

"No," Carson said. "Don't be sorry. I was just making conversation." She jerked her thumb at the television. "You got Netflix on that thing? I'm sure we can find something fun to take our minds off things for a while."

For the first time since Carson arrived, Nicole smiled. A feeble, exhausted, half attempt, but it was a smile nonetheless. "That would be nice." She grabbed the remote, turned on the TV and started scrolling.

There was nothing Carson could do to affect Ian and his less than admirable choices but there had to be something she could do for Nicole. She would be there until just after New Year's to be with Lucy and Drew so Nicole could keep her store open extended hours.

Surely there was more Carson could do. Something tangible.

Tom

Tom Wyatt accepted the half-full shot glass from his friend's outstretched hand, held it to his nose and breathed in the sweet scent of maple. He raised his eyebrows and looked at Will over the rim of the glass.

Leaning back in the leather chair like he was getting comfortable in his own home, and not sitting in Tom's living room, Will looked back and grinned then nodded as a way to tell Tom to take a sip.

Closing his eyes to focus his concentration, Tom tipped the glass to his lips and let a few drops of the maple whiskey coat his tongue. The distinct sweetness of the maple complemented the slight burn of the alcohol, and after a few seconds, he picked up a subtle hint of smoke. *Damn, that was good.*

"Donny Weaver really made this?" Tom said, still savoring the exquisite taste of their friend's first batch of small still whiskey. "That little bastard really made something as good as this?" Holding up the shot glass in the soft light of the table lamp, he admired the amber liquid inside.

The hockey game played on the TV opposite the couch where Tom sat, the warmth of the room in direct contrast to the crisp winter evening outside. Leather furniture and wood floors absorbed the heat from the woodburning stove in the corner and kept the temperature comfortable.

With his ever-present smile, Will nodded. "It's good, isn't it? I told you it would be."

It was more than good. It was fucking brilliant. And the fact that their buddy was able to grow from a small scale winery to a small still distillery that crafted the maple whiskey in his hand in such a short time only fueled Tom's desire to do the same.

"It's way better than good," Tom said, tipping the glass and emptying it in one swallow. He grabbed the bottle from the coffee table and refilled both his and Will's glasses before he took a closer look at the label. "Shit, even the label looks good," he said taking in the clever illustration of Donny himself sitting in front of a weaving loom on the cream-colored label. "His wife did that?"

As if Tom needed another reason to be jealous of Donny, who'd found a great woman, while Tom's divorced ass worked all alone day after day. Working with Will was great but it was not the same thing. At all.

"She did," Will said.

Tom took another sip, savored the taste all over again. "You said he did this in only a year?"

Will leaned forward, rested his elbows on his knees. Both men had lost any interest in hockey as they focused their energy on the potential business venture in front of them. "Yep. Took him just under twelve months to get from nothing to that," he said, pointing to the bottle. "So... what do you think? Are we doing this, or what?"

Tom had been the sole owner of the Whispering Hills Winery for the past six years. Technically, five, since his ex-wife was co-owner for the first year. Since she'd gone, most of his time had been devoted to learning and perfecting his craft and producing the best wines possible. He primarily used grapes from his own vineyard combined with a variety of fruits from local growers.

The addition of a distillery to the property, even with Will coming on board to help, would add a whole other dimension to the business. Increasing production from strictly wine to include a selection of whiskeys and other spirits would be no small undertaking. It would be expensive. And time-consuming. And a hell of a lot more work than he was currently doing.

After tossing back the rest of the shot of whiskey, he thumped the glass on the table and held Will's gaze. "I submitted the application to the state two weeks ago. We should be hearing back before the first of the year," he said. "If Donny Weaver can do this, we can sure as hell do this."

Will's face went slack before he clapped his hands together. "Yes!" He jumped up from his chair, spun around in a half circle as if he was looking for something. Not finding whatever it was, he plunked his butt back in the chair, his eyes wide and round. He clenched his hands into fists then released them and clapped them together again. "Fuck yeah!"

Despite the calming effect of the alcohol, Tom's heart rate ticked higher at the thought of the opportunity—and the work—before them. "You think we'll still be friends if we partner up on this?" It was a stupid question; the two of them had been working toward this exact moment for the last four years, at least. They were about to embark on the natural next step of their journey toward becoming small still distillers.

"Hell yeah," Will said. "You know how it goes. You're the brains, I'm the brawn. Together, we're going to give Donny Weaver a fuckin' run for his money." With a laugh, he added, "But not for at least another year or so."

"And we'll be able to get enough people on board to help harvest?" Tom asked, mentally running the numbers again. Knowing how much of an outlay this distillery was going to be, he couldn't forget to factor in some additional labor costs.

The play-by-play guy on the television yelled when someone scored a goal. Will flicked a glance in that direction, but even that bit of good news couldn't distract him for long. "We'll figure it out," he said, turning back to Tom. "Even if it's me and you out there to start. Hell, I've got five brothers with wives and kids. I'll put all their asses to work." He tipped back the remainder of his shot glass. "Even the babies!"

How Will's parents raised six boys would forever be a fascinating subject to Tom. Coming from a family of two, with just one older sister, a house with that much testosterone must have been chaos from sunup to sundown. For years at a time. He shuddered at the thought.

"We've also got to find a local supply of apples, plums, and, obviously, maple syrup," Tom said.

Will's legs bounced like he was waiting for a starting gun to sound. "Don't worry about it. We'll find all that stuff. I've done a little looking around and we should be able to work with some farms in New York and Vermont. There's even a couple in New Hampshire if we need them. Whatever it is we've got to have, we'll find it. And, hey, who knows? Maybe you can buy a few bar stools and take advantage of the liquor license you already have and don't use."

Will knew that was a sore spot and he chose to poke it anyway. "Seriously?" Tom said.

"What? You've got the license. You've got the bar. All you need is someplace for people to sit, and they might actually use it."

Tom bristled, his shoulders getting tighter by the second. "Yeah," he said. "But who the hell's going to work it?"

Will threw his hands in the air, obviously exasperated. "Who knows! Hire someone. Or open once a week for a few hours and do some wine tasting. Then when the distillery's up and running you can add the whiskey too." He dropped his head back, stared at the ceiling. "Why are you so against doing more with that place? You could make a killing over there."

The idea of more customers sounded good in theory, but with the winery, the distillery, and then throwing in the potential of a tasting room, Tom was quickly running out of hours in his day. He left his job back in Boston because he'd burned out on it—big time. The niggling worry snuck into his brain that he might be courting the same disaster all over again.

On the flip side was all the learning he'd get to do. Adding the distillery to his current business was a puzzle he couldn't wait to dig into. But would it be worth the headache of an increased customer base? There were just so many things to think about.

Slow-moving tires crunched over the snowy gravel of the dead-end road outside. Aside from Tom's house and the winery next to it, he also owned the small ranch house directly across from the winery. About six months ago, he had rented out the house to a woman and her two kids. Whenever there was traffic on the road at night, it was always them and he'd learned to ignore it.

Will, on the other hand, never missed an opportunity to take a peek when he heard the car drive up.

"You expecting company?" Will asked. Approaching the window, he pulled the heavy curtain back to get a better look.

"Just you," Tom said. "And since you're already here..."

"Don't be a smartass." Will angled his head, staring harder out the window.

Tom shook his head. "Why don't you just ask her out?" Will's crush on the woman across the road was a secret to nobody—except the woman across the road. "She seems like a nice enough person."

Visibly shocked, Will dropped the curtain back into place as he turned to Tom. "I'm not asking her out. I've never even talked to her." He pulled the curtain open and peered out the window again. "Besides, that's not her."

From his seat on the couch, Tom said, "Yeah? Who's out there then? Some other guy finally ask her out because you're too chicken shit to talk to her?"

"Fuck you, dude, I'm not afraid to talk to her. I just haven't happened to bump into her yet."

It didn't matter that Will was at the winery or Tom's house at least three or four times a week and they'd seen her out there countless times. Tom laughed as Will craned his neck to keep watching his neighbor's visitor, most likely hoping it wasn't some guy.

"Ha!" Will said, throwing a satisfied glance over his shoulder. "Fuck you again, it's not a guy. It's a girl."

Finally standing to watch the goings-on outside his window, Tom followed Will's line of sight to a woman approaching the small house across the street, her silhouette outlined by the yellow front porch light.

"She's kinda bundled up," Will said. "But she's got hips and probably a nice ass from the looks of it."

Pulling Will away from the window with another laugh, Tom said, "Brother, you can't even ask out the one woman you like. Take a breather from adding new ones to the list." He grabbed the whiskey bottle, topped off both their glasses, and sat back down to watch the rest of the game, relieved to be done with the conversation about expanding his business.

"Who do you think she is?" Will said, without removing his gaze from the television. "You don't think Nicole's into girls, do you?"

Tom almost choked on his drink. "Jesus, Will, just say hi to the woman the next time you see her. She's out there with her kids all the time."

His eyes fixed on the screen, Will ignored Tom's suggestion. Instead, he asked, "How come you never asked her out?"

Tom rested his head against the wall behind him. "You mean aside from the fact that she's my neighbor and technically my tenant? Or the fact that she has two kids? Oh, and let's not forget about my track record with women being zero for one." He tipped his glass and emptied it in one mouthful. "And one failed marriage is more than enough for me."

Will skipped over Tom's comment about his failed marriage to Heather and focused on one of his other reasons. "You really aren't interested because she's got kids?" he asked. "I think kids would be pretty cool."

To say he spent exactly no time thinking about his neighbor would be an understatement. They said hello to one another occasionally, and she had been into the winery for a bottle of wine a couple times or to drop off her rent check, but there was never any spark of anything between them.

She was polite. He sold her a bottle of wine or accepted her check. End of story. The only time he spent thinking about her at all was when Will showed up and wouldn't stop talking about her.

"Kids are fine, I guess," Tom said. "I got nothing against them." Since he had to work in the morning, he stuck the cork back into the whiskey bottle. "Just not really interested in any of my own." At one point, he and Heather had talked about having kids, but that was before his abrupt career change from bio-tech researcher to small town vintner, and their subsequent divorce.

He had always thought of the move as a way out of his career burnout, but rather than understand how miserably unhappy he was doing that kind of work, she often accused him of simply giving up on their life together, and she'd said she wasn't willing to do that.

ONCE THE FINAL BUZZER sounded and the game ended, Will took off, leaving Tom to think over everything they'd talked about that night. As he walked by the living room window, he couldn't help but take a peek across the road. The new car was still in the driveway, meaning his neighbor's guest was probably there for the night.

Not that it mattered. What happened over there was none of his business. Whoever the newcomer was, she meant nothing to him. Even if her silhouette was intriguing, making him think she probably did have a nice ass. It was still none of his business who she was or why she was there. He had enough to worry about.

Carson

D ESPITE SLEEPING IN A bed that wasn't her own, Carson had slept well and the warmth and coziness of the pile of comforters had her clicking snooze a few times before the aroma of coffee wafting in from the kitchen was too much to withstand.

"Cell service isn't the best here," Nicole said as she scribbled directions to the kids' school on a piece of notebook paper. "And don't forget to follow the line of cars around to the front of the building. I already left a message with the front office, so they won't think you're trying to steal my kids or anything." The relief on Nicole's face was a welcome change from the tension Carson had seen there the night before. "You're sure you don't mind picking them up so I can stay at the shop a little later?"

Carson waved away her sister's concerns. "As long as nobody thinks I'm kidnapping these two and I don't get arrested, the rest of my day will be cake." She winked at Lucy, who stood by the door with her backpack on, holding Drew's hand. "Right, Luce? We got this."

Lucy smiled and nodded, so Drew did too.

Once Nicole and the kids left, Carson finished her coffee, then spent a couple hours getting some work done. Anderson would be checking in most days, if not every day, and she didn't want to give him anything to complain about.

Reopening a browser window, she did a quick search through a few different website hosting providers, none of which looked particularly difficult to set up. Most of them had built-in functionality for opening an online store that could be up and running within an hour.

Feeling confident in her ability to get Nicole set up with a retail site before she returned to Savannah, Carson ate a quick bowl of cereal, threw on some warm clothes, and headed out to the garage to get started on her big day of decorating.

Stepping into the attached garage, she suddenly understood why Nicole parked her car in the driveway. Piles of boxes and plastic bins, loads of black trash bags and random art supplies filled the entire space where the car should be parked. She steeled herself for the work that lay ahead of her.

Carson thought about texting her sister to find out which of the containers held the Christmas lights but decided against it since she wanted it to be as much of a surprise for Nicole as it would hopefully be for Lucy and Drew.

Not wanting to completely invade her sister's privacy, she felt around a few of the trash bags, which all felt soft but heavy, like they were filled with blankets or off-season clothes, and moved them off to the side of the garage to make some space in the middle from which to sort decorations.

A couple of boxes had been labeled with heavy, dark marker in handwriting she didn't recognize as Nicole's. Clearly, Ian had labeled the contents of those boxes. His books and CDs filled one box while some hand tools and random crap filled another.

Barely quelling the urge to carry those boxes to the back yard and set them on fire, she shoved them along the wall next to the trash bags and continued her search for Christmas lights.

Having not had much luck with the cardboard boxes, she decided to start opening and looking through the plastic bins. Along the back wall, a steel shelving system had been loaded with bins and she scanned them to see if any had been labeled with their contents. With the exception of one on the very bottom labeled *Nicole's Art Stuff*, the rest were as much a mystery as Nicole's taste in men.

Storing the Christmas lights on the bottom shelf would have made her life far too easy, so she wasn't surprised when all she found there were some old baby clothes, more art supplies, and a container with what looked like Ian's shoes. Why the hell Nicole had so many of Ian's belongings was beyond her, but it wasn't her place to throw it in the garbage can any more than it was her place to use his things to start a bonfire that might finally warm her frozen bones.

But it wouldn't take much to convince her.

Shoving Ian's things to the side, she made space to place one foot and hoist herself up to grab hold and yank down a bin. It was surprisingly heavier than she expected it to be. "Shit!" she yelled as the weight of the bin launched her backwards from her perch and sent her sprawling onto the concrete floor, crashing onto her hip with a painful thud.

After slowly getting back to her feet, she gingerly moved her leg, checking to make sure she hadn't broken anything. Certain she'd have a bruise on her ass cheek by the end of the day, if not by the end of the hour, she briefly entertained the thought of going back into the house for an ibuprofen, or four, and skipping the whole decorating the house thing. Until she saw what spilled from the bin onto the floor beside her, and her heart lifted.

Dark green strings of lights lay tangled in a big ball, some wrapped among green, plastic garland, and some in tight messes of chaos. Her quick high crashed as she realized how much work it was going to be getting all those strings separated out.

With a sigh, she set to work. After what felt like an hour, she managed to get one whole string freed from its captivity and hurried to get it out to the front yard. She would have run it out there, but her hip was aching so much it was more of a fast hobble. Which wouldn't have been so bad except she tripped over another of Ian's boxes and, with another loud curse, crashed down onto her knees, not using her hands to catch herself so she didn't break her recently liberated string lights.

"I am too freaking old for this," she said, pushing herself up to standing and brushing dust from her pant legs. With one foot she swept the contents of the box into a pile, not caring if she broke things that belonged to Ian, but careful not to break any bulbs. As she squatted down to shove Ian's belongings into the box, another bin caught her eye from the third shelf up on the right. *Santa*. That looked promising.

With one bruised hip and two smarting knees she navigated the maze of Nicole's garage, gently stepped onto a lower bin and reached for the *Santa* box. Pulling it down without any additional injuries, she laid it on the floor and smiled when she saw the contents; several coils of rope lights and a sign that read, *Santa! Stop Here!*

Taped to the inside of the lid were the instructions for setting up a landing strip on the front lawn for Santa Claus. In Ian's scrawl were written the words, "Front yard! Next year!"

"I can do you one better. Jerk," she said as she read the directions, then stood, grabbed a ladder, and took her newfound treasures to the yard.

Getting the ladder situated safely against the house took longer than she anticipated but once she was sure it wasn't going anywhere, she climbed up, put the rope lights on the roof and tossed up a box of clips to attach them to the shingles.

Carson had never been afraid of heights but climbing on the roof in twenty-five-degree weather with a stiff breeze was perhaps not her favorite thing. But if Ian wasn't there to do it, someone would have to, and with Nicole working and their father on the way to Aunt Peggy's house in Pennsylvania, that someone would have to be her.

With a deep breath for extra courage, she popped a quick antacid and climbed up onto the roof, crawling slowly on sore knees, dragging her decorations along with her.

"There's a reason I have a crew to do this stuff," she mumbled as she crawled to the far end of the house, making a mental note to thank her crew profusely when she got back to Savannah... assuming Anderson didn't actually follow through on his threat of firing her if even one thing went wrong on the two events she'd left in Vanessa's charge. But that was a problem for another day.

Creating the landing strip would have gone faster if her fingers hadn't been stiff from the cold, but even so, it looked pretty cool. The low slope of the roof made a perfect landing spot for the big man when he made his appearance, and the strips of red and green lights would no doubt excite the kids.

She'd been feeling pretty good about herself until she realized she'd neglected to bring up an extension cord to plug it all in.

As she neared the edge of the roof to climb back down the ladder, a gust of wind blew up and threw her into a mild panic. She dropped flat on her belly, legs dangling over the edge, terrifyingly aware that she couldn't feel a ladder beneath her feet. Flailing her legs, she sought the sturdy aluminum frame she needed to get off the roof. Then, with a loud ping that only comes from a plastic boot heel against aluminum, her only way off the roof drifted in slow motion away from the house, landing flat on the lawn.

"Dammit!" Carson scurried back onto the roof; eyes wide as she looked down to where she wanted to be. On the ground. Not on the roof. Grabbing her cell phone, she scrolled to Nicole's contact info, but her finger hovered over the call button. The whole point of Carson being there was to be helpful, not cause more stress to her already overwhelmed sister. Unless there was absolutely no other option, she would put off making that call.

The only problem was that she didn't know anyone else to call. Which meant she would have to call the local police. *Ugh*. Not how she wanted to spend her day. Resigned to the humiliation of needing to call for help, she readied herself to dial.

The wind gusted again and, afraid of getting a quick and painful trip off the roof, Carson laid flat on her back. She felt her phone slip from her frozen grip. Frantic to keep it from sliding straight off the roof, she threw herself after it but wasn't fast enough. This time it wasn't in slow motion. It was the blink of an eye, and her phone was gone, making a soft whooshing sound as it landed in the snowy shrub below.

Tom

THERE WAS STILL ALMOST a month before Christmas and the seasonal uptick in customers kept Tom busy inside the store, but that didn't stop the chores he had to keep up with outside as well. By early afternoon, the store had quieted down and from experience he knew it would likely stay that way until the early evening. Throwing on a hat and a heavy coat, he went outside to dump crushed stones into the holes that had formed in the gravel parking lot.

His tenant's house was normally quiet during the day, so the slight commotion of the woman in the yard carrying armloads of Christmas lights caught his attention, but only for a few seconds. With a noticeable limp, she staggered across the yard, dumped the lights onto the ground and turned back, still limping, toward the garage.

Leaving her to her work and ignoring his own curiosity about where the limp came from, he returned to the task at hand. Rounding the back of the barn-turned-storefront with a five-gallon bucket, he dumped a few shovelfuls of crushed stone into it. As he carried it back to the parking lot, he couldn't help but notice the ladder propped against the house and the limping woman crawling around the roof.

As the owner of the property, he wasn't sure if that would put him at a liability if she somehow managed to fall off. Judging by the shakiness in her movements, that wasn't an impossibility. In fact, it was more like a certainty. Looking closer, he wondered what she was doing clipping straight rows of lights on the flat surface of the roof; it was an odd way to hang lights to be sure.

Bracing himself against the gusting wind, he pulled his collar higher around his neck and his hat lower over his ears. He heard the clang as her foot hit the ladder. From his vantage point leaning against his porch railing, he watched the woman scramble away from the edge of the roof, the ladder now flat on the ground. To make matters worse, she pulled out her cell phone and just as quickly watched it slip out of her hands, down the slope of the roof, and land in the small evergreen bush in front of the house.

His eyes may not have been as sharp as they used to be, but he knew it was not his tenant crawling around the roof, so that left nobody but her visitor.

Work as a small business owner was never ending. Chores didn't do themselves, wine didn't bottle and sell itself, and clearly his tenant's guest couldn't save herself. With a grunt, he dropped the bucket, leaned the shovel against the porch, and stomped across the road to prevent himself a lawsuit.

The woman's head lifted as Tom's boots crunched through the snow. "Oh, thank God," she said, crawling closer to the edge. "Can you—"

"Stop!" he yelled. "Back up, please. That's technically my house you're crawling all over and I can't have you flying off it like that cell phone over there." He flung his arm in the direction of the evergreens. "Not interested in having a lawsuit on my hands."

"Right," she said as she stilled her movements. "This is so embarrassing. I'm really sorry. If you could just put the ladder back."

Already moving toward it, he lifted it from the yard and propped it against the edge of the roof. Without saying anything, he braced the ladder and held it while he waited for her to begin her descent.

After scooting on her ass across the roof toward him, she flipped onto her hands and knees. She hissed out a quick breath, as if she was in pain, and her limp came to mind, which he summarily dismissed because none of what was happening was any of his business. Getting her off the roof was his only concern.

"You don't have to hold it," she said as her first foot landed on the top rung. "I can get down from here."

"Sorry. Remember the whole lawsuit thing? This ladder is sitting on hard snow. If it slips and you fall, I'm liable." Bracing one side of the ladder with his boot, he held the sides steady as she continued her way down, step by step until her ass was at his eye level.

He reminded himself that once this woman was on solid ground, she was no longer his concern, despite the enjoyment of seeing her ass up close. With his focus where it shouldn't be, he lost his grip on the ladder and it slid a little to the side, causing the woman to scream and him to reach out to steady the whole mess by grabbing the ladder with one hand and her ass with the other to keep her from falling off.

Like her body was on fire, he yanked his hand from her as she hopped off the last rung. "You all right?" he asked, hoping she wouldn't sue him for sexual harassment now. "Didn't mean to grab you like that. Just didn't want you to fall."

"Right," she said, yanking her coat down to cover her hips. "No lawsuits. So you've said."

The discomfort between them hung heavy in the air. She didn't seem the type to suffer strange men grabbing her ass, even if said man was trying to prevent her bodily injury. And he certainly wasn't the type to go around grabbing women by the ass, but how could he explain that to her after that was exactly what he did?

"So, who are you?" he finally said as he pulled the ladder away from the house. "And why were you climbing on the roof?" As he carried the ladder back toward the garage, she hurried behind him.

"I'm staying here with my sister for a little while. She lives here. Nicole Jensen? She and her kids rent this house and I'm just here to help them out for a few weeks. I'm just lending a hand, helping her get through the holidays, you know?" Her voice was cheery and friendly and trying way too hard. As if she hadn't been seconds away from falling off a roof on his property.

"Well, Nicole's sister, I own this house and I need to ask you to refrain from climbing on the roof anymore." He entered the garage and stepped over and around an incredibly chaotic collection of boxes and bags to stand the ladder against the wall.

"I was just putting up a runway so that Santa would know where to land. It's so dark up here at night, I wanted to give my niece and nephew one less thing to worry about without their dad here." Still cheery but laced through with a trace of something else. Anger? Frustration? Didn't matter. None of it was his business.

Leaving the ladder where it was, he turned to leave and get back to his own work when the woman grabbed the ladder and started carrying it right back out of the garage.

"Where are you going with that?" Tom asked, his irritation with this woman steadily rising.

"Well, since lights need electricity to work, I have to hook up the extension cord," she said, her own irritation now dripping from every word.

Taking the ladder from her hands, he said, "I can't let you do that." He made it two steps back into the garage before her grip on the ladder stopped him in his tracks. She wasn't giving up on this project and he begrudgingly admired her spirit. Even if he couldn't let her go through with it.

"Are you for real right now?" she said, both hands gripping the rungs of the ladder. "I'm not going back onto the roof," she said. "I just have to bring the extension cord up and plug the lights in. And I need the ladder to reach." This time there was no forced cheer in her voice, only challenge.

For the first time, he held eye contact with her, each of them daring the other to say or do something. Her pink nose and cheeks almost overshadowed the intensity of those eyes, brimming with fire, and he had a feeling this was a woman used to getting her own way when she wanted something. But this was his house and giving in to her held nothing but the potential for trouble.

He answered her the only way he could. "You grab the extension cord. I'll go up the ladder." When he tried to walk, her grip on the ladder held it, and him, in place. "What now?" he said.

"I am perfectly capable of climbing up a ladder to plug in some stupid Christmas lights." One hand was fisted on her hip as she stared at him, challenged him. "I don't need you to come along, being all chivalrous to keep me from hurting my delicate little self."

He sucked in a quick breath and huffed it out, suppressing the grin that threatened. "My house, my insurance, my rules," he said, as he dislodged the ladder from her hand and walked toward the open garage door. "Besides—" he grabbed the coiled-up extension cord from the shelf with his free hand on his way out, "didn't anyone tell you; chivalry is dead."

Carson

"I'M SORRY I DIDN'T get any of the new lights up this afternoon," Carson said to Nicole as they sat down together in the living room in front of a crackling fire. After her ridiculous encounter with the guy across the street, she'd hopped into her rental and gone to the nearest Target. It hadn't been her original plan, but it turned out to be so much easier than untangling the rat's nests of lights still in the garage.

The dishwasher whirred from the kitchen, the sisters had changed from daytime clothes to end-of-the-day sweats, and after conning Carson into reading four bedtime stories, Lucy and Drew were finally asleep.

"I really wanted to have them all up and shining to surprise the kids but it's amazing how fast you run out of time when you have to pick them up at three o'clock." She left out the part about being stranded on the roof and then rescued by the stupidly handsome neighbor.

"Tell me about it," Nicole said with a laugh. "I can't wait to see their faces when they get to see the house all decked out once you're done."

She took a sip of wine. "Thank you, Cari," she said, her voice soft. "For coming all the way back here to help me like this."

"No need to thank me, Colie," she said. "It's what I do." It's what she'd done for as long as she could remember. Taking care of people was kind of her thing.

Swirling the blackberry wine in her glass, she admired its deep purple color then raised the glass to her nose. When she took a sip, it was like biting into a ripe blackberry with just a hint of vanilla. "Oh my God, Nicole, this is delicious," she said, and took another, bigger, sip.

Nicole sat curled up under a blanket on the couch, her wine glass resting on her folded knee. "Isn't it amazing?" She sipped again and said, "I bought it across the street."

"Across what street?" There was no way something as wonderful as that blackberry wine came from the winery fifty feet from where they sat.

Laughing, Nicole said, "My street." She lifted her glass and pointed toward the front window. "Obviously you've seen the vineyard, but inside that big old barn he runs a small store front. Actually, it's a pretty big storefront, though he doesn't do much with it. Anyway, it is one hundred percent my favorite winter dessert wine."

"You're telling me the guy over there made this?" Carson said.

Her sister nodded. "Yeah, isn't it great? And he's such a nice guy."

Carson choked on her wine and had to wipe the dribble that ran down her chin. "Nice guy?" she echoed. "That guy over there? You think he's a nice guy?"

Nicole looked at her the way she did when one of the kids said or did something she didn't approve of. "Carson, what did you do to Tom?"

"Me? What makes you think I did anything to him? Maybe he was a total jerk to me. Did you ever think of that?"

Unable to hold her smile back, Nicole said, "No, I didn't think of that. He's never been anything but nice to me." She paused long enough to take another sip of wine. "I think he's super painfully shy, but he's never ever been a jerk to me or the kids." She held Carson's gaze and said in her best Mom voice, "Tell me what happened."

Sparing only the parts that didn't reflect as well on herself, Carson gave Nicole the brief rundown of her roof fiasco. Unable to stop her laughter at Carson's expense, Nicole had to put her wine glass onto the end table to keep from spilling it.

"You've got to be kidding me," Nicole said, wiping tears of laughter from her eyes, when Carson ended her tale. "I'm still waiting for the part where he turns out to be a jerk, though."

"What? Were you even listening to me? The only thing he cared about was making sure I didn't fall off the roof and sue him for everything he's got. Where's the nice guy in that story?"

"Aside from the parts where he held the ladder for you, kept you from falling off it—"

"By grabbing my ass!"

"—And then finishing the job himself," Nicole continued, ignoring Carson's outburst. "It sounds like he was a really nice guy."

Not willing to concede her position on Nicole's neighbor, she asked, "Has he ever offered to help you with anything around here?"

"No—"

"Has he ever said anything at all to you when you're outside?" She was getting heated thinking about his complete lack of manners. Certainly no Knight of the Round Table, that was obvious.

"It's not his job to take care of me or help me do anything in my house, Carson. He's my landlord and he takes care of the property. Aside from that, he's my neighbor and he has a life and business to run, and I have my life and my business to run." Nicole's eyes narrowed a fraction, making Carson shift her gaze toward the fireplace and away from her sister. "Oh... you think he's cute, don't you?" Nicole said.

"What? No, I don't think he's cute," Carson said, a little too emphatically. "I mean, he's got a nice face, if you're into that kind of thing, but he's such a jerk that he's not even cute." The way Nicole always managed to know what was happening inside her brain made it difficult to keep secrets throughout their lives, and apparently living a thousand miles apart for the past almost fifteen years hadn't dimmed Nicole's Sisterly Magic.

"It's alright, I know you're lying," Nicole said.

"How?" Carson was indignant.

"Because he's got more than a nice face, you dummy. The man in insanely hot."

The women broke out into a fit of giggles that was only partly inspired by Tom's blackberry wine, and mostly inspired by Tom himself.

Nicole got quiet first and let out a small sigh.

"What's up?" Carson asked. "Afraid to ask him out?"

It was Nicole who choked out a laugh that time. "Holy shit, no," she said. "I said he was nice to look at, not that I have any interest in him. At. All."

It shouldn't have made Carson happy that Nicole wasn't interested in Tom, but the traitorous little flutter in her belly meant that it absolutely did.

"Then what's that sigh all about?"

Without looking up from her glass, Nicole swirled it in small circles. "I wish I could be interested in him. It would be nice to have someone to flirt with again. But Tom is definitely not it." She paused. "He's actually a little intimidating."

"That's a good word for him," Carson said. "Though I'd probably call him something else entirely."

Nicole's lips curved into a slight smile that didn't reach her eyes, and Carson's heart broke all over again for her obviously hurting younger sister. For someone used to working hard and getting things done, Carson felt virtually useless in any meaningful way.

Looking at her sister, the artist, snuggled up on the couch and then at the glass of wine in her hand, a plan started forming in her head.

She sat in silence for a few minutes, thinking, scheming, formulating a plan. A plan that just might work.

"Have you ever done one of those paint and sip things?" Carson asked. "With your friends or coworkers or whatever? You know, where you drink wine, and everybody works on doing a painting of some sort?"

"I have," Nicole answered with a smile. "I've done them as a participant and I've also—sorta—taught one."

It was exactly the response Carson was hoping for.

"Really? How'd it go?"

"Which one?" Nicole asked.

"Either. Both."

"The one I did as a participant was a total blast. The wine was decent, and the project was fun; we did palm trees by a beach, if I'm remember it right." She giggled. "There was a lot of wine. But I'm pretty sure the painting still lives in Mom and Dad's garage."

"How did you like teaching the other one?" Carson asked.

"That was actually more of a paint without the sip. It was pretty fun though. It was a kid and grownup thing with Lucy's class at the school's end of the year field day last year. All the adults came and sat with their kids, and we all did a painting of a stuffed teddy bear sitting on a blanket. They came out so cute and everyone seemed to love it."

Watching how animated Nicole became as she remembered the fun of those events was all the encouragement Carson needed. As long as

Nicole said yes, her idea was as good as done. Being a mom and sole provider for her family was enough for Nicole to worry about; Carson had just found a way to be helpful in a concrete way. Nicole could take care of her store and Carson would take over the rest.

"What would you think about hosting a Christmas-themed paint and sip? If you already led one for a bunch of kids, you could probably lead one for a bunch of tipsy grownups, right?"

"For real?" Nicole said. "I honestly don't know." She lifted her free hand to her lips and bit her thumbnail, the surefire sign that she was excited but scared. Carson knew the gesture well. "Do you think I could do it? But most of all, do you think we could pull it off before Christmas? I mean, that only gives us about three weeks and..." Her body began to slump again. "Who am I kidding? I don't have the bandwidth to add another big thing, this month of all months."

Carson practically jumped out of her chair. "No, Colie, you wouldn't have to do anything. I literally plan events like this for a living. I've never had a deadline I couldn't meet." She took another sip of her wine, because it was just too good not to. "And I've worked for some serious pains in the ass. This would actually be a fun one to plan."

"I couldn't ask you to do that, Cari. It's enough that you even came to help with the kids."

"Oh, my God. The kids can totally help me plan this. Obviously, I'd do the actual work, but they could help me hang flyers and talk to people around town and tell them what we're doing. You can't tell me they wouldn't love it." Carson was getting more excited by the second; more excited than she'd been about any event she'd planned for Southern Charm Events in years, including the epic Hatch Family Holiday Bash.

Nicole twisted her fingers into the blanket draped over her legs. "They would love to help you." Her voice got a touch louder as she started to catch Carson's excitement. "You know, Tom has that beautiful building over there and it would be absolutely perfect to host something like that. Ooh, we could sell tickets and he could do the wine part." She squeaked and Carson laughed out loud, despite her reluctance to involve the grouchy man across the road. "It would be perfect for both of us. And I wouldn't even have to worry about the kids because they could just come over with me."

Before she could suggest a different location, Carson thought about Nicole's point about keeping the kids close to home. As much as she didn't want to ask Tom about hosting their big event, sure he'd say no anyway, she at least had to ask.

While she debated the best way to approach him, a quick checklist formed in her mind. Aside from securing the space, she'd have to gather supplies, secure permits, and then advertise the event.

She'd found the perfect intersection of her happy places; taking care of the ones she loved combined with planning fun events that everyone else would love. As awesome as her idea was, it would be nothing but a plan without a place for it to happen.

Step one would be to go talk to Sir Lancelot across the road and convince him what a great idea she'd had and why it would be in his best interest and the best interest of his business to go along with it.

Tom

Though Tom wasn't much of a holiday decorator, Will insisted on it being good for business. Tom wasn't sure if the decorations had any direct effect on the increased sales or if those sales just went along with the season. Either way, his regular customers seemed to enjoy it when he put up some of the seasonal décor Heather bought for their first, and as it turned out, only, Christmas together at Whispering Hills.

He made a face as he pulled the items from the bin. Setting the ceramic Christmas tree on the counter, he looked at all the places where it had been cracked and glued back together. Three lines were immediately obvious, and they only highlighted the little chips of white around the otherwise green edges. The garland that always hung in loops along the bar was threadbare at best, the intertwined lights having stopped working at least two Christmases ago.

Squinting at the lighted wreath that hung on the wall was the only way to make it look good. The wiry branches were flat and all the green, plastic "needles" had been crushed, as if it sat at the bottom of the decorations bin the other elven months of the year—which, of course, it did. It all needed to be replaced but every year he told himself he'd do it next year.

Tilting his head to the side and squinting harder at the wreath, the blinking white lights almost made it look acceptable. Although, he'd be the only person willing to put in the work to look at the wreath and not see a relic hanging on the wall. Climbing onto the step ladder, he unhooked it and carried it back to the decoration bin. He should have tossed it directly into the garbage can but couldn't quite bring himself to do it.

The tinkling of the bell above the door startled Tom into awareness as he dug through the bin to see if the window clings had survived to see another Christmas.

It wasn't like him to miss the crunch of tires outside. Needing to be able to work from different areas of the winery meant his ear had been fine tuned to hear potential customers approach. Then it dawned on him that he didn't hear any tires because his latest customer hadn't driven. Lady Guinevere, the delightful pain in the ass from across the street had obviously walked over.

"Morning," she said, as she tiptoed along the low racks of wine bottles, eyes cast downward, and hands tucked into her coat pockets. Tom closed the decoration bin and placed it behind the bar.

"Morning," he replied. He focused on the way she moved, looking at the bottles of wine like they were art pieces on display, not touching any of them. Then she shifted her gaze, taking in the building itself.

At first, he wondered if she was there to pick up their fight where they'd left it the day before, but her body language spoke more of apology than antagonism. To his surprise, the surge of excitement zinging through his body let him know he was ready for either.

"Wow," she finally said, pulling her knitted hat off and smoothing down the flyaway hairs. "My sister was right about this place. It's stunning in here." She looked in every direction, her eyes wide and admiring. "You do all this work yourself?"

"I did," he said. His gaze stayed fixed on her as he tried to guess what she wanted from him.

She spun in a slow circle, looking all around again. "We had some of your blackberry dessert wine last night," she said. She stopped moving and locked eyes with him. His heart beat an extra time and he dropped his eyes to the bar top in front of him.

Women were in his store all the time. A good number of them flirted with him, yet none of them caused his heart to do the two-step like that.

"It was so delicious," she said. "I told her I might need a bottle or two to bring back to Savannah with me." Though her eyes were round and bright, her smile felt off, not entirely false, but maybe uncomfortable, as she caught his eye.

"Would you look at that," he said. "Who would've guessed the Lady Guinevere actually knows how to say nice words, too." Evidently, he was hoping for a continuation of their encounter yesterday. He wanted to see that spark of challenge in her eyes again. His mouth tipped into a smile, inviting her to the dance.

Her face contorted as she bit back whatever snark she was ready to unload on him. To her credit, and his mild disappointment, she remained silent, though she kept her odd smile in place while she turned another slow circle around the room, assessing it. He didn't stop himself from staring at her ass again beneath the edge of her short jacket. How the hell she didn't freeze to death in that thing was a mystery to him.

His memory from the day before had been correct, though; she did have a nice ass. Not that it mattered, but she did. And long, dark hair that framed her naturally pretty face. Which also didn't matter. But he sure did enjoy looking at both.

Turning to face him, she blew out a soft breath, her body relaxing before his eyes, and said, "Carson."

"I'm sorry?"

"My name is Carson. Not Guinevere." Taking a few steps closer to the bar, she said, "And I'm sorry for yesterday. I was having a really bad day, and I took it out on you." She shrugged. "It wasn't nice to take my frustrations out like that. You were kind enough to help me down," she said with a laugh. "I would have been up there until my sister got out of work. And then I would've had to stay up there because I would have missed pickup time at my niece and nephew's school and Nicole would have wanted to kill me." She made an "oh shit" face and laughed again.

"Glad I could help," he said. "Certainly wouldn't want you getting in trouble when you just got here, right?"

"Right."

Her fingers were twisting in knots and when she became aware of what she was doing, she shoved them into her coat pockets again. She stomped up to the bar, pulled one hand free, thrust it toward him. "Hi, I'm Carson Everett. It's nice to meet you." Her weird smile had been firmly reattached to her face.

He stuck his hand into hers, feeling her soft, cool skin. "Tom Wyatt," he said. "Nice to meet you too."

Finally, her smile reached her eyes, and he was unnerved by how striking the difference was.

She shifted from one foot to the other. "Hi, Tom."

As intriguing as standing there in silence would be, he had more work to do. Aside from the stupid decorations, there was distillery equipment to price out and floor plans to be looked over. "Is there something I can help you with?" he said.

Her smile shifted again, closer to conspiratorial. "Tom, how difficult would it be to move all these wine racks?"

Carson

H E SHOOK HIS HEAD, as if he hadn't heard her correctly. "Sorry," he said. "What? What do you mean move the racks? Why would I do that?"

She felt a little guilty ambushing him the way she did but with only a few weeks before Christmas, there was no time to lose. Quickly guessing at the square footage of the building, she figured they could fit about thirty people at a paint and sip event, no problem.

What she couldn't guess was what gears were turning in Tom's head.

"Have you ever done a paint and sip thing, where you drink wine and paint a picture with a bunch of people? They're really fun."

"I know what they are," he said. "I've never done one, but I get the idea."

The way his eyes fixed on her, Carson wasn't sure if she wanted scrap the whole idea so she wouldn't need to work with him anymore, or pray that he said yes so she could spend more time getting to know him.

The corner of his mouth tipped up. "But what does any of that have to do with me and my store?"

Blowing out a quick breath and squaring her shoulders, she said, "Funny you should ask."

"Is it?"

"Yeah," she said. "It is." She stepped up to the bar, all the while aware of his eyes on her, eyes that watched her like a hawk. But if her plan to help Nicole get her store a little more business, and hopefully build its reputation, was to succeed, Carson needed to stop feeling like a mouse under his gaze. She needed to be the professional event planner she was and get this shit done.

While she laid out her plan to him, he listened politely but didn't say anything or ask any questions. She pulled out her phone and brought up her calendar, showing him the timeframe that each piece of the event would require; website creation, flyers up around town, rearranging the interior of his store, and everything else that went along with running an event like that.

His eyes began to glaze over as she ran through the details of the night, and she feared she was losing him. He needed reassurance. "If you're willing to do this," she said, full of hope that diminished by the second. "I think it could be just as big a benefit to you as it would be to Nicole. I mean, think of all the people that would come in and taste your wine."

Out of nowhere, a vision of her sipping wine from a small glass as Tom held it just out of reach of her lips barreled into her mind. Not sure where the hell that came from, her cheeks flushed and she had to force her brain to stay engaged in the conversation and not on the image it had just created.

Trying her best to ignore her burning cheeks and hoping he didn't notice, she continued. "I mean... you know... think of all the new customers you could get."

He stared across the bar at her with a bemused expression, his forehead creased in confusion and, she hoped, curiosity.

Without answering, his eyes traveled around the interior of the store, like he'd never seen it before, or maybe like he'd never given any thought to seeing it other than how it was.

"It's such a lovely space," she said, hoping to say the magic words that might help convince him to let the paint and sip move forward. Mentally she made a note to start searching for other possible locations. Just in case. "How long ago did you renovate the interior?"

The inside of the old barn looked like a Nordic ski resort, golden knotty-pine walls and ceiling, rough wood floors, and large, bright windows. The air held the delicate scent of pine forest, and she imagined how beautiful the space would look with tables and art easels set up where the wine racks currently sat, and a big, gloriously decorated Christmas tree with a bright red skirt beneath it lighting up the corner.

Doing some quick mental math, she added an additional fifty dollars to the budget to replace the sad looking decorations he had hanging from various surfaces. If he decided to say yes. Even if he didn't, she might buy him the new decorations purely to put the current ones out of their misery.

"It's been ongoing over the past few years," he said, his pride in his work evident in his face. Thinking he was on the verge of saying yes, her heart lifted and she sucked in a breath. "But I'm just not sure. I need some time to think about it," he said. Her heart sank as her breath seeped out.

She knew what that meant, and she couldn't let that be his final answer. Event planning was her calling, her career, her life. Surely, she could manage to pull off a simple Christmas paint and sip in this sleepy little Massachusetts town in the next three weeks.

"If you're worried about the logistics, you don't need to be," she said, desperate to keep the conversation going. "We have all the tables and the easels and everything else. You would just have to have a permit that lets you serve alcohol." If he didn't have one of those, the plan was dead in the water because he'd never get it in such short time.

"It's not the license. I've got that." He regarded her with thoughtful eyes that had the unexpected effect of stirring up a swarm of butterflies in her belly. His gaze drifted around his store, then back to her and she crossed her fingers inside her coat pockets, hoping he would pull the trigger and say yes. "I'm just not sure that kind of event would work here. Like I said, I've got to think about it."

Her heart wanted to keep pushing to get him to come around to see the possibility of what could be if he said yes. To see how wonderful and energizing and plain old fun this could be for all of them. But her gut told her to let it go. Tom Wyatt didn't appear to be the kind of guy who would be pushed into a decision he didn't want to make.

Before she made a mistake and kept talking—or worse, let her swirling imagination and emotions talk her into asking him out on a date—she pulled her hat onto her head, stuffed her hands into her coat pockets, and took two giant steps backward, smashing her already bruised hip into one of the solid wood and iron wine racks.

She yelped and winced but forced a smile through the pain, focusing on the trio of small ceramic angels on the shelf above the window to stop herself from letting fly with a string of obscenities.

Tom's face immediately changed as he hurried out from behind the bar. "You all right?" he asked, reaching toward her but stopping just shy of contact, letting his hand hover over her ass. "Did you hurt your... uhh... hip?"

"I'm totally fine," she lied. "I hurt it the other day when I was getting my sister's Christmas lights untangled, and bumping it again reminded me it was there, that's all." She backed away, trying to keep the threatening tears at bay. "Well, I'll leave you to think about what we talked about."

Placing one foot in front of the other, she forced herself to walk as normally as possible across the wide plank wood floors, pushed the door open, and stepped out into the cold December afternoon with a wave. "Bye, now!"

Limping back to the house, she focused her mind away from the pain in her hip and onto the problem at hand. If Tom wasn't willing to host Nicole's event, she'd have to find someplace else that would.

Tom

THERE WAS NO WAY to have gotten her to understand why he wasn't interested in her idea. Most people probably wouldn't understand his lack of desire to grow his business strictly for any financial gain. Having made a fortune in technology years ago, he lived off of that, using the winery to keep his body working and his brain engaged.

Originally, he thought Heather would have loved it out in the western part of the state, but as it turned out she wasn't willing to leave Boston to open a small business with him in the quiet mountain town. Every day since, whether he cared to admit it to himself or not, was an attempt to keep his heart away from the world and the pain it could inflict upon him.

So, why did Carson Everett both scare and excite him in a way he wasn't prepared for? It was easier when she was simply the angry, stubborn visitor across the street. Then she had to go and be sweet and excitable and energetic, and, God help him, cute as hell.

The way she'd explained her plan to help her sister's business, and his own, by setting up this whole painting thing pulled at him. Her enthusiasm had been contagious, and he'd been able to see everything just as she described it to him; wine racks lining the walls, tables and art easels in the big, empty space, Christmas music playing softly in the background. He'd even seen the giant tree, decked out in white lights and red ribbons with the red skirt underneath it.

Watching her hobble out the door, Tom wrestled with the idea of what to do next. She'd presented him with a problem and there was nothing he liked more than a good problem to solve. But he wasn't sure if the problem to be solved was the event she wanted to plan, or if it was Carson herself. Letting her host her event in his store would mean spending time with her. And that scared the hell out of him.

Setting the decoration bin on the bar, he went back to work looking for window clings but couldn't get his mind away from Carson. And that wasn't good. He couldn't be interested in getting to know her and spending time with her. Or anyone else for that matter. No, in order to keep his business and his life on track, it would be best if he told her to find another place for her event.

He enjoyed Whispering Hills as it was. All the changes that adding a distillery would cause would be enough for him. Bringing more people through the doors would happen on its own; he didn't need to force things.

The year after Heather had moved back to Boston, and Tom still hadn't been interested in dating anyone new, Will's sister-in-law said she suspected he was trying to keep his heart closed off from new people by hiding away in the winery. He hadn't given it much credence at the time, but her words came back to haunt him as he let himself wonder what it would be like spending time alone with Carson.

Then he wondered the best way to tell her he wouldn't be hosting her Christmas painting thing.

It was going to kill him a little when he had to crush her idea and tell her no. He mentally prepared himself to watch the smile that lit her whole face fall into a frown that would sting his heart. Unfortunately, there was no way to avoid that. His place just wasn't the right one to host an event like that. Besides, he had work to do and a distillery to plan. There was no time for adding extra projects to his already lengthy to-do list.

B Y THE TIME WILL got there after work, Tom had figured it out. He'd head down to Nicole's shop in the morning and break the news, then move on with his life. That twinge of guilt he kept pushing down would go away for good once he actually said no to them. Their plans were not his plans, nor were they his problem.

"You don't think that could be fun, though?" Will asked when Tom told him about his visit from Carson earlier in the day. He cracked a grin. "I could always come over and lend a hand and do all the heavy lifting and then Nicole will see me as a hero and be indebted to me forever."

Tom laughed. "Or you could just ask her out and save yourself, *and me*, the trouble."

Daylight was fading and they only had a few minutes to get their outdoor work done before the sky faded completely to black. Tom held one end of the string in place while Will dragged it to the opposite side of the yard.

Part of the licensing to get the distillery set up and running meant they'd have to construct a building separate from the current winery. They'd had plans drawn up and floorplans sketched out, but Tom had been on edge, and the cold, brisk air outside normally helped him clear his head as they worked.

Will positioned the last stone in place to mark the northwest corner. "I *could* ask her out and be all boring about it," he said. "But where's the fun in that? How is that a story worth telling the grandchildren about?"

Tom threw his head back and laughed, blowing out puffs of air. "Grandchildren? Jesus, bud, you've never even spoken to her and now you've got grandchildren together?" From nowhere, his brain brought Carson front and center in his thoughts. That had to stop. Quickly. He barely knew the woman. Scratch that—he didn't know her at all, outside of the ten minutes he'd spent with her over the course of the last two days.

Will grinned and tapped a finger to the side of his head. "I'm always thinking ahead, dude. You just never know what life is going to throw at you. Gotta be ready for anything."

"If you say so." The chill of the early evening wasn't doing its usual mind-clearing magic and Tom needed to get his focus back on his business. "Wanna give me a hand in the shop for a few minutes before the game starts?"

Back inside, Will moved the bottles of Greylock Red from the bottom of the racks to the empty spaces at the top. "This one's a good seller. We should probably think of making extra next year," he said.

"I was thinking the same thing." Tom worked on the other side of the room, moving bottles of their dessert wines. "I've had some great feedback on the blackberry and the peach, so maybe up production on those too?"

Will stood up from his crouch and leaned against the wine racks. "You give any more thought to opening a tasting room?" he asked, pointing toward the bar with no stools. "You've got the setup for it. You have the permits for it. You have a built-in customer base to tap into to get it rolling."

No matter how the conversations started lately, they all seemed to lead down the same road. "You sound like my visitor form this morning, trying to expand my business whether I want to or not."

"Nope," Will said. "Not what I'm doing at all. Just telling you what Donny Weaver did. He started with wine tasting and had a pretty reliable clientèle—mostly female." His mouth tipped into a lopsided grin. "But now that he's got the distillery, he's bringing in just as many guys as he'd been bringing in women."

Tom had gotten the permit as part of his and Heather's original plan for the business, but she was supposed to be the customer-facing personality of the pair. He had no interest in standing around talking to people all day.

Carson, when she turned on her charm, would be a natural fit for a position like that. Carson in a few other *positions* presented themselves to his imagination and he had to scrub her from his mind. Again. "I don't think so."

"Really upped his income is all I'm saying. I know you don't need it but figured I'd throw it out there," Will said. "You do whatever you want with the place."

"Sorry," Tom said. "Not trying to be a dick. Just still thinking about that woman from across the street wanting to come in here and mess up my store for her Christmas painting thing."

Will looked up from where he was stocking new bottles, a knowing look on his face. "She's cute, isn't she?" he asked.

"What? I don't know," Tom said. "I didn't notice."

"Bullshit, you didn't." Will came closer without getting in his space, but just barely. "You know she's cute and it's killing you that you even noticed someone that isn't Heather."

The old, familiar spark of anger flared in the base of his brain. Heather left him and there was no denying it, but it didn't mean he still had any kind of feelings for her. She chose to go back to Boston. Just like he chose to stay out in the Berkshires. "That's not true and you know it."

"I don't know it," Will threw back. "I'm serious. It's been like five years. It's OK to look at someone new." His face pulled into a frown. "It's not like she died, and you're stuck here having to honor her memory."

"Will..." Images of Heather crying as she told him she was leaving flooded his memory. Her heartfelt promises that it wasn't because of the guy she worked with—even though they ended up together less than a month later—still sounded hollow.

"No, man, she was fucking cheating on you—*you know she was*—and left you... for some douche in Boston."

"*Will...*" Tom wasn't a physical guy normally, but his friend was walking a dangerously fine line between leaving with a black eye or not. He wished Will would just stop talking. Bringing up all the memories Tom worked so hard to ignore was a dick move.

"She's not even worth the energy you want to spend kicking my ass, Tom." Will glanced down at Tom's fisted hands before he looked him in the eyes again.

Realizing the truth of Will's words, Tom unclenched his fists, blew out a deep breath. "You're right." She was long gone. Ancient history. But the memory of having his heart stomped on and discarded was still a painful one. Not something he was eager to experience again.

"Damn right I am," Will said.

"But that doesn't mean I need to rush right out and find someone new." Tom needed to make sure Will understood he was not interested in Carson. At all. And maybe—a little bit—he was trying to convince himself of the same.

"Oh, yeah, I get ya, man. Wouldn't want you to rush into anything." Will laughed and Tom gave him a playful shove before he turned his attention back to the store.

ONCE THE HOCKEY GAME ended and Tom was alone again, he reached for one of the books he'd purchased when he first started toying with the idea of adding the distillery. Hand-written notes had been scribbled in the margins of nearly every page.

He added questions to his ever-growing list inside the front cover. Even if it would be a year or more before they had any alcohol to sell, his excitement grew more and more at the prospect of making it all work.

In his imagination he saw himself adding new racks to display the cinnamon apple liquor he hoped would be their masterpiece, and the chocolate mint he imagined his favorite customers would buy for their book club.

As the Tom in his imagination restocked bottles, the sound of people chatting began to fill the space. He turned around and the racks of wine that normally took up the main part of the store had been rearranged, high top tables and chairs in their place. Behind the small, polished bar, the cutest brunette stood talking up customers and pouring samples of Whispering Hills' wines and liquors. As he watched her, she looked up at him, smiled from ear to ear. It was a smile meant only for him and it found its target.

Shaking his head to clear the vision from his mind, Tom sat back in his chair, pushed the book to the side and wondered where the hell thoughts like that had come from. He barely knew her and his brain had already planted Carson firmly into thoughts of his future.

That wasn't an option, and it would be best for his heart if he squashed those thoughts before they had time to take deeper root. In the morning, right after breakfast, he would go down to Nicole's store and tell her the paint and sip was a definite no-go. It would be easier to tell Nicole because seeing the look of disappointment on Carson's face might be enough to cause him to fold.

No, it would be best to cut ties with her as cleanly, and as quickly, as possible.

Carson

Hazelton captivated Carson's imagination. The ten-minute trip from Nicole's house to her store turned into a forty-five-minute meandering drive through the scenic mountain roads. Up hills and down, through twisty turns and straight roads, with snow-covered fields and hillsides in every direction.

It had been more than a decade since she'd moved away, and she'd forgotten how picturesque and idyllic this part of the country was. And how quiet.

She hadn't heard from Tom the night before, which meant he probably wasn't on board with letting them use his space. It was unfortunate for him, she thought, because it really could have been a boon to his business. She sighed as she turned from a small back road onto the main street through town. The inside of the winery would have been absolutely stunning if she'd been given the chance to get her hands on it.

Ahead of her on the right side of the road, stood a large barn-like building with a huge fenced-in yard. The sign said Mountain Tap

Brewery. With nobody driving behind her, she slowed down and pulled to the side of the road so she could do a quick search online.

It was too early in the morning for anyone to be there, but judging from the outside, the space could work for a paint and sip. The building itself was a large square with huge doors that looked like they would open more like a garage than a restaurant. The parking lot was suitably large and since it was a restaurant that presumably sold alcohol, there wouldn't be an issue with licensing.

Round, stone firepits dotted the fenced-in part of the property and she imagined there were most likely picnic tables or something similar in the warm weather. It looked like a cool place to hang out and have a beer and some good old fashioned pub food.

Despite the early hour, she dialed the restaurant's number and was greeted by a message that the Mountain Tap Brewery was closed for renovations until their big New Year's Eve bash and grand re-opening. She was directed to their website to make reservations for New Year's Eve.

She disconnected but was undeterred. Even if the paint and sip couldn't happen there, she made a note that she'd like to come back and try it anyway once it reopened. Maybe she'd see about coming back up to see Nicole during the summer.

Continuing through town, she saw a sign with an arrow and followed it to another location that held promise. The Faraway Inn was a beautiful old, yellow Colonial that had clearly been expanded upon. The sign out front said they offered lodging and dining. Dining meant they had a restaurant that hopefully Carson would be able to rent out.

Three steps into the building, she worried that she may have chosen the wrong place. If they held the paint and sip at Tom's winery, they could break even at ten participants. If the interior of the Faraway Inn told her anything, it was that they might not break even with twice that.

"How can I help you?" a young woman asked from behind the counter, her glasses perched on top of her head and her hair pulled back into a high ponytail. Garlands of evergreens draped the countertop, with clusters of glass baubles evenly spaced along its length. It was tasteful and elegant. Red ribbons and bows edged with gold added an extra touch of charm to the look.

Carson briefly explained what she was looking for.

The innkeeper frowned. "I'm sorry," she said. "Our restaurant is still relatively new, and it's almost entirely booked out for dinner throughout the whole month of December. But come in earlier next year and we can try again," the woman said as Carson breathed a silent sigh of relief. "It really does sound like fun."

Before she pulled out of the parking lot, she searched for the nearest chain hotel—which was almost fifteen miles away. "Ugh," she said, tossing her phone into her purse before shifting her car into drive. Her throat pinched as she fought off tears. Nothing was working in her favor. As it stood, her "brilliant" idea to help her sister was turning into a great big bag of nothing.

There were benefits to living in small towns like Hazelton, but there were also drawbacks, and a lack of function space was turning into the biggest hurdle Carson had faced in a long while. Back in Savannah it was easy to plan events, both big and small, and find the perfect place to match the mood. In western Massachusetts? Not as much.

Back out on the main road through town, the brightly painted sign for Happenstance, Nicole's art consignment store, came into view. The yellows and reds of the sign were warm and bright and stood in stark contrast to the white snow and bare trees all around.

She would have to tell Nicole that they might need to think of a backup plan if Carson couldn't find an available venue. Imagining the look of disappointment on her sister's face brought a lump to her throat that she tried to swallow around.

There were only a few open spaces to park, so Carson pulled into a spot right outside The Daily Grind, a small coffee shop two doors before Happenstance. Coffee shops usually sold pastries. Pastries would make a good "I'm sorry" gift. She cast a quick glance at the Happenstance sign, then pulled open the door to The Daily Grind.

Because of the cold outside, the street was devoid of people, but inside the coffee shop, life was definitely happening. The red vinyl booths along the wall were full of chatting customers. The sounds of clinking silverware amid the din of conversation and laughter welcomed Carson like a long-lost friend.

Every available surface of the place had been adorned with red and green sparkly garland, gold stars, jolly Santa wall hangings, and every other manner of kitschy Christmas-themed decoration. It reminded her of Christmas season at her grandparents' house growing up.

"Come on in," said the gray-haired woman from behind the counter. Pouring coffee into the waiting cups of the customers seated there, the woman smiled at Carson and pointed to an empty seat. "There's space for you right here."

Unsure what to do with her coat, she thought about keeping it on, but the diner was so warm and cozy she ended up taking it off and draping it over her lap.

"Coffee?" the same gray-haired woman asked, placing a cup and saucer on the counter. Her reindeer earrings dangled above her collar, and she hovered the coffee pot until Carson gave her the go-ahead nod.

"Yes, please."

"Welcome to The Grind," the woman said. "I'm Delores." She smiled and the gesture added to the already homey feeling Carson had. "Haven't see you here before." Delores reached down a few seats and grabbed a cream and sugar caddy, placed it in front of Carson. "You're a little early for ski season. You here visiting?"

"I am," Carson said and took a sip of coffee. "My sister owns a shop down the street, and I was on my way there but thought I'd stop in here and grab some breakfast to bring to her."

"Oh yeah?" Delores said. "Which shop is hers?"

Carson pointed over her shoulder in the direction of Nicole's store. "It's called Happenstance. It's a—"

Delores threw her hand over her heart. "Oooh, I love that store," she said. "She has the cutest stuff in there." Shaking her head to make the reindeer earrings jangle, she said, "That's where I got these from." Then, looking somewhere behind Carson, Delores called out, "Emma, you've been in there, right?"

"Been in where?" a voice responded. Carson turned around to see a booth with four women in it, all of whom were looking at Delores.

"Happenstance. That cute little place a couple doors down."

All of the women smiled and nodded. One woman responded, "I sure have. Bought my granddaughter the cutest earring and necklace set from there just last week. Why do you ask?"

Delores dipped her chin toward Carson. "Our new friend here—"

"Carson."

"Our new friend, Carson, is the owner's sister."

"Is that right?" the woman said. "Well, it's nice to meet you, Carson. I'm Emma Sheehan and this is Janice, Olivia, and Tina," she said, pointing to each woman around the table. They all waved hello in turn. "Welcome to Hazelton."

"Yeah, welcome," Janice echoed. "Oh, I love your sister's store. The stuff in there is so cute and your sister is such a doll."

The other women murmured their agreement and Janice continued. "She's such a sweet person, it makes it fun to shop there."

Carson's heart swelled. Nicole had only been in town for six months and she already had such loyal customers. She wondered if Nicole was aware of how highly these women thought of her.

A few other people in the coffee shop looked over as the conversation continued. One woman looked at Carson and nodded, as if she too had similar things to say about Nicole.

"I hate to admit I haven't been in there yet," Carson said. "I've only been in town a few days, and this will be the first time I go in." She looked at Delores. "That's why I wanted to come in here and grab some coffee and muffins or something to bring down there when I go."

Delores smiled down at her. "I've got you covered," she said. "I know the perfect thing." She turned and typed something in the point of sale and then returned to refilling coffee mugs and delivering food to the other customers.

Carson casually glanced around the room, suddenly thinking that maybe their event could happen there. Except she was in a coffee shop, not a bar. Coffee shops didn't normally have liquor licenses. *Damn*. It wouldn't have been ideal but at least it would have been a place, which is more than she had now.

Carson had already found the beginnings of the list of people to invite. Rather than scare them away with an immediate ask, she tucked away the warm feelings they had for her sister and made a plan to come back to The Daily Grind again.

All she had to do now was find a location.

Carson

Walking into Happenstance, armed with two coffee cups, a bag of assorted muffins, and a couple of antacids, Carson's mood wasn't entirely bleak but wasn't overly optimistic either.

She took a sip of coffee and swallowed down the disappointment and frustration of her morning and tried to hold onto the good feelings she'd picked up at the diner.

The store itself was freaking adorable. The pale peach walls gave it warmth, despite the biting cold outside. The worn wood floors added a comfortable, lived-in feel and all the items for sale were displayed on bookshelves and dressers and armoires.

There was no commercial shelving anywhere, just pieces of real furniture being repurposed. No wonder Delores and Emma and their friends all loved the store so much. How could you not?

Despite everything Nicole had gone through over the past couple of years, she still managed to be a great mom and keep her store running, if not at a huge profit, at least enough to give her kids a roof and enough food to eat. And her ability as an artist and a small business owner was what made it all possible.

A pang of envy stirred in Carson's gut. Not that she wanted to own her own store, but that Nicole was able to execute on her vision and was working to make her dream come true.

Somehow, they'd managed to flipflop their roles. Carson had always been the one to take charge and get things done. Nicole had been the flighty one, the one to chase butterflies and rainbows while other people did the hard work.

And now it was Carson who couldn't scrape together a tiny painting party and Nicole who had been doing more than one person should have to do by themselves.

Pride and delight quickly overtook the envy she'd felt, and Carson hurried past shelves of jewelry and homemade bowl cozies and handmade picture frames, toward the counter where Nicole was working.

"Thank you!" Nicole said as Carson approached and put the breakfast goodies down in front of her. "I love that place. They have the best blueberry muffins," she said, pulling open the bag and smiling in satisfaction when she saw the contents.

She lifted out a blueberry muffin and sighed as she bit into it, catching the crumbs with a hand under her chin. "You have to try one of these," she mumbled through a mouthful of muffin.

The sisters spent a few minutes talking while they ate their second breakfast and Nicole gave Carson a quick tour of Happenstance. "Mostly, right now, I'm selling other people's things, but I really want to be able to sell more of my own work too," Nicole said as Carson took in the eclectic mix of pieces for sale.

"How's the planning coming together?" Nicole asked as she returned to work, taping up a small box of snowman ornaments to be shipped out later in the day.

Carson sipped her coffee and put the cup down on the counter, trying to hide the disappointment in her voice. "It's coming along," she said. "I already found some people to invite."

Nicole tipped her head in a questioning gesture. "You did? Where'd you find them?"

Carson pointed to the bag. "Evidently, your business neighbors are crazy about you and your store."

A look of emotion flashed over Nicole's face before she sighed and said, "But we have nowhere to invite them to, do we?" She sighed again. "Maybe we should just call it quits on the whole thing. I mean, it was kind of ambitious to think we could pull something like this off three weeks before Christmas."

Nicole finished sealing the box and stashed the roll of tape beneath the counter. Her hand trembled slightly but then she pasted a big, forced grin onto her face. "At least we'll be together for Christmas this year. We haven't been together on Christmas in so long."

"You always did see the bright side of everything," Carson said, squeezing Nicole's hand gently. "One of your greatest traits, I think."

Carson wanted to make things better for her sister and she was once again at a total loss as to how to do it. Nicole would be amazing leading a class like that and people would have a blast. There had to be a way to make it happen.

"Have you heard from Tom, then?" Nicole asked. "Did he definitely say no?"

"I haven't heard back from him one way or the other," Carson said, the tiniest glimmer of hope still alive in her heart. "So, technically," she said, "he hasn't said no so it could still be a yes. You know if we move all those racks around in his shop, we could probably fit upwards of thirty people in there. Maybe more."

Carson willed cheer into her voice but Nicole wasn't buying it.

"There's no way he's going to say yes," Nicole said, grabbing another muffin from the bag. Breaking it in two, she handed one half to Carson, who accepted it gratefully.

She hated the look of defeat on her sister's face. "I was planning to go over this afternoon and follow up with him. Even if he says no, *which he hasn't*, there has to be some place to do it." Desperation burned her stomach, and she popped a couple antacids into her mouth, washed them down with another bite of blueberry muffin.

"Do you know anyone else who could do the wine part of the night?" She looked around the small footprint of the store and knew it wouldn't be ideal. "If we had to, we could do it here. We couldn't fit more than four or five people, but four or five is better than none."

Nicole shook her head. "I don't think it would be worth it for only four or five people but I don't know of any other places we could do it."

"We just need a bigger space. And a caterer with a liquor license, then we can do it wherever we want. What about the community center?" Most of the towns in the area maintained large, open buildings that played host to any and all types of functions. Both girls had their proms in their hometown rec center back in the day, so she knew the general layout of one.

Nicole shrugged. "It would be the perfect size." She looked up. "Maybe even a little too big. But it doesn't matter because you can't serve alcohol there, so never mind." Her shoulders slumped.

The bell above the door jingled and a blast of frigid air whipped through the small space. Not wanting to be in the way of Nicole and her customer, Carson stepped to the side.

Nicole looked at the newcomer then flashed a quick, hopeful glance at Carson, before rising from her stool to greet the man. "Hi, Tom. Cold one out there today."

Carson turned to see Tom Wyatt standing inside the shop, bundled from head to toe against the cold, his eyes looking everywhere but at Carson. The women exchanged a look and Nicole moved around to the customer side of the counter.

Cold radiated off Tom's body and Carson took notice again of how solid a body he had. His hair touched his collar, his dark beard was sprinkled with silver and his shoulders filled out his coat perfectly.

Tom pulled off his hat, glanced from Nicole to Carson and then quickly back to Nicole. "I didn't realize you'd both be here," he said, twisting his hat in his hands. If she didn't know better, Carson would have said he was nervous. Shy, she could believe, but nervous? That was a surprise to her.

The question remained whether it would be a good surprise or a bad one for them.

"Carson wanted to see where the magic happens, you know?" Nicole smiled in her direction. "It's not as big and busy as Savannah, but Hazelton is still fun, right, sis?"

"It is," Carson answered. "It's certainly not as warm as back home, but it's nice."

Tom looked down at the floor and Nicole sent Carson a look. Carson shrugged, her eyes wide, not knowing what on earth Tom had come down to the store for, but hoping it meant he was feeling the Christmas spirit.

"How are things at the winery?" Nicole said. "Looks like it's pretty busy this time of year."

"Yeah," he said. "It's going pretty well." He ran his hand through his hair and looked from Nicole to Carson again, on the verge of saying something. Finally, he huffed out a breath and said, "That's why I came down here. I gave the whole painting night thing some thought."

Carson's stomach tightened waiting for him to get the words out. His body language certainly gave off 'hell no' vibes, and she steeled herself to keep an even tone while she thanked him for giving it some thought. Just because she didn't live there didn't mean she could be unprofessional.

The man was about to put the final nail in the coffin of their grand plan, so why was she thinking about how good looking he was? And why did she want to run her hands over his chest and down his arms and up to his face?

And what the actual hell was wrong with her?

Tom

T HE TWO WOMEN STOOD surrounded by handmade art pieces and paintings and sculptures and all manner of things that screamed *female,* and they looked perfect there. The soft peach-colored walls and the dark wood floor fit these two, but Carson especially. Her long hair was almost as dark as the stained wood of the shelf beside her, her body looked soft and touchable.

He needed to get the hell out of there.

Carson held his gaze and the look in her eyes spoke volumes. She'd told him that she was in town to help her sister and she was trying to expand the reach of Nicole's business. As a small business owner himself, he understood that. But Nicole's success was neither his business nor his concern.

Except it was, after all., wasn't it? If she didn't succeed, she couldn't pay her rent. If she couldn't pay her rent, he would be forced to evict a single mother and her children. Nobody wants to do that. That would be a no-win situation for all of them.

The women were waiting for him to say something while he rationalized and justified his decisions to himself. Each second that ticked by only made his silence more uncomfortable.

"If you think you can pull it all together and make something work with only a few weeks until Christmas, who am I to be Scrooge and say no?"

Both sets of eyes that had been watching him grew wide with disbelief. Clearly, they had been positive he was going to say no. Because he was going to say no. He'd been ready to say no since Carson hobbled out the door the day before.

Nicole clapped her hands. "Oh, my God, Tom, for real? That's amazing. Thank you so much."

Then, before he knew what was happening, Carson jumped into his arms and pulled him into a death grip of a hug. Instinctively he hugged her back and she smooshed a kiss into his cheek. "Thank you, thank you, thank you," she said.

The feel of her breasts against his chest, her cool fingers on his suddenly overheated cheeks, and the soft strip of skin that was exposed when she lifted her arms to hug him sent his imagination into overdrive.

The scent of her shampoo fit her, flowery and sweet but with a hint of spiciness to it, and he wondered, by her reaction, if there was a hint of spiciness to her as well.

Quickly, Carson recovered herself and took a few steps back from him, straightening out her shirt and leaving his body aching for her to hold him again. She hid her face behind her hands and peeked out from between her fingers. "Tom, I am so sorry. I... I have no idea what came over me. I can't believe I did that!"

"Don't worry about it," he said, watching the blush of red climb into her cheeks. "I've certainly been treated worse."

She cleared her throat and took a step closer to her sister. "This is really so awesome of you to agree to this." Carson bounced on the balls of her feet, and he could almost see the wheels in her head start turning.

"OK," she said. "First, we need to get the word out and let people know what we're doing. Then we need to make sure we have all the supplies we need. And we need to know exactly how many people we can fit in the winery, and—"

He'd hung a 'be back soon' sign on the winery's front door and the clock was ticking. "How about this," he said, interrupting her. "When you ladies are done here for the day, why don't you come by the store, and we can talk more about what needs to be done. I close up around eight. Does that work for you?"

Nicole frowned. "I can't tonight. There's a Christmas party at the community center and I promised to take the kids. We probably won't be home until close to ten."

His heart skipped a beat when Carson told her, "Take the kids to their party. I can go over and deal with all the planning stuff." She hugged her sister and said, "Remember? This is what I do."

"You really don't mind?"

"Isn't that what I came here for? To help out so you could enjoy your children and not be completely stressed out about everything, even for a few weeks?"

The reality of the situation stung him again when she said she'd only be around for a few weeks, but he pushed it aside, instead thinking about all the things in his shop that would need to be moved for their big event. He would definitely be calling in Will and maybe a brother or two for help with the heavy lifting.

"You're amazing, Cari. Thank you." Nicole hugged her sister and Tom averted his eyes to keep from intruding on a special family moment.

The tension broke when Carson looked back at him. "Don't eat dinner," she said. "I'll bring a pizza and I'll be there ready to go at seven fifty-five."

His balls ached at the thought of Carson being 'ready to go,' and before she and her sister knew it too, he said, "Great. Sounds like a plan. See you tonight," and, yanking his hat back on, he pushed through the door and out into the cold, which was exactly what his overheated body needed.

Tom

THE CLOCK ON THE wall ticked by as slowly as a clock ever had while Tom trudged through the rest of his day. He'd never actively tried to convince himself of anything the way he tried to force himself to believe he wasn't looking forward to Carson Everett showing up with a pizza once he closed the store.

One of his favorite and most loyal customers, an older woman who hosted a monthly book club as well as a weekly knitting group, stood across the bar from him as he loaded up the case of mixed reds with a couple dry whites for her.

"Emma, you need me to carry this out to the car for you?" Tom asked as they waited for her credit card to process.

"That would be great, Tom, thank you." She smiled and said with a wink, "If only I had you at home to help me get it into the house."

It always cracked him how unabashedly the woman flirted with him. As far as he knew she was happily married, but that hadn't stopped her yet. "One of these days I'm going to take you up on that, Mrs. Sheehan. Then what are you going to do?"

Emma laughed at his joke, tucked her card back into her wallet. "I would tell Mr. Sheehan to find somewhere else to be for a little while, Tom. That's what I'd do."

Together they carried eight bottles of wine out to her waiting Explorer. "Enjoy your wine, Emma. We'll see you next week?"

"Absolutely," she said as she climbed up behind the wheel. "Thank you, Tom."

As the black truck rolled down the hill, another car made its way up. He was only ten minutes away from closing, but he'd certainly wait for anyone who made the trek this late at night to buy from him.

The car pulled into the parking lot and once they turned their headlights off, Tom saw it was Carson. She took a knit beanie off her head and finger brushed her hair then reached over to grab a couple of white pizza boxes from the seat beside her.

"Hey," she said, holding up the boxes when he opened the car door for her. "I forgot to ask what kind of pizza you like, so I got one cheese and one pepperoni. Is that OK?"

Damn, she was cute. "I'm not picky. Whatever you brought is just fine."

Every time she smiled her whole face lit up. "Are you closed for the night? I know I'm a couple minutes early."

"You passed my last customer a few seconds ago."

Once they were inside, it only took her a minute to get the pizzas set up and her laptop opened, ready to take notes.

"Can I take your coat?" he asked.

"No thanks. Not yet. I've been here for a week already and I still haven't figured out a way to keep warm."

A few ideas of how to keep her warm flitted through his brain but he chose to click the thermostat up a few degrees instead.

The forced hot air heating system warmed the space quickly and after a couple minutes, Carson finally took off her coat. Turning to him with furrowed brows, she said, "Do you mind if I turn on a Christmas playlist? I think it might help me get in the right mood." Without waiting for an answer, she grabbed the phone from her back pocket and started scrolling.

"There's not much reception up here; don't know if that's going to work."

Waving off his concern, she went back to scrolling and said, "No worries. I have it downloaded all year."

"Of course you do," he said as the soft drum beat of "The Little Drummer Boy" began streaming from her phone.

There was an energy that radiated from her as she walked around his store, throwing out ideas on how they could rearrange the racks, how many tables they could set up, where the supply table would be, and every other thing that popped into her head. "I'll organize this all on my laptop later," she said as she scribbled notes onto a sheet of paper.

"If we moved these racks out of here and lined them up against the wall, we could open up space for at least four more easels," she said, then spun around and pointed to the small room attached to the main store. "What's in there?"

"Nothing yet." The original intention had been to use the space as additional sales floor but so far, he hadn't needed it. Will had convinced him to make it look more inviting in the meantime. It currently held a couch, a low coffee table, and a small bookshelf.

Her eyes narrowed and she chewed absentmindedly on her thumbnail as she thought. "It's perfect. That's where we'll set up the snack tables and we can set you up right there to man the wine table and help people top off their glasses."

Her body nearly vibrated with excitement as she spoke, and she started bouncing on her toes as she turned to him. "This is going to be so amazing, isn't it?"

He wanted to bottle even half of her enthusiasm to keep for later. Being around a whirlwind like Carson had him being pulled into her nonstop motion. He wasn't sure if he liked it or not, but he was absolutely sure he was intrigued enough to stay a little longer and find out.

Although maybe that wasn't a good thing. She lived so far away and wouldn't be staying in Hazelton long enough to make this something he should pursue. It would probably be for the best to simply let her use his space and then they could both move on with their lives.

"It's going to be great," he said, though he had no idea if it would be good, great, or a complete train wreck.

"Do you have any banquet tables? I think Nicole has some decorative tablecloths we could use for the snack table." Her eyes grew wide. "I haven't thought about food yet. We're going to need snacks and stuff." She started to worry her bottom lip. "I have to ask her what she wants to do about that," she said, mostly to herself. "No, I can't bother her with that stuff. This is on me. It's what I do. I've got this."

Tom went to the counter, flipped open the cheese pizza box, pulled a slice and put it on a paper plate then held it out to her. "Here," he said. "Let's have some dinner and then we can keep talking."

"Oh! You go ahead and start eating," she said. "I forgot something in the car." Like a flash of lightning, she was out the door. Tom ate a few bites of his pizza waiting for her to come back. After a few minutes he decided to go take a look in case there was something she needed help with.

When he opened the door, she was leaning against the trunk of her car, arms wrapped around her middle, staring up into the dark night. "Carson," he said. "Everything OK out here?"

Without moving, she said, "Have you seen this sky?" Her voice was quiet, almost reverent. "It's so dark. And the stars... there are so many stars."

He descended the porch stairs and went to do a little stargazing with her. Raising his eyes, he saw a night sky that should have taken his breath away every time he looked at it. It was magnificent. When had he gotten to the point of taking that view for granted?

"Isn't it the most beautiful thing you've ever seen?" Carson asked through slightly chattering teeth.

"Almost," he said.

She turned to smile at him, and her entire body had begun to shiver.

"Come on," he said, reaching down to take hold of her hand. "Let's get you back inside and warmed up again."

"OK." She started to walk with him then pulled up short. "Hang on, I almost forgot why I came out here." She opened her car and reached in to grab something from the back seat. "Check it out," she said pulling out a stack of white canvases. "You get to choose the painting Nicole's going to teach!"

He took them from her arms, grabbed hold of her hand again. "We'll bring them inside and you can show me my options while we eat some dinner."

He grabbed his plate with the half-eaten slice of pizza from the counter while Carson picked up the canvases and laid them on top of a wine rack.

Even through the fuzzy fabric of her sweater, the outline of her cold nipples caught his eye, and he shifted his footing to ease the growing ache that seemed to gnaw at him whenever he was near her.

Thankfully she hadn't seemed to notice the extra glance at her chest as she fussed over the canvases, making sure they were in a nice, neat line.

Like a gameshow hostess she stood back and waved her arm along the row of kitschy paintings. "So... which one do you like the best?"

"I don't know," Tom said walking over to her. They all look nice."

She rolled her eyes and laughed. "But you have to have a favorite."

He stepped closer to the row of paintings and took an extra inhale to get the sweet scent of Carson into his mind. The first painting, a Christmas gnome sitting on a present inside a snow globe, made him smile. A gingerbread house decked out with tons of brightly colored candy was also nice, but the next to last one had his vote; a smiling snowman, wearing a flowy scarf around his neck, leaning against a green-garland-wrapped light post.

"I'm no Bob Ross or anything," he said, pointing to the snowman painting. "But I kinda like this one."

"Me too! That was my choice!"

Her stomach growled so he took hold of her hand again, tugged her toward the pizza. "There's plenty of time for planning. Now, we eat."

He pulled a chair from the small office behind the bar so Carson could sit down. She decided to hop up onto the bar top instead, and again he felt himself being drawn to her and enthralled by how open she was.

After eating a couple of slices, she leaned back onto the counter, giving him another tempting view of her breasts, but this time he wondered if she was doing it on purpose. He sure hoped so. A wistful look came across her face, and it slowly transformed into a genuine smile.

"What's that look?" he asked.

"I'm trying to think about the last time I ate pizza and didn't need any of these." She reached into her pocket and pulled out a small roll of antacids. "Honestly, I can't even remember but it had to have been before I started my job at Southern Charm."

"What's Southern Charm?"

"It's the event company I work for down in Savannah."

"Don't like the job? Because from my side of things it looks like something you love."

She breathed out a hard sigh. "That's the thing. I do love it. It's the best thing I've ever done. I just work for this guy—well, let's just say he and I don't necessarily see things eye to eye. On pretty much anything. Ever."

Maybe there wasn't as much for Carson to go back for as Tom had originally thought. Unless, of course, there was some*one* for her to go back to. It didn't feel right to ask, so he let it go.

Eventually she pushed back to sitting upright, scanned the room from one side to the other. "Oh, well," she said. "How hard will it be to get all this moved?"

"Not terribly," he said. "But it will be time consuming. All the wine has to come off the racks. The racks get moved. Wine has to go back on the racks." They were quiet for a second until he asked. "How many people do you plan on having at this thing?"

"In order to break even, we need about ten. But I'm hoping to get twenty. Maybe even thirty," she said hopefully.

"Thirty people?" He chuckled. "There aren't even thirty people living in this town." He was exaggerating, but only slightly. "How are you going to bring thirty people in here?"

Her back stiffened noticeably. "This is what I do for a living. I know how to get people in here. Don't worry about that."

"Sure, maybe in Savannah it would be easy to get thirty people for a last-minute thing like this the week before Christmas. But how the hell do you plan on getting that many up here? Specifically?"

Carson

"I DON'T KNOW," SHE said. "Specifically. But don't underestimate the power of good, old-fashioned charm and a nice smile." She grinned at him, showing her best professional pose. "Besides it's so boring up here, I'm sure I'll be able to get people to flock in here just for something to do."

He looked at her as if he was trying to figure her out, his face serious. "I like it here. I don't think it's boring."

She may have hit a nerve. Growing up in the area, she knew there were more than a few 'lifers' who had no intention of ever leaving and it appeared Tom might be one of them. "Have you ever lived anywhere else?" she asked.

"Downtown Boston. Almost twenty years."

Not what she expected him to say.

"And you came here from Boston?" she said. "On purpose?" She tried to hide her shock but wasn't entirely successful, judging by the way his eyebrow rose and his mouth twisted into a half smile.

"I told you; I like it here."

She reached back into her memory, of days growing up in the area. She thought about the beauty of the snow-covered scenery when she walked out the door each day. Thought about how stunning it was every Autumn as the lush green of summer gave way to the deep reds and oranges and yellows before the hibernation of winter.

Maybe she missed it.

A little bit.

Carson had never been a big believer in love at first sight. Chemistry? Absolutely. How that chemistry worked was something she had no clue about. You either felt the sparks and got along with someone and wanted to spend time together, or you didn't.

But sitting on the bar across from Tom, the attraction, the chemistry she'd been feeling the past few days was only growing stronger by the minute.

If she'd been thinking clearly and not caught up in the nostalgia of New England scenery and the way the stars twinkled—literally twinkled—in the winter sky, she would have remembered that she was only in town for a few more weeks. No matter what she felt for Tom Wyatt, it only held a future that was three weeks long.

Even still, she wondered what it was like to be him, what made him tick.

"What's your favorite thing about making wine?" she asked.

"That's easy." He hopped up onto the bar next to her, his thigh resting snugly against hers and his hands clasped in his lap. "It's hard work, and a lot of it, to be sure, but it's also the year-round nature of it. It's like life in microcosm. There are things that need to be done depending on the season, and there are things that you can't do even if you want to if the timing isn't right. There's a rhythm to it that can't be forced and there's a certain peace in that."

Carson wondered if he was speaking strictly about wine or if he was including her in his seasonal philosophy. Was spending time with her something he considered poor timing?

Although, maybe that was a better way to look at her feelings for Tom. They were seasonal. Like all seasons, it would come to an end, but maybe there was the chance to spend some time together enjoying each other's company in the meantime.

"There's something to do every day," he said. "Whether it's in the vineyard, down by the fermentation tanks, or around the buildings, there's always a job to be done and there's great satisfaction in that. Testing the wine as it ages, making sure the acidity is correct, and honestly, even the paperwork that goes along with running this business keeps me busy."

"Wow," she said, impressed with all that was involved in his business, sure he was only telling her a fraction of everything he did. "And here I thought making the wine was the hard part."

He laughed. "Keeping those vines alive and healthy is a job in itself but when harvest season comes, you get to transform all those grapes into something else entirely. It's chemistry. It's biology. And it's a little bit magic."

That's kind of how it felt being so close to Tom as he shared the passion he obviously had for his work, not to mention the heat of his body as it mingled with her own.

"Is that what you did in Boston?" she said. "Make wine?"

"Nope," he said, shaking his head. "I actually worked in biotech for a long time."

Another surprise answer.

"How on earth does a tech guy from Boston end up in the far reaches of the Berkshire Mountains running a winery?" She bumped shoulders with him. "That's a seriously sharp career shift."

His sigh was so deep it was like it came from the bottom of his soul. Slipping off the bar, he said, "You and your sister liked the blackberry wine, right?"

"Yeah."

She followed his steps and admired the way his body moved when he walked. The confidence in his steps, the tiniest hint of swagger in the sway of his arms. Crossing to the far side of the room, he grabbed a bottle from one of the racks and brought it back to where she waited.

The low light in the room lent a surreal, almost romantic feel to the night. Pitch black and cold outside contrasted against being warm and cozy inside with Tom. He grabbed a couple small tasting glasses from under the bar and put them down beside her.

Her eyes were fixed on his hands and the working muscles of his forearms as he uncorked the bottle. She couldn't help but imagine what else those hands could do. A tiny noise escaped her throat and Tom's eyes flicked to hers.

Did he know what she was thinking? Was he thinking it too?

He poured a couple inches of wine into each of the glasses and handed her one. "Try this," he said.

Accepting his offering, she lifted the glass to her nose to breathe in the sweet aroma then put it to her lips and took a sip. Tom did the same.

The taste of dark chocolate melted over her tongue followed by the mellow tones of some kind of spice. It was sweet and delicious and sensuous, and it blazed a trail of warmth from her throat to her belly, straight down until it sparked that tingle of desire between her thighs.

She all but moaned out loud as she took a second sip. "This is delicious, Tom. Seriously, I thought the blackberry was amazing, but I think this might be my new favorite." She leaned over to see what type of wine it was, and Tom's eyes very clearly traveled from her eyes to her breasts to her legs, though not lingering anywhere too long, and that growing desire became an insistent, begging need under the heat of his gaze.

"Glad you like it. I figured you probably would. And that's the magic in doing what I do out here. People enjoying the wines I make. Reactions like yours? That's what makes it all worth it."

Their faces were close together and the urge to reach over and touch his beard, to kiss him just to taste the wine on his lips, drew her hand from the counter. But before she made a terrible mistake, she diverted its path and picked up the bottle of chocolate port. Grabbing her phone, she opened the camera. To Tom's questioning look she responded, "I want to remember what it's called so I can get a bottle for Nicole."

His eyes searched hers as he leaned in, took the bottle from her hand and placed it back on the bar. Her heart thumped as he positioned his body between her legs, cradled her face in his hands, and pressed a gentle kiss to her lips.

Intoxicated by the taste of the sweet chocolate wine on his lips, she needed more. Taking in a deep breath, she inhaled the masculine scent of him, angled her head and extended the invitation to kiss her again, which he wordlessly accepted.

He slipped his tongue into her mouth, she parted her lips, granting him access, as the rest of her body responded with a thrill of sensation from top to bottom. Energy pulsed from her fingertips to her toes as the kiss deepened and she braved reaching up, touching her fingers to his soft beard.

Tom's hand brushed gently over her breast, sending waves of sensation throughout her body. He wasn't rushed or hurried in his movements. Instead he seemed to be taking his time, learning her body and savoring her kisses just as much as he seemed to enjoy her body's reaction to his caresses.

A tiny moan escaped her lips as his kisses traveled from her mouth to the side of her neck, just below her ear, and she felt his lips quirk up into a smile against her skin.

Then, just as quickly as the kiss had started, it ended. Pulling in a shaky breath, Carson opened her eyes and saw Tom staring down at her with the softest smile on his face. It was the most peaceful she'd seen him since meeting him; granted she'd met him less than a week ago, but something was noticeably different about him.

"Your smile suits you," she said, adjusting her legs on the bar and trying to shake out the pins and needles that stole feeling from one of them. "You should wear it more often."

"Your smile has been stuck in here," he said, pointing to the side of his head, "since the very first time I saw it."

"I guess that means our children would have million dollar smiles then!" Her heart skidded and her belly dropped as Tom laughed at her unrestrained thought. "Holy crap, I don't know where that came from," she said. "It's just that, you know how when you see two people, and you think how cute their kids would be, or..."

Her words were swallowed by Tom's mouth on hers again, more urgent this time, bordering on demanding, and she was on board with all of it. Sleeping leg be damned, she broke the kiss just long enough to hop down from the bar before grabbing his face and taking his mouth with hers.

Blood pounded through her veins as his hands slid beneath the hem of her sweater, pressing into her low back before trailing around her midsection and working their way to her breasts. Her nipples craved his touch when he brushed over her satin bra, and she wished he would take the damn thing off already.

As the intensity of their kisses grew, his hands roamed with increasing freedom, from her breasts down to her ass and back again, stroking and igniting everything he touched in between. She didn't even try to stop the moans that escaped with every new sensation.

He broke his kiss long enough to take hold of both sides of her face. "Are you OK with this? If you want to stop, I'll walk away from you right now."

For the first time she'd arrived in Massachusetts, her body was fully warm, through and through. "Don't you dare."

Tom

CARSON'S BODY FIT PERFECTLY against his, her desire for him as strong as his for her. Tom's head swam with thoughts of things he wanted to do with this woman, kissing being only the starting point.

Her fingers curled into his hair and pulled softly as she leaned into him. He moved slowly, giving her time to tell him whether he could continue. Having already grabbed her ass once, he reached down and took two handfuls, loving the way she moaned against his mouth in response.

She'd allowed him to touch her ass and her breasts through her clothes, but he needed to feel skin again. He needed to touch the warm, smooth skin of her belly as he slid his hands beneath her sweater, the silky fabric of her bra hiding nothing from his touch.

Just as he slipped one finger inside the cup of her bra to tease her already hard nipple, a loud series of knocks at the front door made them both jump.

"Cari? Are you still in there?" Nicole called through the front door, her voice echoing around the wood walls of his store.

"Holy shit!" Carson fumbled with her clothes while he adjusted his rock-hard erection inside his jeans. "What is she doing here?" she whispered. "Shit, she's going to know what we were doing." Running her fingers through her hair, she stood straight and squared her shoulders.

As she turned quickly toward the door, he grabbed hold of her hand and pulled her to a stop. "Hey," he said. "It's fine. You're fine." He touched the side of her cheek gently, and she sucked in a quick breath. "We're both adults. We're allowed to do things that make us feel good. And kissing you made me feel really good, Carson. Better than I've felt in a long time."

She stared at him, and something flickered in her eyes.

Another sharp knock. "Cari?" Nicole yelled through the door. "Tom?"

Carson reached out and took his hands, gave them a reassuring squeeze. "It made me feel really good too," she said. With a sweet smile, she turned and walked to the door. Pulling it open, she said, "Hey, Colie. Sorry it took me a minute to get to the door but I'm here."

Tom couldn't see Nicole's expression, but he heard the humor in her voice. "Oh, no problem," she said. "We just got home, and I didn't see any lights on in the house, so we came over to see if you were still here." There was a slight pause. "And here you are."

He opened the door wider. "Why don't you come in for a minute and get out of the cold," Tom said. The little girl ran directly inside, so Nicole, holding her sleepy little boy, followed her.

Carson squatted down to be at eye level with her niece and said, "Hey, Lucy, how was your Christmas party?"

Lucy held up a tiny doll for Carson to see. "Santa was there, and he gave me this. Well, I know it wasn't really Santa. It was just Mr. Bradshaw dressed up in a Santa suit," she said, and Tom suppressed a laugh. Of course it was Ben Bradshaw playing Santa. From his shock white hair and beard to the big, boisterous voice and round belly, nobody else in town could do the jolly old elf justice. "Real Santa is too busy getting ready for Christmas, but it was really nice of Mr. Bradshaw to do that, wasn't it Mama?"

Nicole rested her hand on her daughter's head. "It sure was, sweetheart."

Not to be forgotten, the little boy squirmed out of his mother's arms, stepped up and thrust a pack of play dough into Carson's face, knocking her slightly off balance. "San—I mean Mr. Bradshaw—got me this. Isn't it awesome?"

"That is the coolest, Drew. You guys are super lucky to have someone as nice as Mr. Bradshaw." Both kids nodded and smiled and then Drew's eyes started to droop as he yawned again and leaned a little heavier against Nicole's leg.

Knowing Carson had to leave, Tom went and closed up her laptop for her.

Carson ran her hand softly over her nephew's cheek then stood to talk to Nicole. "Why don't you all head home. I just need a minute to help clean up the pizza and grab my laptop and stuff. I'll be over in like five minutes."

Tom stood holding the laptop in one hand with her coat draped over his arm. "Here," he said, handing her her belongings. "You head home, and I'll clean up in here." Walking back to the counter, he grabbed the leftover pizza and handed the box to Carson. "Now you can all have cold pizza for breakfast."

Her eyes softened as she smiled at him. "I can't leave you with this mess. Let me stay and help."

Glancing around the shop, he said, "What mess? It's a few paintings and a couple paper plates. I'll throw away the plates and bring the paintings over in the morning."

"Thanks, Tom," Nicole said. To her children, she said, "OK, let's head home and get some sleep. Say goodnight to Mr. Wyatt."

The kids said sleepy good nights as Nicole hoisted Drew up into her arms and Lucy walked beside her out the door. Carson zipped up her coat and paused, waiting for her family to make it to the bottom of the stairs. She looked at Tom as if she wanted to say something, but the words weren't coming.

"Thanks for coming by tonight," he said. "And for the pizza. It was nice having someone to eat dinner with. And, God help me, I might actually be looking forward to your painting party." Her laugh warmed his insides all over again and he knew it would be hard to watch her leave, even if she was only walking across the road. He didn't want to think about what would happen after Christmas when she would be leaving for good.

"Night, Tom," she said. "I had a good time having dinner with you too." She paused with her hand on the door. "I'll see you tomorrow?"

"Absolutely," he said. "You know where to find me. Wait," he said. "You forgot something." He jogged over to the bottle of chocolate port and pushed the cork back into the top. "Here."

"You don't need to give me this," she said.

"Didn't you like it?"

"I loved it."

"Then take it," he said. "That's why I do this job, remember? The things I create make people happy. Bring it home, enjoy it with your sister."

She finally accepted the bottle from his outstretched hand. "Thank you," she said. "For everything." With that, she turned and walked out the door, meeting her waiting family at the bottom of the stairs.

Watching Carson retreat with her family tugged at his heart, as she scooped Lucy off the ground and hugged her close while they walked. The kids chattered the entire way across the road, but he couldn't make out the words, only saw their hands moving as they showed off the toys Ben Bradshaw had given them.

He stood in the doorway and waited for them to go inside Nicole's house. Carson turned around and gave a little wave before she closed the door.

By the time he made it from the store across the yard to his house, his mind and body had calmed down from the unexpected high of kissing his new neighbor. He hadn't planned on kissing her, could never in a million years have predicted that the evening would have taken that turn, but somehow it felt right. Being around her felt right. And it felt good.

After a quick shower, he lay in bed, thinking about the way the night had turned out, wondering how it moved from, "which painting is your favorite?" to talk about his business and the things that mattered to him. He hadn't talked to anyone, aside from Will, about any of that. And some things he'd never even told him.

Being around Carson was like being around an old friend he hadn't seen in years but with whom things easily returned to the way they were within minutes. But that wasn't the truth of it. She was a virtual stranger to him. They had no past, no shared experiences, no memories made together. So, why was it so easy and comfortable being near her?

Carson

NICOLE TUCKED THE KIDS in while Carson stuck the bottle of wine on the counter then hurried down to her own room to get ready for bed. The thought of a shower had crossed her mind but the sooner she retreated into the safety of her room; the sooner she could escape the questions she knew Nicole would have for her.

She had just clicked off the bedside lamp when Nicole knocked gently. "I know you're awake," she said. "I saw the light turn off from under the door."

Sighing, Carson sat up and clicked the lamp back on. "Come on in."

Nicole sat on the edge of the bed, her hands folded in her lap and Carson noticed how eerily similar Nicole's posture was to that of their mother when she was *not angry, just disappointed.*

"Are you seriously going to make me ask?" Nicole said as she looked from the floor to Carson's eyes and then back again. "Because it was pretty obvious there was something going on over there."

"I'm really sorry, Colie," Carson said. "It wasn't supposed to go that way, I swear it." Tears pricked her eyes as she struggled with the knowledge that she had let her sister down again.

"Did you even talk about the paint night?"

"Yes! We made all kinds of lists, and we picked out the painting that he liked the best and we talked about where we could set up all the tables and he let me try a different bottle of wine that we can serve and..." Her enthusiasm petered out and her heart ached for her sister.

"How far did you go with him? Did you have sex?" Nicole's tone was clipped.

Pulling her blanket tighter across her, Carson sat up straighter. "What? Oh, my God, Nicole, we only kissed. I swear it." She made a crisscross sign over her heart. "How could you think I had sex with a guy I've only known for a week?"

Nicole arched one dubious eyebrow in her direction. "Seriously? How many guys have you slept with that you've known less than a week?"

"Lately?" Carson said with a laugh. "None. But that's because I haven't slept with anyone, no matter how long I've known them, in like a year!"

The sisters laughed together the way they used to when they were teenagers. Back then they were children laughing and giggling and talking about boys. Now they were adults, laughing and giggling and talking about grown men. But the vibe was still the same.

"I'm sorry I showed up and ruined it for you," Nicole said when their laughter subsided.

Carson scooted closer. "No! You didn't ruin anything. I was wrong, Colie. I never should have let things go that way. When we kissed, I should have stopped it. I know I'm here to help you and it probably looks like I was only helping myself tonight. But I promise you we made actual progress on the paint and sip. I'm really excited about this thing. I think it could be a big deal for you and for him."

Nodding slowly, but without looking at her, Nicole said, "Is he a good kisser?"

"Yes," Carson admitted. "But I won't do it again. I won't kiss him anymore. It will be strictly business from now on. I know the kids are out of school now and they are my primary responsibility while you're working. As long as you don't mind me putting them to work, we'll get this paint and sip night pulled together and they'll have fun doing it." She ventured to put her arm around Nicole's shoulder and pulled her in for a hug.

"You can really keep your hands off him? After whatever it was you were doing tonight?"

Carson nodded eagerly, hoping to convince her sister, but secretly hoping she and Tom would somehow be able to find time to be together again.

"He must have been a really good kisser," Nicole said. "Because it took you a long time to open the door."

"You really want to talk about this?"

"I haven't had sex with anyone since Ian left." Nicole laughed as she leaned into Carson's hug. "Not so much as one friggin' date. So, yeah, I really want to talk about this."

Carson toyed with the edge of the blanket. "We kissed and then we kissed some more." She looked up and caught Nicole's eye. "He's a really good kisser."

"That makes sense. He's got a nice smile, nice lips."

Tom did have both of those things and Carson found she couldn't wait to kiss him again.

"What else?" Nicole asked.

"He totally felt me up," Carson whispered. "And it was awesome."

With a wistful sigh, Nicole flopped back onto the bed. "How pathetic am I that I'm totally jealous of you right now?"

"It's not pathetic." Carson poked her rib. "But you absolutely should be jealous. It was the best kiss I've ever had."

A frown overtook Nicole's face, but it didn't carry any real disappointment. "I'm sorry we wrecked your night. I almost didn't come over, but I just got kind of nervous with your car over there and no lights on in here."

"You didn't wreck anything," Carson said, though they both knew it was at least a partial lie. "It's actually nice having someone who cares enough to come looking for me. Back in Savannah I don't know that I have anyone who would've done that."

"Oh. That sucks," Nicole said, turning her head to look at Carson. "Still not a ton of friends there?"

She thought about the group of friends she normally hung around with on a Friday night. Most of them were couples, and somewhat younger than she was. She spent time with them solely as a way to keep from always being by herself. And up until that moment, she hadn't given any of them a second thought since she'd been in Hazelton. "I have a group I'm friendly with, but no real *friends* to speak of," she said.

Nicole gave her a sympathetic smile. "Sorry."

"That's OK," she said. "I'm used to it. It's just how it is."

"No boyfriends either? Nobody coming to defend your honor and beat up Tom Wyatt?" Nicole giggled.

There were only a few single guys in her circle, and she had no interest in any of them outside of the casual friendship they shared.

Carson sighed. "Most definitely no boyfriend. I dated a couple guys over the past few months but nothing serious." Not only were they nothing serious, she didn't even bother going on second dates with two of them, and then ended things with the third right after the second date. She hadn't had sex with any of them.

"I guess I'm not the only sister going through a bit of a dry spell then?" Nicole asked and both women started laughing at the ridiculousness of their lives at present.

"Colie, I promise I won't see him again. At least not in a way that involves kissing." Carson crisscrossed her heart again.

Nicole sighed and pushed back up to sitting. "Don't be silly. We're grownups now, Cari. If you want to kiss him, kiss him. Just do me a favor and take a break every now and again and do a little of bit of work on the paint night."

"Promise," Carson said, laying a hand over her heart.

Nicole's lips pulled into a sad smile as she stood from Carson's bed. "Tom doesn't have any friends, does he?"

Tom

NICOLE WAVED AS SHE pulled out of the driveway on her way to work. Tom waved back then climbed the stairs to Whispering Hills, noting how things had changed in such a short time.

Even the store had a different feel to it than it normally had. Now, everywhere he looked he saw Carson; standing among the racks, sitting on the bar, leaning into his arms as they kissed.

The paintings sat on the bar where he left them, waiting to be returned to Carson before he opened for the day. But in much the same way that the store felt different, Tom himself felt different. He'd slept more deeply than he had in recent memory and for the first time in years, he hit snooze on his alarm, not wanting to give up that peaceful feeling.

He should have gathered up the paintings and walked them across the road in the few spare minutes he had but he wanted more than a few minutes with her, so he left them where they sat.

The front door opened and, even though the slow crunch of tires on gravel made clear it wouldn't be Carson walking in, he couldn't deny the disappointment that accompanied his first visitor. "Hey, Alex," Tom called. "How's it going this morning?"

The older man wiped his boots on the black welcome mat as he entered. "Still kickin', Tom, so no complaints from me."

"You here to buy wine or talk business?"

Tom had already contracted with Alex to be the contractor in charge of building the new distillery. Hopefully they'd be able to start construction as soon as the ground thawed in the spring.

Alex looked around the store as he approached the bar. "Maybe both," he said with a smile. "My intention was to talk about the distillery with you, but, no lie, that chocolate port is good stuff."

"You're a man of excellent taste," Tom said.

Taking off his coat and laying it across the bar, Alex tipped his bearded chin in the direction of Carson's paintings. "Finally putting up some new decorations this year, huh?"

With a laugh, Tom said, "I probably should, but no. Those belong to my neighbor. She and her sister are going to be using the store to put on some kind of painting and wine tasting thing and those were the options for the painting."

Brows drawn in, Alex thought about it for a few seconds. "Yeah, I heard of those things. Jenny took Grace to one of those I think." He flipped through the paintings. "What'd you choose?"

"The snowman with the scarf."

Alex nodded. "That looks like something Jenny and Grace'd like." He looked up at Tom. "When is this thing?"

"Friday night, the eighteenth," he said.

With a hmpf, Alex nodded again. "I'll tell 'em."

Tom wasn't entirely sure, but he thought he'd just gotten Carson her first two attendees. Alex's wife and daughter were absolutely the kind of people who would love something like that.

"All right," Alex said. "Let's talk about those plans you had done."

The meeting with Alex helped to reset Tom's equilibrium. He was back in his element, dealing with his store, his plans for its future. For the first time since he met her, his mind was distracted from thoughts of Carson.

Once Alex left, the steady stream of customers kept his mind occupied. By the time he locked the front door that night, he congratulated himself for making it through the day without rushing over to see her every time there was the slightest lull in business.

With his arms full of canvases, he stepped onto Whispering Hills' porch and his line of sight drew directly to the clear sky above. An idea sprang to life in his mind as he looked at the sparkling stars overhead. Rather than walk across to return the paintings, he hustled up to his house, suddenly a man with a plan.

B Y THE TIME HE made it back to Carson's door, the back seat of his truck cab had been filled with blankets and hats and scarves and his cold weather sleeping bags.

"Auntie, it's Mr. Tom," Drew yelled when Nicole opened the front door. "He's here to see you!"

Nicole rolled her eyes at her son's assessment of his intentions and opened the door wider so Tom could enter. "Oh, thank you," she said accepting the canvases from him. "I forgot we were supposed to go pick those up from you today. Thanks for bringing them back." He breathed in the warm scent of homemade cookies.

"No problem," he said. "I was in the neighborhood." It was a lame joke, but Nicole was polite enough to laugh.

"Hey, Tom," Carson said, coming into the room from down the hall. "What are you—" She looked at the stack of paintings in Nicole's arms and her eyes went wide "Oh no. I'm sorry I never showed up for those. The kids and I were busy making Christmas decorations and stuff, and I never came by to get them."

"It's all good," he said.

Nicole looked at her kids, playing a board game on the table. "OK, you two," she said, walking away from Tom and Carson. "Time to wrap it up and call it a night. It's getting late."

"Good night," Lucy and Drew said to them as they trudged out of the living room.

"So," Tom said, once he and Carson were alone. "I, uh, I was wondering if you were busy now or if you wanted to come see something really cool with me." Why was he so awkward around her? He had a case of nerves like he was a teenager trying to ask a pretty girl to the school dance.

To his astonishment, she immediately said, "Sure. What is it?"

"It's kind of a surprise, if that's OK?" She was prettier than any girl he'd ever asked out and when she smiled at him, the worry that he was entirely out of his league swamped him. Reminding himself that he wasn't a seventeen-year-old kid anymore, he said, "I think you'll like it though."

"I'll go tell Nicole I'm leaving and grab my coat."

"**H**OW FAR AWAY ARE we going?" Carson asked as they rumbled down Vineyard Hill Road toward the big open field at the edge of town.

"Only about ten minutes or so."

"Can I be DJ while we drive?"

"Of course."

She fiddled with the radio, trying to find a station she liked though not having much luck. After a minute she clicked it off and pulled out her phone. Starting up her Christmas playlist, she said, "I hope you like Mariah Carey."

He didn't. "Yeah, she's great. This is one of my favorite Christmas songs."

Beside him, Carson laughed. "Wow, you are a terrible liar." She scrolled through her phone and changed the song. "How about Bing Crosby? Everybody loves Bing, right?"

"What's not to love? If he's good enough for Great Grandma, he's good enough for me."

Carson laughed again, the sound filling the small space. "Did you just call me old?"

Tom was drawn into her good mood. "Hell no. Just saying your taste in music is... eclectic." He reached over and squeezed her hand. "It's a compliment, I swear."

Once she stopped laughing, Carson said, "Where are we going, anyway? You never did tell me." Bing Crosby finished singing "White Christmas" and a bluegrass version of "O Christmas Tree" started.

"Now that's a mood switch," he said. "But I have to admit I kind of like this one." He pulled the truck to a stop at the end of the gravel road. "And we're going right here," he said, shutting off the ignition.

Carson looked around. "There's nothing here."

"You're looking in the wrong direction," he said, leaning forward and angling his head to see the sky through the front windshield.

She let out a little gasp as she followed his lead. "Can we get out and look from outside?"

"I was hoping you might say that." He opened his door and stepped down. While she got down and came around to his side, he opened the back door of the cab and grabbed out the sleeping bags and a couple of heavy blankets. "Here," he said, handing her a fluffy scarf. "You might want to wear this to keep your face and your neck warm."

Looking past him into the truck, she said, "Did you bring all those blankets so I wouldn't be cold?"

Smiling back at her, he said, "There's no way you won't be cold, but I was hoping these would keep you less cold." He hoisted the sleeping bags into the bed of the truck then tossed a couple blankets on top of them. Cold from the aluminum truck bed seeped through his jeans as he knelt to unzip one of the sleeping bags and set it up for them to lie on.

"Come on up," he said, extending his hand to help Carson into the bed.

Tom unrolled the second sleeping bag, spread it on top of the other one. "I know it's not the most comfortable place to stargaze, but I figured it was better than lying on the ground," he said as they adjusted themselves under the heavy blankets.

Above them, the inky sky had been spattered with white stars as far as they could see. Their line of sight was limited by the towering evergreens surrounding the field but even with those giant sentinels standing guard over them, the sky still felt endless.

Carson had pulled her hood up and wrapped the scarf around her neck and cheeks, the rest of her body tucked beneath a blanket. Her eyes darted from place to place before she settled on the section of sky to their right. "Oh, man," she said through the knitted scarf. "This is amazing."

"Not too cold?" Tom asked.

"Oh, no, I'm pretty well frozen to the bone," she said with a laugh. "But what else is new?"

"We can leave whenever you want," he said, hoping he hadn't ruined any chance of spending more time with her.

"OK," she said. "But not yet." She wriggled closer and snuggled against his side. Extending his arm, he offered his bicep as a makeshift pillow. As she stared into the sky, she said, "Do you know anything about constellations? I learned a few of them when I was a kid, but I don't remember much."

"I know a little bit," Tom said. "Not enough to navigate a ship over the ocean or anything, but I can find the North Star."

"I used to lie out in the grass in my front yard when I was a little girl," she said. "There wasn't really much light pollution, and I could see so many stars, but I never knew what they were. Only that they were pretty." She pressed her body closer to his. "Which one is the North Star?"

With his free hand he pointed up. "That's easy," he said. "See the Big Dipper right there?"

Following the line from his finger toward the sky, she nodded. "Yeah, there it is!"

"OK, look at the star on the top right of the cup of the dipper."

"Got it."

"Good," he said. "Now, just follow it straight from there until the line meets the tail of the Little Dipper."

"Oh, I found it."

"That's it. That really bright star at the tail of the Little Dipper is what you're looking for. That's Polaris. It's the North Star."

"Oh my gosh, really? That was so easy! What other ones do you know?" She lifted her head and turned to look at him, only her bright eyes visible between her hood and her scarf.

"That's as much as I know. My granddad taught me how to find Polaris so I would always know which way was north."

"So, maybe you could navigate a ship on the ocean," she said. The corners of her eyes crinkled, hinting at the smile hiding beneath the scarf.

"Hey, if the navigation system broke and every other person in the crew fell overboard, I'm your guy."

Soft laughter shook her body and Tom settled in with the peaceful feeling. Lying next to her, covered in blankets, looking at constellations and making goofy small talk in the back of his truck felt good. It was easy and comfortable.

Instead of resting her head against his arm again, she laid it down on his chest. He wrapped his arm around her and held her, sinking into the warmth of the moment.

"Do you ever do this in the summer when it doesn't feel like you're in the Arctic?" she asked.

"No, not too often. I get up super early to work in the vineyard and it stays light pretty late. So I'm usually either already sleeping or getting ready for bed when the sky is this dark."

"It's so beautiful here," she said, her body relaxing against him. "Thank you for doing this." Turning her face to his, she tugged the scarf from her chin and reached up to place a soft kiss on his lips.

"Thanks for indulging me and being a good sport about hanging out in the back of a pickup truck with me in twenty-degree weather," he said.

"Thanks for taking me."

If they ever made it past the making out stage, he'd be more than willing to take her anytime, anywhere, and any way she wanted. "You're welcome."

Time passed in the silence, each of them looking at the sky above until her body shivered against his. She curled herself against him, instinctively making herself smaller to conserve body heat. "You ready to go home?" he asked.

"Yes and no," she said, though her teeth chattered slightly. "I'm so cold but I really love being out here like this." She was quiet for a second. "I like being around you. And I like that you didn't try to get me naked in the back of your truck on a night this cold."

His whole body shook with laughter. "You're welcome. I guess," he said. "Though I'm not sure what to make of that."

When she laughed too the spell of the evening dissolved, but left in its place was the deep desire to spend more time with Carson before she went back home.

Carson

IN THE MIDDLE OF her second full week in Hazelton, Carson focused solely on Lucy and Drew while Nicole worked. At night while they slept and Nicole worked on new art for her shop, Carson kept busy by setting up an online event, designing flyers, and ordering supplies.

Once the kids woke up, she made them pancakes for breakfast and they stayed in their pajamas watching Christmas movies until lunch time. Once they finished their own sandwiches, they would pack up another one with some chips and a bottle of water, and Carson would drive them all down to Happenstance to drop off Nicole's lunch.

Carson had never spent any real time with her niece and nephew and found that, aside from their inability to stay quiet during movies, they were interesting people to be around, as young as they were.

Lucy was incredibly curious about Carson and asked endless questions about what Nicole was like growing up. Lucy was excited to learn that she had strikingly similar passions to her mother around the same age.

Drew loved animals with the entirety of his being. His section of the bookshelf was stuffed end-to-end with stories about dogs and cats and snakes and every other manner of creature you could imagine. Because they were unable to have a dog in a rental house, Drew made up for it by being the world's foremost collector of stuffed animals.

With only two weeks until the big event, the pressure had begun to build. Between working her own job remotely, taking care of the kids, and creating lists and buying supplies, she hardly had any time to spend with Tom. Though, as she did most days, she sat near the picture window at the front of the house on the off chance she might catch a glimpse of him working outside.

On Wednesday, the kids slept in, so Carson took advantage of the early morning hours before sunrise catching up on work emails, making sure her events in Savannah were still on track. There was a small snag with one of the caterers, but her co-worker Vanessa managed to find another one who had a last-minute cancellation, so the crisis had been averted before Carson had to make any panicked phone calls.

Able to focus on the present, she found a print shop two towns over and sent over the file for them to print out a hundred flyers. In a town as small as Hazelton, one hundred might have been a tad excessive but Carson had high hopes for this event, and she knew not all of the flyers would turn into attendees.

Just as she was about to shut her laptop and get a refill on her coffee, an email from Anderson hit her inbox. Whatever her boss wanted at five-thirty in the morning with a subject line of OPEN AT ONCE couldn't be good. She definitely needed that second cup of coffee to deal with him and whatever 'emergency' had caused the all caps subject line.

Before she could get her coffee back to her laptop, Lucy and Drew padded out of the bedroom in need of food. Anderson would have to wait.

"What do you say? You two want to go pick up the flyers from the print shop? Then we can drive around to some of the shops in town and see if people will let us hang them up."

As they bundled up and headed out to Carson's car, she looked up the road to see Tom carrying wood across his front yard. She waved to him and was delighted when he smiled in return, unable to wave because of the firewood stacked across his forearms.

That smile did things to her. Good things. Perhaps dangerous things.

Because she'd be leaving to go back to Savannah at the beginning of the year, it would be in her best interest to keep a little distance from him. Kissing him had been one thing. A momentary lapse in judgment brought on by a mingling of desire and loneliness. It had caused her to make an irrational decision.

But lying with him under blankets to stare at the stars? That was a one hundred percent conscious choice. And it was the nicest, coziest, safest and most secure she'd felt in a man's arms. Ever. If she could hold onto those feelings while keeping her heart safely hidden away, she was set to have the best Christmas season of her entire adult life.

Once the kids were buckled into their car seats and Carson's heart was officially fluttering, the trio set off to get some work done.

E ACH WITH THEIR OWN stack of flyers and a roll of clear tape, Carson walked with the children into several of the businesses they found on their drive back to Hazelton. "I wish the ice cream stand was open," Lucy said as it flashed by the window as they drove.

"Me too," added Drew.

Carson peeked into mirror to catch their eyes. "Are you hungry again already?" she teased.

"Yeah," they said in unison.

"I'm still growing," Drew said. "So I need to eat lots of food."

"Uh huh," Lucy said. "Me too."

"Say no more," said Carson. "I know the perfect place." She turned onto the main road through town and headed toward The Daily Grind.

"Carson!" Delores called as they entered the coffee shop. "Welcome back." She looked down at the kids. "And you brought friends with you."

"We're working," Drew said to Delores. "So now we're hungry again."

Delores, as well as a few of the surrounding patrons, laughed good-naturedly. "Well, why don't you grab a seat and I'll bring you over some hot chocolate. How's that sound?"

Lucky enough to find an open booth, Lucy and Drew ran over and slid into one side while Carson sat across from them. Delores returned with two hot chocolates loaded with whipped cream, and one coffee. "What can I get for you this morning?" she asked.

The kids looked at Carson expectantly.

"It doesn't matter to me what you get." That was the beauty of being the aunt and not the mom; she could say things like that and truthfully mean it.

While the kids devoured their second breakfast of waffles with strawberry sauce and whipped cream, Carson spent a few minutes talking with her new friend, telling her about the paint and sip. "Would you mind if we hung up a flyer somewhere to try and drum up a few people?"

"I don't see why not," Delores said, taking a flyer from the stack by Drew's arm. She read it over and said, "Honestly, this looks like a lot of fun."

"You should come to it," Lucy said.

"Oh, I don't know. I'm not very artistic."

"That's OK. You don't have to be. My mom's a really good teacher." Delores and Carson both smiled at Lucy, who was turning out to be a natural salesperson.

"How about this?" Delores said. "I'll take a couple of these, and I'll hang one up and I'll give out a few to some other people I think might be interested in this kind of thing." She looked at Carson. "It's a busy time of year but I think folks could probably use a no-pressure distraction like this."

She looked one more time at the flyer before taking a step away from the table. With her brows furrowed, Delores looked back, Catching Carson's eye. "Whispering Hills?" she said. "You're having this inside Tom Wyatt's store?"

Carson looked at Lucy and Drew then back to Delores. "Yeah," she said, suddenly unsure of her decision to have him host the event. "Why? Is that weird?" Her stomach lurched thinking the local woman knew more about Tom than she did and that she was about to hear something she probably didn't want to know about him.

Delores shook her head. "Oh, no," she said. "Not weird, just un-expected. He usually just keeps to himself up there and really likes his peace and quiet. I can't believe you got him to agree to something like this. In fact," she continued, "My book club does a lot of business with Tom. I mean, what's a book club without a nice bottle of red wine, right?"

Delores's words and her laughter eased the tightness in Carson's chest. "Hmm," she said, starting down at the flyer in her hand. "You know, there might be more than a few people interested in this."

Carson paid the check, and they took the rest of their flyers out into the cold. She looked up the street and gave some thought to each of the storefronts she saw. "Maybe we could see if some of those businesses would let us hang up a flyer or two?"

The three of them trundled from store to store speaking with cashiers and managers and small business owners, most of whom were happy to hang the flyers. "Anything to help other local businesses," said the owner of the local movie theater. "What helps one, helps all."

Eventually they had canvassed the entire length of the road, both sides, and they pulled open the door to Happenstance. The kids loved being able to enter their mom's store and get her permission to hang up flyers, the same way they had with all the other business owners they'd just met.

"It's going to be a fun night with friends painting a fun snowman picture. I'll bet your customers would love to attend," Lucy said, an event planner in the making.

"That sounds quite lovely," Nicole replied in a business-like tone. "I would love it if you would hang up a few flyers around my store and maybe leave me a stack of them to give to people who come in?"

"WE HAVE DONE AMAZING work today, you two," Carson said as they sat around their kitchen table eating lunch later that afternoon. "I think the rest of today is for taking a hard-earned rest."

"Can we go outside and make a snow fort?" Drew asked. "Lucy said she wanted to make one too."

"Sure," Carson said, then asked, "Do either of you know how to make a snow fort?"

Both children shook their heads. "Daddy said he would help us, but he hasn't been here since it snowed," Lucy said.

Carson bit back the unkind words that jumped to the tip of her tongue at the mention of Nicole's cheating, jerk of an ex-husband, instead doing a quick search on her phone: *how to build a snow fort.* The results ranged from a scooped-out mound of snow to a giant snow room with a slide.

Surely, they could cobble together a decent snow fort somewhere in between. "We've totally got this." She nodded at their half-eaten sandwiches. "Eat up. We're going to need all the energy we can get for this project."

While the kids went to put on their snow clothes, Carson threw on a coat, hat, and heavy ski gloves and headed out to the garage. "Meet me in the front yard when you're ready," she called out to them as she went to find something to use to make snow bricks.

Tom

Tom hadn't stopped thinking about Carson since he dropped her off at Nicole's place a few days back. When she kissed him, his heart skipped a beat and he'd wished they'd been someplace warmer so they could have kissed a little longer.

Having a woman freeze into an icicle in your arms was no way start a relationship. Only they weren't truly starting a relationship. She'd only be around for a few more weeks. Maybe it would be for the best if he thought about it as an affair, or a whirlwind fling. It sounded a little melodramatic, but it was the truth of the situation.

Giggles and shouts from outside drew his attention away from the wine racks he was dusting. He went outside and stood on the store's front porch, spending a few minutes watching her trying to make a snow fort with her niece and nephew using brightly colored beach pails. The three of them stood inside a circle of snow piles and each time they tried to add a second layer everything collapsed, sending the children into fits of laughter.

Behind them, a string of lights had been abandoned on one of the bushes, obviously not as fun a pursuit as the snow fort.

His heart twinged when Carson turned around in the circle trying to figure out what to do next and her eyes locked onto his. Time limits be damned. He needed to be near her, to spend time with her.

Walking down the steps, he yelled over, "Lady Guinevere! May I offer my assistance in your noble pursuit?"

Lucy and Drew giggled again. "Why did he call you Lady Guinevere, Auntie?" Lucy asked.

"That's not your name," Drew said as he busted up laughing.

Tom grabbed a shovel and carried it across to the fledgling snow fort. "OK, you two," he said to the kids. "I'm going to pile up some snow around your circle. I need you to use your hands and shape it into a wall, like this." He squatted down and patted mounds of snow into the pile, forming the beginning of a solid wall, then helped each of them in turn so they knew what to do. "Can you do that?"

They nodded and sat back on their heels waiting for each scoop of snow he dumped for them. Once he'd given them enough snow to keep them busy for at least three minutes he went over and stood beside Carson. Shoving his hands into the pockets of his flannel jacket, he said, "Haven't seen you much this week."

She averted her eyes to watch the kids. "Sorry. Between taking care of the kids and issues with my job back home, I've been really busy. And with the painting night coming up, we've had a lot to do, so..."

"What's going on with your job?" he asked.

Carson rolled her eyes. "Everybody wants everything. They don't even understand what it is they're asking for, but they all want it. And they want it *right now*." She shrugged one shoulder. "I have an email from my boss that came in before breakfast this morning and I haven't brought myself to open yet."

"Oh," he said. "Maybe it's good news?"

At that, she laughed. "When Anderson Spencer sends an email with an all-caps subject of 'Open at Once,' it's never good news." She laughed again but it was the sound of someone who wasn't entirely comfortable with the joke she was telling. Turning her back to Lucy and Drew, she lowered her voice and said, "For all I know, there are three more waiting for me and the last one is probably telling me I don't have a job anymore."

"Jeez, Carson, that's kind of a huge thing. Maybe you ought to check what he wants." Having an overbearing boss was something Tom could relate to. It was working for a company full of those types of people that drove him to the edge of breakdown and what eventually landed him as the sole proprietor of Whispering Hills Winery.

"Yeah, I will," she said. "But not until later tonight when I have time to think about how to respond. And maybe I'll have a small glass of the chocolate port to help me get the words just right." She sighed. "I even left my phone inside just so I didn't see any of the notifications come through."

Everybody dealt with stress in their own way, so he didn't push her to keep talking. Instead he wondered if she'd be up for a distraction. "Who's ready to take a break from all this work?" he said.

"We did work for Mama's painting class today," Drew said as he patted another handful of snow into place, his entire body swaying with the effort. "This is our resting."

Tom smiled down at the kid. "Rest is important," he said. "You know what else is important?"

Both kids looked at him expectantly, as did Carson, and he swallowed down the urge to grab her face and kiss her senseless. "Candy."

Drew was the first to jump to his feet. "I like candy!"

Lucy was a little slower to join the fun. "Mama doesn't like us to eat too much candy," she said.

"How about if you make it yourself?" Three sets of eyes searched his. He said to Carson, "Give me five minutes and then bring them over to my place, if that's OK with you."

"What are you planning?" she said as he turned toward home.

"I told you—candy."

Back in the house, after rooting through his cabinets, he pulled out a couple cookie pans, two glass measuring cups, a candy thermometer, and a pack of wooden lollipop sticks that his sister's kids left behind when they came for a visit last winter.

It was his sister who taught him how to make candy from maple syrup and he was ready to share his favorite sweet with his new friends. Grabbing the fresh maple syrup from the refrigerator, he slid it across the counter next to the other supplies.

Five minutes later, Carson, Lucy, and Drew showed up at his front door. Before they could take their coats off, he handed the kids each a cookie sheet and said, "Go out into the yard and fill these up with nice fresh, clean snow. There's probably a lot of clean snow around the side of the house toward the back. It has to be clean because this is where we're making our candy. Can you handle it?"

They nodded and took off to find the cleanest snow they could. Carson tried to walk out the door behind them, but Tom reached out and took hold of her elbow. "Carson, wait."

Her eyes moved from his hand on her arm up to his face, and before he knew what was happening, she threw her arms around his neck and pulled him in for a deep kiss, her tongue licking and toying with his, her bright red nose leaving little cold spots on his face.

Following her lead, he didn't hold back, kissing her just as hard as she was kissing him. Their tongues tangled, mirroring the way his hands worked through the thick brown mane of her hair. Stepping her backward, he pushed her against the wall, parting her legs with his thigh. Moans and grunts met his ears as she ground herself against his leg.

Long before he wanted to stop, little voices approached the outside of the house.

"Damn," he said as he and Carson untangled themselves. She quickly adjusted her clothes and finger brushed her hair while Tom adjusted himself through his jeans. "I thought they'd be gone longer," he said with a laugh.

She giggled and he captured it with one more stolen kiss before she pushed him back with a playful shove just as the door flew open.

"Mr. Tom, we got the snow," Drew called as they stomped through his hallway toward the kitchen where he should have been heating the maple syrup—instead of mauling their aunt against a wall—while they were running their errand.

He stood by his decision.

He and Carson followed the kids to the kitchen and helped them out of their snow gear. Carson took the wet coats and gloves and boots and left them on the waterproof mat by the front door while Tom set a small saucepan on the stove and filled it with maple syrup from one of the local sugarhouses.

"What is that?" Drew said from his seat on the counter between the stove and the sink.

"It's maple syrup," Tom said. "Like you'd put on pancakes."

"I like pancakes," Drew said. "And I like to put butter and syrup on them too."

Carson and Lucy put the snow trays into the freezer then sat at the kitchen table waiting for Tom to finish heating the syrup. Once it reached the right temperature, he poured it into a couple glass measuring cups. "We've got to give these a few minutes to cool," he said, suppressing a smile as he felt a certain familiarity with the need to cool down.

"OK," he said to Carson. "Want to grab the snow trays?" He handed the kids a few wooden sticks and then he and Carson each helped them pour lines of thick, sticky syrup into the snow. The look on the kids' faces as they rolled up the syrup into their own lollipops was fantastic.

Large eyes, open mouths and then giggles of pure kid joy. He definitely needed to tell Will he was right about kids being kind of fun. Still no interest in kids of his own but *fun uncle* could be a cool title.

"Can I eat it yet?" Drew asked as he licked the maple sugar stickiness from his fingers.

"No, you have to wait until Mama gets home and says it's OK," Lucy said.

"Bummer." Drew's shoulders slumped.

"Here," Carson said, scraping a few drops of syrup to set in the cold snow. "This piece won't be too big. You can test it and make sure it's good."

"Can I do that too?" Lucy asked and Tom obliged by scraping the glass cup for her.

As the kids savored their sweets, Carson looked at the clock. "OK, you two, let's help Mr. Tom clean up. Mama's going to be home in about five minutes."

It felt as if they'd only just gotten there; he didn't want them to leave quite yet. At least, he didn't want Carson to leave. He'd waited days to see her, and he hoped to get a little more time with her.

The kids carried the spoons and glass cups to the sink while Tom set the pot and candy thermometer to soak. Carson carried the trays with the rapidly melting snow and dumped them into the sink as well. The three of them put their coats back on and Tom pulled Carson aside as the kids held onto their maple candies and headed toward the door. "Any chance you can come back tonight?"

"I'm not sure. I think we're supposed to go to a Christmas party at one of Nicole's friends' houses tonight."

"No chance you can skip? I was thinking maybe we could make some dinner, talk about what else needs to be done for your paint night." He knew he was asking her to put him before her family but kissing her again had reignited the fire in his belly and he couldn't think of a better way to burn.

She worried her lip as she considered his offer. "It's not like she really cares, I don't think. It's just—I don't know. Maybe this isn't a good idea," she whispered so the kids wouldn't overhear. "I'm only here for a couple more weeks."

There wasn't much to say in response to that. She was being upfront and honest with him, and she was right. Maybe it wasn't a good idea. Maybe it would be best if they stayed away from each other, rather than get hooked any deeper by this woman. But Tom hadn't been interested in anyone since Heather left. Even if it was only for a couple more weeks, the need to be near Carson was as strong as anything he'd felt in a long time.

Lucy yelled, "Mama's home," and as she and Drew took off out the door, Carson followed directly behind them. "Thank you, Mr. Tom," Lucy called over her shoulder.

"Thank you," Drew echoed.

"Welcome!" Then to Carson, "If you change your mind, you know where to find me."

She smiled back before she followed the kids across the yard.

He reminded himself that he didn't know her well enough to be as disappointed as he was when she didn't accept his invitation to come back. Yet, there he was, disappointed as all hell.

Carson

"Y OU BROUGHT THE KIDS into his house with you?" Nicole said as she stirred the spaghetti pot with an unnecessary amount of force then dropped the spoon onto the counter with a thump.

"Relax, nothing happened," Carson said from her seat at the kitchen table. "Seriously. He came over to help us with our snow fort, which is *awesome*, by the way, and invited us over to make maple candy. Which we did. Then you came home. Beginning and end of story."

Nicole eyed her suspiciously. "Nothing happened?"

Carson made a crisscross over her heart. Then her conscience forced her to blurt out, "Just one kiss! But the kids were outside getting snow!" She clamped her hands over her mouth and waited for Nicole to start in on her about being a responsible aunt and how she needed to make better decisions.

Instead, Nicole started to laugh. "He kissed you or you kissed him?" she finally said.

In a quiet voice, Carson said, "I kissed him." She felt the need to explain but the right words wouldn't come. She was quiet while she thought of the best way to describe what was happening. "I couldn't help myself. I've been thinking about him all week and when I saw him, I was completely undone. But I promise it was only one kiss and the kids were outside getting snow, so they didn't see anything."

Nicole leaned against the counter, staring down at Carson. "What is it about him that gets to you?"

"I don't know how to answer that," she said, honestly. "Obviously I think he's good looking but there's something about his face that I can't stop looking at, you know? I always want to touch him and every time I look at his hands, I get antsy because I want to know what they feel like on me."

"So, it's purely physical?"

Carson didn't have to think about that at all. "It's absolutely physical," she said. "Almost primal. I don't know if it's a pheromone thing or what. Is that even a real thing or did I just make that up?"

Nicole laughed. "I wouldn't know."

"But it's like when I'm around him I feel different. A little spark of something lights up when he looks at me." She pointed to a spot directly above her belly button. "And I like it. It's not something any other guy has ever done."

"You're sure it has nothing to do with how good a kisser he is?"

"Oh, it absolutely has something to do with that, but not all of it," Carson said with a laugh. "I'd be lying if I said it didn't." She looked up at Nicole. "You must know what I'm talking about, that feeling of lust and longing and need all wrapped up in sweetness and sugar. You were married for five years."

Nicole shut off the burner and placed a colander in the sink. Carson figured her sister wasn't going to respond but then noticed the telltale shudder of crying. She jumped up and pulled Nicole into a tight hug, letting her cry while the spaghetti waited in the pot.

"I've never felt that," Nicole squeaked out between sobs. "Not ever. Not even when we were dating."

"What's wrong with Mama?" Lucy's voice broke into the scene as she entered the kitchen.

"She's just a little bit sad right now, and crying makes her feel better," Carson said over Nicole's shoulder as she tried to wipe her own eyes which had started to water too. "Doesn't crying help you feel better sometimes?"

Lucy nodded and ran over to her mother. "It's OK to cry, Mama. I cry sometimes too." She wrapped her arms around Nicole's waist and the three of them stood there crying together in one big tangle of arms and tears.

"ARE YOU SURE YOU don't want to come to Sherry's with us? You are more than welcome. Sherry invited you, so it's not like you'd be crashing."

"I think I'm going to skip, if it's all the same to you," Carson said. "I've been so busy working on the paint and sip the last few days that I've been neglecting my actual job." She had finally opened the succession of emails from Anderson and, although she hadn't been fired, the threat was there and would become her reality if she didn't get her butt back in gear and start picking up whatever slack she could. "I think I ought to put a little extra work in tonight while the house is quiet. Thank Sherry for the invitation and maybe next year, if I'm in town, I'll take her up on it."

"OK," Nicole said. "I hate that you have to stay home on a Friday night to do work while we're out having fun at a Christmas party."

"Don't worry about me," Carson said. "Aside from the Christmas part, this is my life every Friday night."

Nicole was stunning in a red velvet wrap dress with strappy heels. Carson had helped her work her hair into a beautiful reverse French braid and it tied the whole look together. "You look amazing," Carson said as Nicole pulled on her coat.

"Me too?" said Drew who was dressed in black corduroys and a red sweater with an embroidered train on the front.

"Absolutely," Carson replied, leaning down to kiss the top of his head. "And let's not forget Miss Lucy, who will be the belle of the ball tonight," she said, pulling her niece in for a gentle hug so as not to mess up her stylishly messy bun. Lucy twirled, flaring out the skirt of her buffalo plaid dress.

Dressed in their Christmas finery, Nicole and the kids disappeared out the door and Carson's shoulders relaxed as she readied herself to get some work done. But first she needed some tea, so she threw a cup of water in the microwave. She also needed to get out of the jeans she was wearing, so while the water heated, she retreated to her room to throw on some comfy clothes.

When she had packed to go to Massachusetts, choosing her wardrobe had been easy; a couple pairs of leggings, some jeans and sweaters, a Christmas dress, and all the pajamas she could fit. Some girls were into shoes, others makeup, but Carson's weakness had always been pajamas.

"What man is going to want to see you always wearing fuzzy pants and baggy tops with those ridiculous slippers?" her mother used to ask her.

That was an easy question to answer. The guy that loved the way she looked and felt in fuzzy pants, a baggy top, and ridiculous slippers would be the one worth keeping. She just hadn't found him yet.

With her pajamas on and maple ginger tea steeping on the table beside her, she pulled her hair into a quick ponytail and settled into the couch with a blanket and her laptop. Her work email took a half hour to get through.

Most of her coworkers knew she was visiting family for the holidays, but that she would still be checking emails and working remotely. She sent off a few emails to clients, ensuring that details were being taken care of to their satisfaction.

One of the musical acts scheduled to perform at a party next weekend had to cancel when their guitar player broke her arm and leg in a motorcycle accident. She'd make a full recovery, but not in time for Yoshida Industries annual winter gala. It took another fifteen minutes of emails to compile a list of potential replacements.

After choosing her words carefully, she hit send on her response to Anderson's latest complaint about her work and her perceived *"lack of work ethic"* since she *"abandoned"* her clients *"in favor of babysitting"* her family.

Her brain and her bruised ego wanted to fire off an "I quit" email, composed of an expletive-laden list of all the ways in which Anderson could fuck right off. Her professional side won out and replaced all the things she wanted to say with all the things she knew she had to say.

The silence of the house was a welcome companion. She loved her sister and the kids to no end, but she didn't notice how much she appreciated a little quiet time until she had it.

Needing to get her head out of the angry cloud of work, she closed her laptop and laid the blanket to the side so she could get a refill on her tea before she turned on the television. It turned out she only appreciated total silence in small doses.

A noise from outside froze her in place. Nicole's house was in the middle of nowhere, which meant nobody should be coming to the house, but there was most certainly someone, or something, in the front yard. She glanced at the clock—it was far too early for Nicole to be coming home, and she never heard the car pull up the gravel road.

With her heart pounding in her ears, she quickly scanned the room, searching for anything she could use as a weapon if the need arose, but the only thing she found was a tiny wooden hammer from the kids' construction playset. *Any port in a storm*, she thought, and grabbed the miniature tool.

Not wanting to be seen, she inched along the wall and stopped at the edge of the picture window before pulling the corner of the curtain aside and peeking through the glass to find... nothing. There was nobody in the front yard; no animal, no human, no nothing.

She blew out a sigh and and cursed her over active imagination as she tossed the hammer back onto the tool bench on her way to the kitchen. Her fingers trembled slightly as she refilled her mug and closed it in the microwave.

As she stepped foot in the living room, she heard it again. That was not her imagination. There was definitely something going on outside. In her panic, she found herself wondering if Tom was looking out his window by any chance, so she wouldn't have to face whatever, or whoever, it was, by herself.

Scurrying along the wall again, she snuck up to the window but crouched down to the floor so she could see the whole yard from her defensive position. She closed her eyes and listened to see if she could figure out what was happening on the other side of the glass. It sounded like a clicking noise. It had no rhythm or any discernible pattern, but it was definitely clicking.

Taking a deep breath, she pushed up onto her toes, grabbed onto the windowsill and slowly raised her head. A pair of eyes stared back at her, and Carson screamed, fell backward onto her still sore hip, arms flailing, and landed flat on her back, feet in the air.

There was something about those eyes. Her brain screamed *Run! Panic!* But her heart butted in, *Not a stranger. Deep breath. You know him.*

Her heart thundered in her rib cage, and she struggled to get back to her feet. Rapid pounding on the front door didn't help. "Carson? I didn't mean to scare you! It's me, Tom!"

The microwave beeped from the kitchen. Tom knocked on the door again. "Are you OK?" he yelled. "Please open the door!"

Carson didn't know what to do first, so she pulled in a couple deep gulps of air to steady her nerves. Then she went and stood with her shoulder braced against the door but didn't open it. "Tom?"

"Yeah, it's me."

"What are you doing out there? Why were you hiding in the bushes looking in the window?" Suddenly she was creeped out beyond measure and thought about running to grab her phone in case she needed to call her sister. Or the police.

He laughed and said, "I wasn't hiding in the bushes, Carson. If you open the door for a second and look out, I'll show you what I was doing."

"Open the door, huh? Isn't that what a serial killer would say?" Maybe she'd been watching too many true crime dramas. Or... maybe all those shows *weren't* a time suck and were about to save her life.

He laughed again. "Carson, if I was a serial killer, wouldn't I have killed you the other day? You know, instead of pushing you against the wall and letting you grind on my leg?"

She whipped the door open. "Ssshhhh! You can't just say that out loud!"

His grin was wicked. "You do know we're the only ones on the street, right? Nobody heard that except you."

He had a point, but still. She stood with one foot behind the door, ready to shut it in his face if she needed to. "Why are you here? And why were you were sneaking around the bushes?"

Instead of saying anything, he stepped down off the porch and held out his hand for her to follow. The night air nipped at the skin of her cheeks, and after checking to make sure the front door was unlocked, she grabbed a scarf, stepped into a pair of snow boots, and followed him out the door.

Tom

H E HADN'T MEANT TO scare her. It was supposed to be a surprise, but then she scared the shit out of him by popping up in the window and staring out at him with those wide eyes. His own shout of surprise was almost as loud as her scream from inside the house and he fell on his ass into the snow.

Now as she stood beside him in the cutest pajamas he'd ever seen, trusting him not to be a serial killer, he told her to close her eyes. It was cold as hell outside, and he assumed she'd have put on a coat, but she made the interesting choice of a scarf and boots instead.

"Keep them closed," he said as he walked over and plugged the extension cord into the outlet at the corner of the garage. The brightly colored string lights he'd spent the past half hour hanging up illuminated the whole front of the house. "No peeking."

Through chattering teeth, with her hands over her eyes she said, "I'm not p-peeking, I promise."

Standing beside her, he wrapped his arm around her shoulders to warm her up, then touched his hand to her frozen fingers. "OK," he said. "Open them."

She gasped, held one hand to her heart and the other to her lips. "Tom," she whispered, taking in the sight of the lights. "It looks beautiful. Thank you so much for doing this." She stepped closer to the bushes. "Are these the lights I bought that first day we met?"

"Yeah, I noticed you and the kids made an attempt to hang them up the other day but didn't get very far. And I thought you guys were all gone tonight, and I'd sneak over and hang them up to surprise you when you got home. I had no idea you didn't go with them." He started to laugh again. "You really scared the hell out of me when you popped up in that window."

Exactly the way she'd done at Nicole's store, Carson jumped up and threw herself into his arms. "Thank you, thank you, thank you," she said into his neck, her cold cheeks chilling him.

Unlike the day in Nicole's store, he felt comfortable holding her tightly against himself, letting his warmth melt into her. "You're welcome," he said, nuzzling against her ear. "You're also freezing."

She nodded, rubbing her face against the scruff of his cheek. "It's my new state of being," she said with a laugh.

Following her up the porch steps, he waited while she tried to open the door.

"What the hell?" she said and tried turning the knob again. "I know I unlocked this." She banged the flat of her hand against the door. "Open up, stupid door!"

"Does your sister have a spare key somewhere?"

She hung her head and mumbled, "Yes."

"Where is it?"

"On my keychain."

"Where's your keychain?"

"On the kitchen table."

The cold was obviously starting to get to her as she shuffled from one foot to the other, rubbing her hands up and down her arms then blowing on her fingers for warmth.

"Come on," he said. "Let's go." He turned away from her and leaned over with his hands braced on his knees, waiting for her to hop on.

"What are you doing?"

"Offering you a piggyback ride. Obviously."

She hesitated for a heartbeat then started to laugh. "Lady Guinevere mounts her trusty steed," she said. Hopping on his back, she threw her arms around his neck.

He hooked his arms under her knees. "At your service, milady." His long strides ate up the distance across the yard and into the street.

"Are you taking me to your house?"

"Nope. I figured I'd set you up in the tool shed. No heat in there but it'll keep you out of the wind anyhow."

She giggled and he kept walking toward his front door. Though it certainly hadn't been his plan when he'd set out to decorate their house earlier, it sure as hell wasn't a terrible way to spend his evening.

"Your house is so beautiful," she said, unwrapping her scarf and hanging it on one of the pegs by the door. She rubbed her arms to warm herself up again. "I meant to say something the other day, but we got busy making candy." She slipped off her boots and he couldn't help but smile at the fuzzy slipper socks on her feet, dark blue and covered with snowmen wearing top hats.

"Those," he said, pointing to her socks, "are fantastic."

Her face softened while her smile widened. "Thank you," she said. "Nobody in my family, with the exception of people aged eight and under, see the beauty in them." She laughed and added, "In fact, my mother hates them. Says they're for children."

"With respect to your mother, she's quite wrong about that." A side of Carson's personality showed through that was different from the things she normally let him see. Getting locked out of the house meant she was stuck wearing whatever she had on her body. And since she was alone in the house, she was wearing what she loved to wear, what made her comfortable.

"I feel exactly the same way." She smiled again and her body shuddered from the cold, despite the warmth of the house. "It's so hard to stay warm up here. It's amazing how acclimated to a warm climate I am."

The desire to pull her close and feel again how comfortable she was in his arms was strong, but she'd only been in his house for two minutes and he didn't want to scare her away—especially since she had nowhere else to go until her sister came home.

"Come on in," he said. "I'll give you the ten-cent tour and we'll get you an extra sweatshirt or something to help you warm up."

It had taken him almost five years, but he finally had his house exactly the way he wanted it. Nights spent sanding and refinishing floors and laying tile, and all those early mornings prepping and painting walls were about to pay off in a different way as he found himself eager to show Carson around.

Aside from Will, only his parents and his sister and her family had ever seen it finished. Even Heather hadn't stayed around long enough to see how beautiful it ended up.

Carson had seen part of the main floor when she was there with the kids earlier, but he showed her the living room with the fireplace, the small bar, and the big TV. "Great for watching hockey," he told her when she looked at the giant television with a hint of skepticism.

"I'm sure it is," she said. "But I can't imagine wanting to watch television when you have a fireplace like that." Her eyes were wide, appreciative of his work. "Did you do all this work too?" She stepped forward, ran her fingertips over the stone mantle then turned to smile at him. He could get drunk on that smile.

"Most of it," he said, leaning against the doorframe, admiring her in much the same way she was admiring his house. "I had help with some things I couldn't do on my own but a lot of it was just me."

Carson narrowed her eyes and a coy smile played at her lips.

"Why are you looking at me like that?"

Shrugging, she said, "It's nothing bad, I promise. I'm just super impressed by you, that's all. A tech guy from Boston with home renovation skills that could rival anything on HGTV, plus you own and operate a vineyard and winery." She walked over and sat against the arm of the big leather couch, nearer to where he stood. "You're one of those people that the rest of us aspire to be like."

Her praise caught him off guard. He'd never seen his carpentry skills as anything more than a fun hobby until he bought the house at Whispering Hills. Heather had never seen those other parts of him as necessary or even particularly useful. But the way Carson looked at him like those things were worthwhile, desirable, felt like a validation that he only just realized he'd been lacking.

"By the time you reach your forties, it's a lot easier to stop caring about what the world thinks you should be doing and how you should be doing it, and to pay attention to what you really want out of life." He looked around the room. "And this is what I want."

She sighed and a small frown played at her lips, but she didn't say anything else.

"Come on. Let me show you my favorite room," he said, reaching out for hand. He led her through the dining room, which she admired, but her mouth fell open when he brought her into his study.

"Tom," she said, her voice almost reverent. "This is stunning." Dropping his hand, she walked further into the room, slowly turned a full circle then approached one of three floor-to-ceiling bookshelves behind his desk. He heard her chuckle as she read the titles on the spines of some of his books.

"Are you laughing at my library?" he asked, walking up behind her to see which books she was looking at.

"Oh, I'm not laughing like that," she said. "It's just that some of these books—" Tilting her head and running her fingertip across the spines, she read, "*Relational Segmentation... Sensory Quality Control*." Her smile was back in place, and she lifted her eyes to his. "I'll bet you pull stuff out of those at parties, don't you?"

She started to laugh again as she looked back at the books. "Here's a surefire way to make friends. Bring up *Yeast Propagation and Optimization*. Pretty sure women go crazy for that kind of talk."

When Carson laughed it did things to him. It made him want to touch her and hold her and kiss her all over again. He couldn't help but laugh along with her.

"I'll have you know," he said, trying to put on his most serious tone of voice. "Those books are instrumental in adding a distillery to the property and getting it up and running."

"Don't worry," she said, gliding closer to him until they were face to face. He rested his hands on her hips as she stepped right into his space. Her breasts brushed against his chest. "I wasn't really making fun of you. I was only playing around." Her eyes started to close, and Tom leaned down but stopped just as her eyes popped open again and darted to the side. "A second fireplace?" she asked.

The fireplace didn't get as much use as the one in the living room, but he was glad to have it on those late nights when he didn't want to go to bed alone, and he stayed up reading until he fell asleep under a blanket on the couch.

He nodded. "Gotta keep warm somehow." It was said as an offhand joke but the way her smile shifted, he wondered if she misunderstood his intention. How he *hoped* she misunderstood his intention.

From the fireplace, he watched as her eyes drifted to the spiral staircase tucked away in the corner of the room. "Where do those go?"

He swallowed hard. "My bedroom."

Carson

"I LOVE SPIRAL STAIRCASES," she said. "My grandparents used to have one in their house, but it was more of a way for the servants to get upstairs without being seen by guests. I don't mean that my grandparents had servants," she said with a laugh at the way his eyes bugged out. "But that was the original intention when the house was built in the late eighteen hundreds."

"Must've been a big house."

"It was. It was huge." Walking over, she rested her hand on the railing and peeked up to see what she could see of his room. Since the only light was in the library behind her, she couldn't see much past the top of the staircase.

She stepped one foot onto the bottom step. "Between my sister and me and all the cousins, we used to have the most epic games of hide and seek in that house. There were all kinds of passageways and little hidden rooms and stuff. One time, my little cousin Wayne fell asleep in one of the closets on the third floor and all the grownups had to help us find him." She laughed at the memory. It was one she hadn't thought of in years. "Can I go up?"

"Absolutely," he said. "Want me to go first since I know where the light is at the top?"

She wanted to spiral her way up from his library to his bedroom and the lack of light didn't deter her. "Nope," she said. "I've climbed these things a million times in the dark. It's almost more fun that way."

When he nodded, she climbed the stairs, getting an amazing view of the library below. There was wood everywhere she looked. From the floor to the walls, to the desk, and the built-in bookshelves. It gave the room an incredibly masculine and incredibly sexy feel. The deep brown leather sofa and glass-topped wooden coffee table in front of the fireplace looked like they belonged on a movie set.

Carson stopped when her feet landed on the plank floor of his bedroom. While there wasn't any artificial light upstairs, her eyes quickly adjusted to the silvery moonlight streaming through the giant windows that made up the far wall of the room. The masculine feel of the library carried over seamlessly into his bedroom.

"Whoa," she said under her breath as Tom reached the top of the stairs behind her. She'd never seen a room like his that wasn't on some home makeover show. The heavy wood bed stood against the wall to her left, flanked by box shelves that hung directly from the wall. To the right was a small sitting area. Two recliners sat at an angle to one another with a small table between them. Two doors flanked a hallway leading downstairs behind the chairs. A closet and a bathroom, she figured.

But it was the windows, and the view overlooking the snow-blanketed vineyard behind the house, that stole her breath. "This is your room?" she whispered.

"For what it's worth," he said, obviously trying to downplay the magnificence of what he'd done there.

Turning to him, she said, "It's worth a lot, I think. I've never been in a room like this before. It's amazing." She walked over to look out the window. The wintry scene below was like looking at a living Christmas card. He approached quietly and stood behind her, looping his arms around her waist.

Resting her body against his, she let her head fall back onto his solid chest and simply enjoyed the moment. The warmth of his body against her back, the softness of the rug beneath her feet, and the gentle strength of his arms around her waist. "This is nice," she said.

"It absolutely is," he said. "But I think the best part of all has to be those slippers." He tipped his body sideways and she lifted one snowman-clad foot.

"You know you're jealous," she said.

"Yes," he said with a chuckle. "I am one hundred percent jealous of those socks." He brought his mouth closer to her neck and she tipped her head slightly to make it easier for him to place nibbling kisses on the sensitive skin.

The woodsy-spicy smell of him sent tingles of desire through her body and a small moan escaped her lips. Reaching her arms up, she clasped her hands above his head, pushing her chest out. Within seconds, Tom accepted the invitation she'd given and moved his hands up from her waist to cup her breasts in his strong hands. She whimpered as his fingers massaged her through her shirt, bringing her nipples to taut attention.

"I like the sounds you make," he murmured into her neck. He flicked her nipples with his thumbs, and she moaned again. "I like that I cause them."

She needed to kiss him, to taste him, to feel his soft, scruffy beard with her fingers. Turning toward him, she stood on her tiptoes and pulled his face to hers. The kiss was deep and passionate as tongues pushed against one another.

She pulled back, slid her tongue along her lower lip and was rewarded by his mouth crushing into hers, demanding and hungry. His hands were everywhere on her body; under her shirt, up her back, over her breasts, down the back of her pants, then inside the front of her panties.

She sucked in a quick breath as his fingers found her, wet and ready for him. He growled low in his chest, slid his fingers between her lips, circled gently before he removed his hand. A crushing wave of need tore through her entire body.

Her breath released in a rush. "Don't stop. Please, don't stop," she whispered as she wrapped her arms around his neck, partly to feel the connection of his body and partly to steady her legs while she waited for his fingers to find their way back.

"Don't worry, I'm not done with you. I really just need to get this off you first." With a wicked grin, he grabbed the hem of her shirt and pulled it up and over her head. Her breasts drew his immediate attention. Lowering his head to her chest, he placed his mouth over one nipple, sucking on it while he teased the other with his thumb.

Looking down at her fluffy pants and snowman socks, she felt more than a little foolish, but he didn't seem to care about any of that. He dipped his hands into the back waistband of her pants again, grabbing two handfuls and squeezing. "God, I love your ass," he said then claimed her puffy lips with another demanding kiss.

"You can take my pants off too, if you want," she said, desperate for him to touch more of her skin, to feed that fire that burned from her lips straight down her core.

"I'll get there, but not yet." Wrapping his arms around her waist, he lifted her straight off the floor. She wrapped her legs around his waist and held her body against his, feeling the soft flannel of his shirt rub against her nipples.

As if he didn't have a fully grown human hanging from his body, he walked to his bed. As she slid down the front of him, her whole body ached with need. He stepped her backward until her knees hit the bed and she sat. "Lie down."

She scooted up the bed then watched as he climbed up next to her, his eyes filled with a hunger she felt in her bones. Dropping his head to her breast, he teased and licked her while he trailed his fingers over her belly and into her pants. When his fingers reached her center, her head fell back, her eyes drifted closed.

"I really want to taste you, Carson," he said, as he released one nipple then took the other in its place.

"You are tasting me," she whispered, her eyes still closed.

He licked and sucked on her while she stayed still and enjoyed every sensation.

"No," he said, sliding his fingers through the wet heat between her legs. "I mean I want to *taste* you, Carson." He lowered his mouth over her breast and sucked again while he slid one finger inside her. "Will you let me taste you?"

With a moan that started deep in her body, she managed to nod her head as her hips began to sway of their own free will, moving in time with Tom's fingers, complementing his movements and his rhythm.

"Are you ready for me to take these off now?" he said, pulling at the fabric of her pajama pants.

"Oh, God, yes, please."

She lifted her hips so he could pull everything off. After he tossed her clothes to the floor, he sat beside her, looked down and said, "You are absolutely stunning. Do you know that?"

Her hips started their swaying thing again and Tom's grin turned her belly to mush. "What are you doing there?" he said, running one finger in an arc from the top of one thigh, over her belly, to the top of her other thigh. "Are you trying to get me to touch you again?" He hovered his hand directly above her but didn't make contact with her skin.

The primal need she had to be touched by this man blazed through her. Every heartbeat fanned that fire until she thought she might combust right there in his bed, leaving a Carson-shaped pile of ashes behind.

"You're sure you want to do this?" he asked.

"Oh yeah," she said. "I'm sure." She'd never been more sure of anything in her life. Her legs dropped to the sides, and he seized his chance. Flipping his body so he was kneeling between her legs, he pressed them apart and leaned in to lick one long, slow stroke through her center.

He groaned against her most sensitive skin, sending vibrations straight through her.

She pulled her legs up, her knees by her shoulders and Tom continued to devour her, sucking, licking, and flicking her with his tongue; and she moaned and whined and whimpered as he did. Every cell of her body hovered on the verge of explosion.

These two people were virtually strangers, yet the chemistry they shared made it feel to her as if they'd known each other for years. There was no shame, no self-consciousness, no insecurities. It was as if he pushed aside all her inhibitions by his steady, calm presence alone.

He continued to work his magic with his mouth and his fingers as the delicious sensations rolling through her body set off sparks in her toes, her legs, her belly, and up into her chest. Her orgasm drew nearer with every exhale.

Suddenly he lifted his mouth.

Her brain was shocked and confused, her body desperate to hold onto that feeling. She grasped with open hands to get him back. "No, no, no," she whined. "Why'd you stop?"

"I need you to promise me something, Carson," he said, trailing his fingers along the heated skin of her inner thighs.

She looked down the length of her body to lock eyes with him. There was nothing on earth she wouldn't have promised as long as he went back to what he'd been doing.

"I need you to tell me what you like and what you don't like, OK?"

She nodded, desperate for him to bring that euphoric feeling back.

"And if there's something you want that I'm not doing, I want you to be free to tell me that too."

"OK," she whispered. If she hadn't been so close to an orgasm seconds ago, she could have thought of all kinds of things that would have been fun to try but her mind and her body were focused on exactly one thing. "Can you finish now?" she asked through choppy breaths.

His wolfish grin was the last thing she saw as he lowered his face and set about very quickly bringing her to her first climax of the night.

Tom

H E COULD HAVE FEASTED on her for hours, but he didn't want to wear her out completely. The night was still young, and they had nothing but time. As she lay, naked and relaxed on his bed, save for a pair of snowman slipper socks, he traced his fingers over her soft, warm skin and let her come down from her orgasm.

Her body was new to him, and he wanted to learn it. He wanted to learn what she liked, what she didn't, what made her feel as exquisite as she looked.

It was exciting to be with Carson for the first time. They'd only spent a few hours in each other's company, but it was as natural as breathing for him to be with her. They got along well; she was fun to be around and had a big heart for helping other people. Not to mention the way she moved, the way she tasted, the way she sounded and felt and looked.

As he lay close to her, Tom imagined all the ways he wanted to please her, to find out what else made her body quiver and her mind reel.

His dick was aching to be where his mouth just was and, as if she knew it, she reached one hand down and worked it inside of his jeans. Quickly he undid the button and zipper and pulled his pants over his hips, allowing her better access. When her cool fingers wrapped around him, he knew he'd need to be inside her soon.

"Can I?" she asked, looking down to where she had begun to gently stroke him. When she licked her lips, he sucked in a deep breath to keep from coming in her hand.

"I'd never say no to that."

She slid down the bed and pushed her long hair over one shoulder, and with another of those amazing smiles, she lowered her mouth to him, kissing his shaft and working her way up to the head. He wanted to think about how wonderful she was, and how sexy and erotic it was to watch her lips touch his cock, but once she took him inside her mouth, his brain forgot how to function.

With his eyes closed, he reached down to wrap his fingers in the silky strands of her hair. Her tongue stroked the length of him as her head bobbed, his mind and body teetering at the edge of the calm before the storm. Slow and shallow at first, her depth changed as she held him firmly, then took him slow and deep to the back of her throat.

His balls ached and tightened; he wouldn't last much longer. Reaching down, he stilled her head. She understood and slowly licked him from base to tip before she looked up at him.

"Can I have you now?" he said, straining to hold back his orgasm.

"Do you have a condom?" she asked. "Obviously I didn't bring any with me when I got locked out of the house."

"In the top drawer of the dresser."

Her smile grew wide. "You have no idea how happy I am that you said that." Leaning down again, she licked him slowly before she took him deep into her throat and sucked him for a few extra seconds of pure brain-melting bliss.

"How do you want me?" she asked, when she finally released him, looking up with those big eyes of hers.

That was a loaded question. He wanted her every way and any way she'd allow.

"I want to make you come again," he said. "How's your favorite way to do that?"

"Normally it's easiest for me if I'm on top," she said, still kneeling with her face between his legs. "But can we try something first?"

His head almost exploded at her simple six-word request. "Carson, honey, we can try anything you want."

She stood up and walked over to the floor-to-ceiling windows. The curves of her silhouette against the glass were fucking perfect. She looked like she belonged in the space, like she was the person the room had been meant for and he only just understood it.

Leaving his own clothes on the bed, he grabbed a condom and rolled it on as he walked up behind her. He wrapped his arms around her warm body again, feeling the weight of her breasts on his forearms, his erection pressed against her ass.

She let out a soft sigh and snuggled back into him as they looked out the window together. After a minute of the most amazing body contact, she disengaged from his arms, took a step forward then leaned over and pressed her hands to the glass.

"Will you take me like this?" she asked.

She was absolute perfection, and he took an extra second to simply admire her before stepping closer. He ran his hands down her sides, glided them over her ass. Gently, he slipped his fingers into her to make sure she was still wet enough. Her hips swayed again as he fingered her, and she pushed back with a whimper, seeking him out when he withdrew them.

Pressing his hips against her, he leaned over, brushed her hair over her shoulder, and placed a kiss at the top of her spine. She inhaled sharply and goosebumps broke out all over her body as he continued placing kisses down the length of her back.

Standing behind her, he held her hips while he slid into her, loving the sound of her gasps. It was the first time he'd been inside her, and he hoped to God it wouldn't be the last.

Carson wasn't shy about enjoying herself. With every thrust, she responded. Gasps, moans, whimpers, sighs, grunts. If lightning struck him dead at that moment, he would die a happy, happy man.

As he picked up his tempo, he focused his gaze on her hands against the glass, her fingertips grasping and clawing at the cold, hard surface. If he wasn't careful, he'd finish before he gave her the orgasm he promised. He slowed down, felt her tighten around him with every deliberate movement of his hips.

The slower tempo seemed to be working for her and Tom moved his hands from her hips to hold her breasts in his palms as he leaned over her. Her moans grew deeper and her back heaved from the deep breaths she pulled in and blew out every time he withdrew and slid back in.

Her breathing quickened and her legs began to tremble. It wouldn't be long before she came undone.

"I don't think I can hold out much longer," he said, bringing his hands back down and looping them under her hips, helping to keep her knees from giving out. "I need to come in you, Carson."

Her rapid breaths gave way to frantic gasps as he drove into her, her hands balled into fists against the glass.

Tom's whole body tensed, and with a deep groan and herculean effort, he held back while he waited for her. With a moan-turned-scream, her body shook, her fingers tapped at the window glass, and she tensed around him like a vise.

With only a second to take in the sensation of her orgasm, his own tore through him like lightning and he dug his fingers into her hips and pounded into her with a roar of pure ecstasy.

Tom

AFTER COMING BACK DOWN to earth, they showered off together and they were able to finish the grand tour of the house. When they'd made it back to the kitchen, Carson's belly growled. After throwing together a quick plate of cheese and crackers, he poured a couple glasses of his favorite apple cinnamon wine.

"If you were able to stay the night, I'd have lit a fire in the fireplace," he said as they took their places on the couch.

"This is nice though," she said, and curled up beside him, snuggling under a blanket. "Your house is so cozy; I wish I didn't have to go back home." Looking up at him with sleepy eyes she added, "But when I do get to sleep here, I will definitely take you up on that fire."

"I'm pretty sure your sister wouldn't be on board with you sleeping at my house quite yet," he said. Resting his hand on the curve of her ass, he rubbed it absentmindedly, as if they weren't newly acquainted lovers and instead had snuggled together every night after having incredibly hot sex.

Her body shook slightly as she giggled. "No, I don't think that would fly." Sighing, she snuggled deeper into his side. "It's funny," she said. "I'm the older sister and have always been the more responsible one but I feel like we've reversed roles over the past few years." She toyed with the fringe on the edge of the blanket, focusing on the strands as they slipped through her fingers. "I guess having a family to take care of by yourself will do that to you."

"You said that you and your sister grew up around here. How is it that you ended up way the hell down in Georgia? That's a long way from home." It sounded like a casual question to make conversation, but he wasn't sure if he meant it to be casual or if he was trying to gauge the strength of her attachment to her southern home.

"That's easy," she said as she scooted her body away and lay back with her head on his lap, her feet extended down the length of the couch. "I followed a guy there after we finished school. Things didn't work out with him, but I'd found a great job and decided to stay down there for a while. That was probably about fifteen years ago."

Disappointed that he couldn't reach her ass anymore, he wondered what to do with his hands.

"Have you ever thought of coming back up this way?" he asked, choosing to rest the flat of his hand on her belly, just below her breasts.

With a deep sigh, she tipped her head back to look him in the eyes. "I've thought about a lot of things, but I haven't done much about any of them."

It was the first serious thing Carson had brought up with him. "What kinds of things?" he said, letting his fingers glide under her shirt and over her breast.

She purred as he barely grazed her. "Oh, you know," she said. "All kinds of things." Her eyes drifted closed and she made little sounds of pleasure as he stroked her. "Like, I always assumed I'd be married by the time I reached forty, but with only two years to go, I'm pretty sure that's not happening," she whispered. "And I've been giving some thought to maybe, someday, opening my own event planning agency. Oh, that feels so good," she added as he traced delicate circles on her responding nipples.

"Why haven't you done those things?" he asked, intrigued by the woman who lay so relaxed and trusting in his lap. "Is something holding you back?"

"Aside from myself, you mean?"

"Hey, I'm not judging. Everybody's life is their own. Everyone makes choices." He shifted his hand back down to her belly and stroked the soft, warm skin beneath his fingertips. "I just didn't know if there was a particular reason you never went after those things... or if life just sort of keeps happening and the time slips by before you know it."

She tipped her head back and looked up at him again. "Are you asking about me or telling me about yourself?" At first, he thought she was teasing him but there was no humor in her eyes, no mischief in her expression, only a sincere question from a kind person.

"Maybe a bit of both," he said.

"Is that what happened to you? Was life passing you by too quickly, so you decided to buy a winery as a way to stave off a midlife crisis?"

"Something like that," he said. Calling it a midlife crisis somehow made it sound more acceptable than actively trying to avoid a breakdown caused by total career burnout at the ripe old age of thirty-six.

Just then the lights of Nicole's car flashed through the window as she turned into her driveway. "I think your family's home," he said, stilling his hand on her belly.

"I guess I'm about to turn back into a pumpkin," she said. Standing up, she folded the blanket and draped it over the back of the couch. "I should probably head back so she doesn't think I've been kidnapped," she said, pulling a face and then laughing. "Though, I have no idea if she's going to believe how this even happened."

Tom hugged her close, kissed her softly, and said, "She doesn't have to believe it, Carson. You're a grown woman. You can do the things you want to do."

She snuggled into the crook of his neck. "Even if you're what I want to do?"

"Especially then," he said with a laugh and a gentle squeeze of her backside.

"Thank you for such an amazing night," she said as he followed her to the door.

She slipped her feet back into her boots. Grabbing her scarf from the hook, he draped it around her neck. "Thank you for coming over and trying the apple wine." Leaning in, he took hold of the scarf and with a gentle tug pulled her in for another kiss. "And, you know, everything else."

"Maybe we can do it again sometime?" she asked as he wrapped one of his heaviest flannels around her shoulders.

"Without a doubt," he said. "Anytime you want to come by, I'd be happy to have you." He meant that in every way it could possibly be interpreted. "Maybe next time we can even have dinner first."

"And a fire in the fireplace?"

Kissing the tip of her nose, he said, "Absolutely."

As he walked her across the street to her sister's house, she slipped her hand into his and they fell into an easy silence. When they reached the front door, she turned to him. "Any chance I can see you tomorrow? I was hoping to swing by the winery to start getting a handle on the paint night setup."

"Come by anytime. I'll be around all day."

Walking back to his house alone in the dark night, as light snow flurries began to fall around him, he looked forward to sleeping the sleep of a contented man.

Carson

O F COURSE IT TOOK all of Carson's most sincere explanations
to get Nicole to stop laughing at her. And then, the only reason
Nicole believed her was because of the brightly lit bushes along the
front of the house and Carson's key ring locked safely inside the house
on the kitchen table.

"He really did that for us?" Nicole said. "Without you asking him
to do it?"

Carson placed her right hand on top of her heart. "Swear to God,"
she said. "He assumed I'd gone to the party with you guys, and he
wanted to surprise us when we got home."

Once the kids were asleep and the two sisters had taken up their
usual places on the couches in front of the empty fireplace, they talked
through each of their nights.

Carson told her sister the whole story of how she ended up locked
out of the house in her pajamas and ended up spending a nice evening
at Tom's house. She even pointed out the discarded toy hammer
and the long-forgotten water sitting in the microwave, and Nicole

laughed all over again. She wasn't angry or judgmental or disapproving. Though, her eyes expressed a deep sadness that her laughter couldn't hide, and Carson would have given anything to take it away. Even if she had to take it on herself.

"He really is a nice guy, isn't he?" Nicole said. "I always figured he was and then he just had to go and prove it." She thumped her hand onto her leg for emphasis.

"Would you rather he was a jerk?"

"No, that's not what I mean." Nicole looked down at her hands then slowly back to Carson. "I guess I'm just a little lonelier than I wanted to admit."

Carson's heart skidded to a halt. "Oh, my God. You said you weren't interested in him." How many ways could she screw up her sister's life? First, she outs Nicole's cheating husband, leading to their divorce, then lets her uncontrolled sex drive throw her into the arms of the guy Nicole likes!

Nicole's eyes went wide for a second, then she chuckled. "Relax, I am absolutely not interested in him," she said. "I just wish there was somebody that I was interested in, that's all." She was quiet for a second, then said, "OK, it's sisterly confession time."

Carson froze, fully expecting Nicole to call her out for having sex with Tom, even though the topic hadn't come up. Yet. "You go first."

Nicole sighed. "I absolutely love having you here but seeing you click with my neighbor, who is also my landlord, makes me feel uncomfortable and envious and really happy all at the same time." She fluffed the blanket she had spread over her lap and said, "I wish I could be more like you."

Suddenly there was nobody else in existence, simply her and her sister, and she had no idea what to do with Nicole's admission. "No, you don't."

With a sigh, Nicole said, "Yes, I really do. Growing up you were always the stable one, the steady one. I could always count on you—everyone could. And then you show up here just because I needed you, no questions asked, and you're working to help me take care of my kids. You are literally the kindest and most unselfish person I know." She brushed a finger along her lower lid, wiping away a stray tear. "And you fit in wherever you are, and you make friends with everyone you meet. How do you even do it?"

Chuckling softly, Carson said, "My turn to confess. So many times through our lives I've wanted to be more like you."

"Yeah, right."

"Colie, I'm not kidding. You've always been so... I don't know what the word is... Impulsive? Spontaneous? Impetuous? All of those things, actually. And all of those things are the things I'm not. Then you grew up and on top of all that, you're dependable and responsible and an amazing mom with a solid head on your shoulders. You are literally the whole package."

"Maybe not the whole package," Nicole said. "I've been living across the street from a really hot guy for like six months and he's never even noticed me. You show up and within two weeks he's giving you piggyback rides after hanging up your Christmas lights as a surprise." Nicole stared with wide eyes. "Who even are you?"

Carson thought about the time she spent with Tom and her whole body tingled. "I might have another confession to make."

"You *might* have a confession?"

"OK," Carson said. "I one hundred percent have a confession to make." It shouldn't have been difficult to say out loud. They were both adults after all, and they'd talked about guys in the past. Perhaps it was her sister's vulnerability holding her back, but it wasn't something she wanted to be a secret. "When I was over at Tom's house earlier," she said looking Nicole in the eyes, "we had sex."

She waited for her sister to react, to show some kind of emotion or response. Instead Nicole sat and stared before she finally said, "Why are you telling me this?"

"Because I don't want it to be some secret thing happening behind your back. I really like him. He seems to really like me and I'm kind of hoping we'll be able to do it again."

Nicole blew out a breath but then was completely silent again while she digested Carson's words. Her lips twitched into a smile, and she started to giggle. "How was it?" she said, then hid her face behind her hands and laughed. "No, wait. I don't know if I want to know. I'm going to have to see this guy all the time. I don't know if I can live with that kind of information."

"Well, you're going to have to live with it, because it was fantastic," Carson teased.

"Oh, I knew you were going to say that!"

It was nice to see Nicole laughing as hard as she was. Some of that sadness had dissipated with the lightness of the conversation.

Once the laughter subsided, Nicole brought up the one thing Carson had been trying her hardest not to think about. "What are you going to do about it?" she asked. "It's not like this can go on if you're leaving in three weeks. Are you going to try the long-distance thing with him?"

"I don't know," she said. "I'm not sure what the right thing to do even is." Even before their night together, she'd thought about him a lot, but her mind was never able to imagine anything further out than New Year's Eve. "We've only known each other a couple weeks, it's not like we have some enduring romance for the ages or anything."

"I'm not sure I could do it," Nicole said. "I don't know if I could sleep with a guy knowing full well there's no chance of a future with him." Her eyes found Carson's. "I guess it would be easier to go for that kind of thing if there weren't kids involved, huh?" The words weren't sharp, and Carson understood them as Nicole's way of trying to figure out what she wanted from life. But she suddenly felt the subtle sting of underlying judgment.

"I guess so," Carson said. "I've never had to give the 'kid' thing much thought. But I guess it's mostly about expectation. If you don't expect anything from the other person, it makes it a little easier when nothing comes of it." One of her legs had fallen asleep so she stretched it out to get the blood flowing again. "I know you think I'm super friendly and all that, but you do know I don't go around sleeping with random guys every weekend, right? Because it might kill me to have you think of me like that."

"No," Nicole said. "I don't think that about you at all." She paused. "Maybe it's more that we never talk about this kind of stuff anymore, so I have no idea what you're like when it comes to relationships with guys."

Carson didn't know what to say. She didn't need to explain herself or her choices to her sister or to anyone else, but she felt like she owed it to her for some reason. "I've had two on-again, off-again relationships since I moved to Savannah, after Eric and I broke up. One was a guy I worked with who had a second on-again, off-again relationship happening at the same time. They got married last year.

"The second one was a friend of mine, Patrick. We met through mutual friends, and we were each other's plus ones for weddings and things. We hooked up a few times and I thought maybe there was something more about to happen." She frowned, remembering the last time they saw each other. "He's engaged to marry a woman he met at a wedding we went to together."

Telling her stories out loud, she felt neither stable nor steady, but more like predictable and inevitable. "I never had the courage to go after either of those guys and I ended up losing them both to women who did."

"Cari, I'm sorry. I shouldn't have pushed. That was seriously not OK of me."

"Don't worry about it. It was a legit question. I wish I had a better answer for you, though."

Nicole was thoughtful for a few seconds. "So, what about Tom?" she said. "Is he going to be another one of those guys or you planning to change things up this time around?"

"What am I going to do? I don't live here, and he would never leave here. Eventually one of the women in this town is going to realize he's there and he'll move on and forget all about me."

With a slight shrug of one shoulder, Nicole said, "Why couldn't you live here?"

Carson had been pondering the same question since she'd been back. Maybe not consciously, but the idea had been percolating in the back of her mind for the past couple weeks. The past couple months, if she was being completely honest with herself.

"Because this isn't my home anymore," she said. It was the same half-truth she'd been telling herself since the day she jumped into Tom's arms at Nicole's store and had to pull herself away from him. Tom wasn't hers. The town wasn't hers. Not to mention she had an apartment and a job to get back to in Savannah.

"So," Nicole said. "Quit your job and come back here and then it will be. That's how that works. Wherever you live is your home."

In Carson's experience that wasn't entirely true. Savannah was a beautiful place, a wonderful place, but it had never fully felt like it was *her* place. It never felt like *home*. The closest she'd come to that feeling in more than ten years was when she was snuggled up on the couch under a blanket with Tom. The familiarity they had with one another only highlighted the empty ache that permanently lived behind her ribs.

"I guess," she said.

Perhaps sensing Carson's discomfort with the conversation, Nicole, thankfully, changed subjects. "Hey," she said. "Have we gotten any sign-ups for the paint night?"

Having been otherwise preoccupied, Carson hadn't checked and re-checked her email for notification of sign-ups since before Nicole and the kids left for their party. She pulled out her phone and clicked through to her inbox. Expecting it to either be empty, or full of angry emails from Anderson, her breath caught when she saw three different notifications. She blinked, convinced her tired eyes were seeing things. When she refocused, she saw the same three notifications.

With only a week to go before their big night, Carson had begun to think it wasn't going to happen. But there they were, staring her right in the eye. Unable to hold back her laughter, she looked at Nicole. "We've got three!"

"No way!"

Carson opened the first reply, saw that it contained payment for two people. "Make that four," she said. Opening the next one, she saw the same thing. "Five." Hoping that the third would turn it to six, she clicked it open and saw it was payment for four people. "Oh my gosh," she said. "Forget five. We're up to eight!"

Electricity sparked through Carson's fingers as her excitement grew.

Nicole jumped up from the couch and did a little victory dance and Carson hopped up to join her. In their pajamas, the two sisters hugged and danced in a silent burst of excitement, so they didn't wake up the kids.

Tom

TOM'S DAY STARTED THE way his days normally started—coffee and breakfast followed by some informational reading at the house, then over to start work at the winery by nine o'clock.

Unlike the way his days normally started however, was the extra bounce in his step and the complete inability to focus on anything he read. Giving up on *Sustainability in the Distilled Spirits Industry*, he tossed the book onto the table and headed over to the winery to get a jump start on his day.

At nine-fifteen, carrying a bag with a laptop sticking out of it slung over one shoulder and a steaming mug in her hand, Carson pushed through Whispering Hills' front door. Following closely on her heels, Lucy and Drew, each with an armful of colorful boxes and books and toys, entered the store and stomped their feet, shaking snow onto the big black welcome mat. They were bundled up so well that Tom wouldn't have recognized them if he hadn't already known them,

"Hi, Tom," Drew called, and he tried to give Tom a quick wave which meant his precariously perched pile of games and books began to topple. Carson and Lucy jumped to his rescue, but they weren't fast enough, and half the stack crashed around him, sending brightly colored plastic game pieces skittering across the wood floor.

"Hey, don't worry about it," Carson said when Drew's lower lip began to quiver. She pulled him in for a quick hug and said, "It's no big deal. We can clean it all up and you'll be good to go in less than five minutes. OK?"

He nodded and looked around for where to put the remainder of the stack in his hand.

Lucy laid her pile on the long wood table at the front of the store where Tom had a basket of corkscrews and an assortment of wine stoppers for sale. Then she turned and relieved her brother of his burden. "There," she said. "Now we can look for all your pieces." She was a gentle kid, quiet and obviously protective of her little brother. Much the way his own sister always was.

Tom met them by the door, picking up the few plastic pieces he saw as he walked over. "Hey, little man," he said, placing the items on the table. "Here you go." From the corner of his eye, he saw a bright yellow thing hiding under the end of one of the wine racks. Before he could reach it, Lucy saw it and retrieved it for him.

"Sorry about all the ruckus," Carson said with a laugh as she crawled on the floor gathering scattered game pieces. Her smile was big and bright, as if there was nothing else she would rather be doing with her morning than climbing around on her hands and knees helping her nephew fix his games.

Tom squatted down beside her to help her look. "Nothing to apologize for," he said. "It's nice to have a little life happening around here."

Her smile hit him right in the gut, almost toppling him over backward.

By the time Carson had the kids settled in the side room, a pile of games and books and toys strewn across the low coffee table between them, Tom had gone back to getting caught up on his paperwork. He sat at the desk in his small office and opened his accounting software to pay some bills.

Carson stood on the work side of the bar and flipped open her laptop. She went back and forth scribbling things on a notepad and typing things into her computer. With her hair pulled back into a ponytail, she was entirely focused on her task, nibbling on her thumbnail, lost in thought.

He had a mountain of paperwork to get through, but staring at Carson as she worked was so much more interesting—and strangely satisfying. She turned to look at him and he quickly jumped back to his check writing, as if he hadn't just been staring at her like she was some exotic creature he'd never seen before.

When he glanced back at her, a small smile played on her lips as she pretended not to have caught him staring. The middle of a workday with children in the building was not the time for him to be thinking *thoughts* about her. But as the saying goes, *it is what it is*. And that day, it was what it was.

"Auntie," Lucy called. "Can we go outside to play?"

Carson paused from her work, a look of uncertainty creasing her brows. "Does your mom let you play outside alone? 'Cause I can't go out with you right now."

Drew piped up, "She lets us play in the yard when she's in the house, but we can't go out of the yard."

"We could just stay in Mr. Tom's yard and make a snowman or something," Lucy said.

Carson peeked over at Tom, who nodded in her direction. "I like snowmen," he said. "It'll add a touch of holiday charm to the place."

The kids bolted for the door, stopping long enough to bundle up in their winter gear. As they flew out the door, Carson yelled, "Stay in Mr. Tom's yard and make sure I can see you if I come look for you!"

They both answered in the affirmative as the door clicked shut in their wake.

Tom and Carson quickly settled back into their work, Carson's Christmas music playing softly from her phone on the bar beside her. Every now and again she would sing a line or two, then look around self-consciously, and stop.

"It's OK to sing out loud," he said from his little office.

"I didn't get the feeling you liked Christmas music," she said without looking up from her work.

"Why'd you think that?"

"Mostly because it's two weeks before Christmas and mine is the only Christmas music I've heard in this store."

He chuckled. "Fair enough," he said. "For the record, though, I do like Christmas music." But it was Carson's singing voice that he liked even more.

An easy quiet settled between them again and lasted until the front door opened. At first, he thought the kids must have had enough of the cold and come back inside. It wasn't Lucy's or Drew's voice he heard say, "Carson? I didn't realize you worked here."

With a look that went from utter confusion to recognition in a blink, Carson looked up from her work. "Emma! Hi," she said. "No, I don't work here. I'm just getting some planning done for my sister's paint and sip night next week and Tom was nice enough to let me work from here."

Tom's brain struggled to keep up. It felt like his two worlds colliding. A person from his personal life and a person from his professional life in the same place—except they already knew each other? It was an odd disconnect.

As he stood to help Emma with her order, Carson waved him off. "Don't worry," she said. "I can help Emma so you can get your stuff done." She shot him an excited smile. "If I need help, I'll call you."

"It's fortunate I ran into you here," Emma said when Carson returned her attention to the older woman. "Can you tell me a little more about that painting thing? Delores tried to explain it to me but I'm not all that sure I understood what she was talking about. I will say I was intrigued though."

"Absolutely," Carson said and hustled to the other side of the bar. The women walked around the store while Carson explained in great detail what the night was all about, and Emma picked up bottles of wine. "And Tom will be set up right over here," Carson said. "He's going to be serving the blackberry dessert wine, the apple wine, and then the chocolate port." She whispered but he could still hear her say, "The blackberry is my favorite."

Emma whispered back, "Everything Tom does is my favorite."

Tom laughed to himself as the women giggled together like old friends.

His phone buzzed, a text from Will drawing his attention away from them as they continued their info session.

> Need help tonight moving racks? Got some free time

> Yeah. There's a lot to move

> See you around 5

The paint and sip was scheduled for the following week and he had planned to start clearing space in a couple of days but since Will was offering the help, he'd be foolish not to accept it.

"You know," Carson said as she and Emma approached the bar with Emma's armload of wines. "This would be a great place for your book club to meet."

"You think?"

"I do," she said. "There's plenty of room over there. Maybe Tom could pick up another couch and you could all meet here. Bring some snacks, drink some wine. And, think about it, nobody would have to clean their house to get ready for it."

Tom's fingers stilled over the keyboard. What was she doing? Emma would never agree to something like that. But even if she did, he had no interest in opening his store as a meeting location for the local old lady book club.

"That's not a bad idea," Emma mused, because *of course* she'd like the idea. "That space over there would be perfect." She was quiet for a second or two and added, "Hmmm... My knitting group also loves Tom's wine, and they might be interested in an arrangement like that too."

Carson came back to the business side of the bar, like she already knew how to ring up an order. As Tom stood to go help, she called in to him, "Anything special I need to do or just start scanning?"

Emma said, "He usually just starts scanning."

"Never mind," Carson said as he approached. "Emma knows how it works." She picked up a bottle of Greylock Red and passed it under the scanner. She repeated it for each of the six bottles Emma was purchasing.

"Only six this week?" Tom said, feeling slightly out of place in his own store.

"The knitting group is a little smaller than usual this week," Emma said. "But I'll be coming back next week to get quite a few bottles that I'll be giving as gifts this year." She held her credit card to the screen and Tom reached under the bar and took out a box to pack up her order.

"That's great," he said and before he could say anything else in response, Carson jumped into the conversation.

"If you come to the paint and sip night, you can pick up all the wine you want while you're here. Save yourself a trip," she said, handing Emma a receipt.

Emma looked from Carson to Tom and smiled. "She's quite good for your business, Tom. You might want to see about hiring her." She tilted her head in thought. "Although, that would certainly be less fun for me." Emma chuckled and lifted the box from the counter. "I'll see what everybody wants to do and see if I can get some of the old fogies to come down for a night out of the house. How do I sign up again?"

Carson ripped a piece of paper from her notebook and wrote down the website address. "Just go to this website and you can sign up right from there!" She folded the page and stuffed it between two bottles in the box. "It's super easy," she said. "Oh, and Tom picked out the painting we'll be doing."

"Well, in that case..." Emma said. "I'll definitely be here." With a flirty wave, she adjusted the box in her arms and headed out the door.

"What was that?" Tom asked, conflicted in his thoughts about the offer of his space for Emma's book club. There was a reason he'd never put his permit to serve alcohol to use. And the reason was that he didn't want to. It was supposed to be Heather doing the customer-facing things, not him.

"What was what?" Carson asked with a self-satisfied grin. "Me taking care of your customer like I've been doing it for years, or...?"

"Well, there's that," he said, rubbing out the back of his neck with one hand before folding his arms across his chest. "But I was thinking more about you offering the use of my store for Emma's book club."

Carson

*S*HIT. IF THE SCOWL on his face wasn't a clear enough indication that he wasn't entirely pleased with her choice to help give his business a little boost, the crossed arms and hunched shoulders spoke volumes.

"I just thought it would be a good opportunity to get you some more customers." It sounded lame when she said it out loud but in her head it made plenty of sense. "I hadn't planned on making the suggestion but when I saw the kids' stuff over in the extra room, I thought it might make a good spot for... say... a book club?" She shrugged one shoulder and waited for him to understand her logic.

The muscles in the side of his jaw clenched and loosened several times while he kept her pinned with an intense stare that both unnerved her and fanned the fire they'd lit the night before all over again. His eyes held her in place while the rest of him did all kinds of wonderful things in her imagination.

Though, this probably wasn't the time to go wandering down memory lane. From the look of it, he was kind of pissed at her. What she didn't know was why?

"If I wanted that space open for things like book clubs and knitting clubs, don't you think it would already be open?" His tone was even but it looked like it was taking effort to keep it that way.

Squirming under the weight of his stare, she said, "I didn't think of that, no." Quickly she added, "But it's such a nice space. It's cozy and warm and it's big enough to fit everybody in Emma's book club."

He sighed and his shoulders dropped, but he didn't uncross his arms. "Yes, I know it's a nice space. I built it. Remember?"

She nodded. "But why did you build it then, if not to use it for stuff like that? What is it even for?"

"It's for me," he said. "I built it because I wanted it. There doesn't have to be another reason." He finally uncrossed his arms and Carson breathed a little bit easier. "Look," he said, shoving his hands into his back pockets, making his stature a little less imposing. "You did a great job dealing with Emma and I appreciate the help. But I need to ask you to stick with your paint night plans and leave the store to me."

She reached into her pocket and pulled out an antacid, tossed it into her mouth as she fought off the urge to cry. All she'd done was try to help him and all he'd done was be an ass to her for it. "Aren't you the one who was advising me *last night* to go after things and to stop being scared?" she said.

"Sure, but unless you're going after Whispering Hills, you had no right making that offer without even asking me." He dragged one hand through his hair and Carson wondered if he was stalling for time or trying to figure out the best way to tell her the paint night would have to find a new home.

Panic spiraled from her belly up into her throat. There would be no time to find someplace new. None of the venues she spoke with were able to accommodate them. If Tom backed out on her now, the whole thing would have to be scrapped.

She'd screwed up. Again.

The door to the shop opened, bringing in a burst of cold air. Carson and Tom both turned as a young couple walked in.

"Hey, fellas. How's it going?" Tom asked as the men rubbed their arms to shake off the cold.

"Hey, Tom," the taller man with the short, neat hair and beard said. "Back for a little more of the Greylock Red."

The shorter man with the clean-shaved face added, "Every time we serve it, there's never any left, so this time we're buying extra."

Glad for the reprieve in their argument, she retreated into his office and stood against the wall so as not to get in the way of him helping his customers. It had been so fun helping Emma, but as much as it stung to be told so, Tom was right. It wasn't her store, and she was interfering with his business.

"Here you go," Tom said as he finished ringing up his customers. After their footsteps reached the door, Tom appeared in the doorway to the office. "You OK?" he asked, as if she'd merely bumped her toe and not been standing there wracking her brain for an alternate plan for the paint and sip, not to mention the best way to save face and get the hell out of there.

"You were right," she said. "I'm really sorry. I didn't have the right to make decisions for your business. I guess I just got caught up in the moment. Planning things and organizing things is just what I do. It can be hard to turn that off and I guess I made myself a little too comfortable."

She stepped away from the wall and attempted to leave the office, but he stood like a brick wall directly in her way.

"Hey," he said, unwinding her arms from around her middle. "Don't go. Please. I accept your apology." Cradling her face with one hand, he brushed the pad of his thumb over her damp cheek. "And please don't cry. It's not as bad as all that."

Leaning down, he placed a featherlight kiss on her lips. "It was an honest mistake, and it came from a place of good intentions. I'm sorry if I overreacted," he said, tipping her head so he could look her in the eye.

"Does that mean you're still going to let me host Nicole's event here next week?"

His head snapped back. "Of course it does. Why would you think I'd go back on that? Because of that?" He jerked his thumb in the direction of the bar, where they'd had their heated conversation. "That was just me being an idiot," he said, pulling her close and resting his hands on her low back. "What do you think? Can we still be friends?"

"I'd like that," she said.

"As a matter of fact," he said. "I'm going to start clearing space for you guys tonight. My friend Will has some free time this afternoon and he's coming by to help me move the racks."

Her ears perked up and she leaned back to look him in the eye. "You *do* have a friend," she said, and a huge, conspiratorial smile overtook her face.

Tom's eyes grew wide and his grip on her loosened as he took a half step backward. "Umm... yeah... that's not actually something I'm into, though..."

Not something he's into? What the...? The gears clicked into place and Carson laughed so hard tears pooled in the corners of her eyes. Tom continued to stare at her like she might explode into a million pieces just as soon as take her next breath. Which only made her laugh harder.

"Clearly, I'm missing the joke," he said, one eyebrow in a perfect arch above his left eye.

"No," she said when she was finally able to catch her breath. "I don't mean a friend for *us*." She swiveled her finger back and forth between them. "This? This is just between you and me." Hooking her hands over his shoulders, she stood on tiptoes and pressed a kiss to his cheek. "My sister and I were talking the other day and she said she was jealous of what we've got going on and she jokingly asked if you had any friends."

Tom's whole body shrunk on the giant exhale he breathed out. "Thank Christ," he said, hugging her close again. "I think you just about gave me a heart attack."

"What's the matter?" she teased. "Don't you have a sense of adventure in you?"

"It's not that," he said. "I'm plenty adventurous. Anything you want to do, I'm down for." He pinched her ass, and she jumped as she giggled. "Except for sharing you with another person. I only get to have you for the next two weeks, and it's hard enough watching you go back to your sister's every night because I already want you all to myself. But I'll be damned if I'll ever want to share you with someone when you're naked."

Carson's cheeks flushed with heat. As did everything below her cheeks, straight down to the tips of her toes. Being wanted like that, being chosen by him was a heady feeling. It was one she wanted to get used to even though it would tear her heart out when it had to end.

"Even thinking about you naked is killing me right now," he said into her hair. "Is there any way you can sleep at my house tonight?"

She shook her head against his chest. "I don't think that would fly with Nicole. She's got two little kids over there and I don't think I'd be much of a role model if I did something like that." She hugged him tighter. "I wish I could though."

"Me too."

"Speaking of those two," she said. "I should probably go out and check on them to make sure they're OK."

Haltingly, he released her and stepped out of the way to let her pass. As she grabbed her coat from the hook by the door, another customer entered and Tom set to work helping them find what they needed.

"That's quite the snow family you've got out there," the young woman said to Tom as she made her way to through the store. It was obvious she and Tom knew each other, and Carson couldn't stop the flickers of sadness and jealousy as she wondered if that woman would be Tom's next interest after Carson went back to Georgia.

"Is that so?" Tom asked. "My neighbor's kids are helping me do a little decorating, but I haven't been out there yet."

The rest of the conversation was lost to her as the door clicked closed and she caught sight of Lucy and Drew surrounded by a veritable army of snow people. "Oh my goodness," she said. "This is amazing!"

The kids ran over to her, each grabbing one of her hands with their mitten-clad ones. "Look, Auntie," Drew said. "We made one for everyone."

"That's Mama, and that's Drew, and that's me, and that's you, and that's Mr. Tom," Lucy said, pointing to a different snowman in turn.

There was one snowman off to the side, a few steps away from the rest of them. Carson's heart broke as she looked at what she assumed to be a snow version of Ian. "Who's that one?" she asked. "Is that your dad?"

Drew's face scrunched up and he shook his head.

Lucy looked at the ground and then said in a barely audible voice, "No. That's someone else that we don't know yet."

"What do you mean? Like a new friend or something?"

"Kind of," Lucy said, digging the toe of her boot into the snow.

"Oh," Carson said, understanding slowly dawning on her. "You mean like a new friend for your mom."

Lucy gave a curt nod then turned toward their house. "Is it time to bring her lunch now?"

"We've got to run in and grab our stuff from inside so we don't leave it a mess for Mr. Tom, but then, yes, we can absolutely bring lunch down to your mom. She's probably pretty hungry by now."

As the three of them went back inside to gather the games and books and toys, Carson strained her ears to hear the rest of the flirty conversation happening between Tom and his latest customer. A certain satisfaction welled up as she realized the flirting was only one half of the conversation. Tom was as professional as ever.

It was only a matter of weeks until Carson left, and he would be free to flirt with anyone he pleased but she appreciated that he didn't do it while she was still within earshot.

"I will definitely be back for the paint and sip," the woman said as she headed toward the door. "Thanks for the info." With a million-dollar smile and a couple bottles of wine, she disappeared out into the cold afternoon. Even the elation at having another tentative sign-up couldn't keep Carson's heart from beating a light shade of green.

Tom

CARSON AND THE KIDS had taken off for the day, which was probably for the best as the traffic in the store picked up right after lunch and didn't slow down again until right before Will walked in a little past five.

The plan was for Carson and Nicole to come back after dinner and together they would all work to get the space cleared out.

While he and Will waited for them to show up, they carried in the box with the nine-foot artificial Christmas tree that Tom had gone out to buy the day after he told Carson they could use his store.

"It's gonna look great," Will said as they set the box off to the side of the room. "What made you decide to put one up this year?"

"Figured it would look good for the girls' painting thing. I already had it out back, so why the hell not, right?"

"You already had this?" Will asked, looking over the pristine state of the cardboard box. "Funny," he said. "I've never seen it before. And I've gone inside those sheds a time or two."

Tom hoisted up his end of the box. "Shut your face. And help me carry this thing over there."

In between customers, they worked to unload bottles from the wine racks, move the racks to the edges of the room, then reload them. It was slow work, but it needed to be done. It also gave Tom a chance to sweep the floor and get all the dust bunnies that had accumulated beneath them.

When the front door opened and the family shuffled into the store, Tom's mood lifted considerably. Not that he was in a bad mood, but now that Carson had shown up, he was in a great mood.

After a quick round of introductions, Nicole set the kids up in the side room again, this time with one game between them instead of the mountain of games they brought earlier.

Will couldn't keep his eyes off her. "Down, boy," Tom kidded. "You don't want to scare her away before you even talk to her." He gave him a playful smack on the arm then turned to help Carson hang up the coats on the rack in the corner.

"I am so excited for this," she said, bouncing on the balls of her feet. She had taken her hair out of her earlier ponytail and twirled it up into a messy bun, and Tom wanted nothing more than to pull the pin that held it in place and watch the soft waves fall down over her shoulders. Looking across the store, she said, "Wow, look how much you've already gotten done." Her eyes landed on the box with the tree. "And you got a tree!"

"You said you wanted one," he said.

"I love it!" Her arms lifted like she wanted to hug him, then she let them drop again, clearly aware that they had an audience. "Can we set it up?"

"I'll help," said Nicole. "That way they can keep moving the wine racks." Nicole looked from Will to Tom. "Is that alright with you?"

"A hundred percent," Tom said, knowing she made perfect sense but still wishing he could have worked with Carson to set up the tree.

"Can we help?" Lucy yelled from across the store.

"Give me and Auntie a few minutes to set it up then you guys can help us decorate it. Sound good?" Nicole said. The kids agreed and returned to their game.

The next two hours went by in a flurry of activity. Carson had turned her Christmas playlist on again and she and Nicole and the kids all sang along. Every time she sang, Tom wanted to grab her and pull her in for a kiss.

Flicking a glance Carson's way, Will whispered, "So, what's going on with you two?"

"Nothing," Tom lied. "We've been doing a bunch of planning for their paint thing, that's all."

"That's all," Will echoed. "Yeah, right, that's all. You're a shit liar, you know that?" Will chuckled under his breath. "I know you had sex with her."

Tom's stomach dropped. "How the hell do you know that?"

A grin broke out across Will's face. "Aside from the fact that you didn't deny it, it's written all over your face every time you look at her." He shook his head and laughed. "Which is every three seconds."

Carson lived ten states and sixteen hours away (he may have spent some time looking that up) and because she was only there temporarily, he hadn't planned on saying anything about her to anyone. Not even Will.

"I'm not that bad," he said, having no other defense. "She's just cute, that's all. Easy to look at."

Tom's eyes never strayed from Carson for long, as Will's once again sought out Nicole. "You're so busy giving me shit," Tom said. "Why don't you say something to her?" He lifted his chin in Nicole's direction.

"Maybe," Will said, lifting his end of the empty wine rack.

Lucy and Drew had moved to hold the ladder while Nicole balanced at the top working to string the lights. "Yikes," she said, wobbling from her high perch. "Oh my God!"

Will dropped his end of the wine rack and bolted to the base of the ladder. "You OK up there?" he asked, jamming his leg against it to keep it from moving. "Need me to take over?"

"No, I'm good," she said with a slight waver in her voice. "If you can just hold the ladder steady, though, that would be great." She smiled down at him, and Tom imagined Will had never been so happy to be holding up a ladder. Though he was probably waiting for her to fall so he could be the hero and catch her.

With a laugh, Tom turned to watch Carson on a small step ladder in the far room, stringing up lights along the long wall. Her ass was perfect as she reached up high and, taking a few steps closer, watched carefully to make sure she didn't need someone to catch her too.

Eventually Will came back and lifted his end of the rack. "Hold up," he said and let his end down gently again. Squatting down, he grabbed something from the floor then held his open hand out for Tom to see. "The hell is this?" A small purple plastic man lay across his palm.

From across the room, Drew bolted to Will's side and grabbed his hand, pulling it close to inspect his find. "It's mine," Drew said. "Mama," he yelled. "That guy found Professor Plum."

Still squatting to be at eye level with Drew, Will turned his hand and flipped the game piece into Drew's outstretched hand. "Here you go, little man. Professor Plum delivered safely."

Nicole approached and rested her hand on Drew's shoulder. "What do you say to Mr. Will?"

"Thank you for finding him," Drew said, stuffing the purple man into his pocket. "Do you wanna play a game with me?"

Will looked from Drew up to Nicole, whose eyes had gone wide and a little bit glassy. He looked back at Drew. "Dude, I love games," he said. "But I don't know what game that guy is from."

"Clue," Drew shouted. "It's my favorite. Do you wanna play it?"

"Can I play too?" Lucy asked, appearing by her mother's side.

"Absolutely," Will said, then looked at Nicole. "Up for a game of Clue?" He turned back to Drew. "You're going to have to teach me how to play, though."

Drew grabbed his hand and Will stood back up. "OK," Drew said, dragging him through the store and over to the coffee table.

Will threw a smiling glance over his shoulder to Tom.

"See," Carson said, walking over to help Tom move the last two wine racks. "That's what I meant when I said I was happy about you having a friend."

Knowing how much Will liked Nicole, he was glad for him as well.

The laughter and noise coming from the four of them playing their game was a double-edged sword for Tom. He was psyched that Will finally had his chance to get to know Nicole, but he was envious of the situation, knowing his own chance with Carson would be short-lived and over before it had time to grow into anything more.

By eight fifteen, the last-minute customers had stopped coming in and Tom finally locked the doors. Lucy had opted out of the last game of Clue, and Nicole had warned Drew it was the last game of the night. Through gaping yawns he tried to protest but Will stepped in to help. "It's all good, man. It's getting pretty late. I've got to get home and take my dog out one more time before she goes to bed for the night."

"You have a dog?" Drew asked. "Can I see her sometime?"

"If Mom says it's OK, I'll bring her back sometime when I come out here again. Sound good?"

Fifteen minutes later, Nicole and the kids were packed up and headed out the door. Will followed soon after.

"Have a good night, Will," Tom said. "And thanks for all the help tonight."

"Yeah," Carson said, giving him a knowing look. "Thank you for everything."

"It was my absolute pleasure," he said, donning his ball cap and heading out the door with a smile that barely fit through it.

Tom re-locked the door behind Will and turned to Carson. "Does this mean you can hang out with me for a while before you have to go home?"

Checking the time, she said with a gentle laugh, "It's barely eight-thirty. I've got some time."

"Good," he said. "Because I've got some ideas."

Carson

S HE HAD SOME IDEAS of her own and she'd had them since the first time she and Tom had sex. Once everybody else took off and they were alone together in the store, it only took him a few seconds to close the distance between them and have his hands on her hips, his mouth crushed against hers.

It scared her how much she wanted him. How much she craved his touch, the heat from his body. They both knew that what they had started wouldn't last and somehow it made the need to be together that much stronger.

"Did you bring any condoms with you?" she asked as he walked her backwards toward the far end of the small side room where there were no windows.

He stopped kissing her neck, her cheeks, her lips, only long enough to say, "Yup." His hands never left her body.

Walking backward, her balance faltered, but Tom's hands on the small of her back guided her until they reached the end wall, tucked away in the corner where nobody could see them. She was doing the same thing to her heart; pushing it into a corner where it couldn't be seen or touched. Except, the more time she spent around Tom, the more familiar his hands on her body became, the more exposed her heart felt.

Tipping her head back, she gave him access to the hollow of her throat, his breath warm and his soft beard tickling her skin. Closing her eyes, she let her hands find their own way around his body, up his arms, over his shoulders, down his back. She angled her head to catch his kisses again, needing his mouth on her mouth, his tongue against her tongue. Touching, tasting, pulling away. Chasing and being chased.

Tom's fingers took hold of the hem of her sweater, pulled it inside out as he lifted it over her head, then tossed it to the floor. She moved her body away from the cold wood wall against her back, but his body stopped her forward movement and gently pushed her backward again. His warm hands rubbed the cold out of her back as he continued feasting on her mouth.

Unable to hold herself back, Carson moved her fingers to his fly, making quick work of the button before she unzipped it and shoved her hand into his boxer briefs.

Tom groaned against her mouth as his hips started to push and pull, causing a gentle friction against the fingers she had wrapped around him. "Oh my God, Carson," he whispered into her ear. "That feels amazing." She closed her fingers a little bit tighter. "Fuck…"

Her back had adjusted to the temperature of the wall behind her, and she leaned back, letting Tom use her shoulder as leverage while he stroked himself through her fingers. The need for him that coursed through her veins grew stronger every time his thigh bumped hers. His face was buried in the crook of her neck, and she turned her head and kissed his cheek every time he pushed into her hand.

A needy hunger wracked her body, and she needed him to be thrusting into her body, not just her hand. "Tom," she whispered.

"Are you ready for me?" he whispered in response, already knowing what she needed.

"Yes."

She kept her fingers wrapped around him while he pushed her pants down past her hips, running his hands over the soft, bare skin of her ass. She was caged between the bulk of his body and the wall behind her.

Taking a step away, he lowered himself to his knees in front of her. "Oh." He spread her legs apart, as much as the restricting fabric of her pants would allow and leaned in to place a lingering kiss against her low belly. Her legs trembled and she grabbed onto his shoulders as he slipped his tongue between her lips and licked a slow, delicious path through her center.

Carson stood, legs spread, eyes closed, and drummed an erratic beat to go along with her erratic breaths. He returned his full attention to savoring her, licking her, sucking her, and then, sliding one hand to the front, slipping one finger slowly inside her. He worked her with his tongue and his finger before he slowly added a second.

The rest of the world melted away as she allowed Tom to bring her this fleeting pleasure. Working the tip of his tongue in small circles with slowly increasing pressure, Carson moaned, needing to experience everything he had to offer.

Tension gathered in her belly and her fingers and her toes, all careening into a giant ball of energy that finally exploded. Her muscles tensed around his fingers, and, with panting breaths of ecstasy, she frantically flailed her hands, grabbing for something to steady herself and ending up with two fistfuls of his hair as her legs gave out beneath her.

"Sorry," she whispered, half-heartedly trying to flatten his hair back into place. "Didn't mean to... You're just... really good at that." She sighed softly and reached down to pull her clothing back into place.

"Are you sure you want to put those back on?" he said, stilling her hands as they grabbed the waistband of her pants.

"Unless you can think of something better to do while they're off..."

He reached into his pocket and pulled out a condom.

"May I?" she said, reaching to take it from him. When he didn't stop her, she ripped open the little foil packet and took out the condom. Stepping forward on slightly wobbly legs, she reached down and rolled it over him, watching his eyes fall closed at her touch.

As soon as she removed her hand his eyes flew open. "Take those off," he said, pointing to her pants.

Quickly, she pushed them down to the floor and stepped out of them, leaving her once again in nothing but a pair of socks. His body crashed against hers in an instant and he pressed her into the wall. Lifting one of her legs, he held it in the crook of his arm as he positioned himself to enter her.

"I shouldn't want you this much, Carson. I shouldn't need to be inside you more than I need my next fucking breath." With a hard thrust, he slid into her with a grunt. As he pulled back, he said, "I can't keep you." He pounded into her again. "So why can't I get you out of my fucking mind?"

The intensity with which he drove into her took her breath away. He crashed into her over and over as he pinned her against the wall with his body. Right before he climaxed, he buried his face into her neck again, his teeth grazing the skin of her collarbone.

"Oh fuck, Carson... Fuck," he whispered. Wrapping her hands around his back, she held him close as she clenched around him. He thrust his hips into her one last time. With a forceful exhale into her hair, he pressed his body against hers, trembling slightly as he finished.

Carson

T HE NEXT FEW DAYS passed in a whirlwind of activity. Between taking care of Lucy and Drew during the day, trying to get caught up on work for Southern Charm each evening, and helping to organize last minute details with Nicole every second in between, Carson barely had time to wave to Tom when they saw each other in passing.

But his words from the other night had been playing in an infinite loop in her mind. *I shouldn't want you this much. I can't keep you.* Those were big words, powerful words. She just had no idea what to make of them. He wanted her...except that he didn't want her. It was enough to make her head spin.

She decided to push his words to the back of her mind and deal with them another time. Or maybe she wouldn't deal with them at all, and she'd consider it a non-issue when she got back to Savannah.

As a hazy morning dawned, Nicole had gone down to her shop to pack up and ship out a slew of last-minute orders. Carson finalized details for one of the events back in Savannah, then she and the kids did some more work on their snow fort before they switched focus to smoothing out a path for their sleds behind the house.

Nicole had explained to her that the small house had been built for the parents of the winery's previous owner. Once they retired and moved to Florida the house sat empty until Tom bought the place and rented out the little ranch house with a small front yard and a small downward sloping hill in the back.

"It has to turn at the end, so we don't break Mr. Tom's plants," Lucy said as she patted down the snow at the bottom of the run.

"I like the way you think," Tom said, appearing from out of nowhere and catching the three of them off guard. "And I certainly appreciate you worrying about my plants."

Drew jumped up and ran over to Tom. "Look!" He opened his mouth and pointed to the hole where his wiggly baby tooth used to be. "It came out in the candy we made."

"It did?"

"Yeah," Drew said. "I saved a little bit of it, and I had it last night and when I bit it, my tooth fell out!" Drew's pink cheeks pulled into a gap-toothed smile and Carson was reminded once more that Ian should be the one to be celebrating Drew's missing tooth.

"Fist bump!" Tom said.

Drew's mittened hand folded over and he crashed it into Tom's big hand then he ran back to work on the sled run with Lucy.

Carson wanted to throw her arms around Tom but wasn't sure if she should. She was well aware of the little eyes that watched everything she did. "Hey," she said as she approached, but kept a respectable distance from him. "What's going on?"

His breath came out with little puffs of steam in the cold air. "Nothing. Just had a few minutes before I have to get back to work and saw you outside over here. Thought I'd come over and say hi. I haven't seen you much the past couple days."

"Sorry," she said. "I've been so busy with these two." She pointed over her shoulder. "I've also been neglecting my real job and I've had so much work to catch up on, so I don't get fired, that I've barely had time to breathe, let alone get out of the house by myself. Not to mention all the little stuff Nicole's needed help with at the store. And then there's the paint night."

"How's that coming along?" he asked. "How many people did you get to sign up?"

"We've actually gotten quite a few. Not as many as I was hoping for but there's still time."

"Was there a Jenny or Grace Valentine on the list?"

"There was," Carson said. "Both of them signed up." She'd been checking for sign up responses every hour for the past week and she knew the names of all the people on the list. "Are they friends of yours?"

"Yeah," he said, a smile pulling the corner of his mouth. "They're the wife and daughter of a friend of mine. I'm glad to hear they're coming." When he stepped closer to her, her instinct was to step away, to keep a necessary distance as well as keep things off the radar of the kids, but she stayed rooted to the ground and found herself welcoming his nearness.

"I was wondering if you had any plans tonight," he said.

"Ummm... Not sure. Why do you ask?"

"The town is doing the big Christmas tree lighting tonight, and I thought I might close up a little early and go check it out."

"We're going to that!" Lucy yelled from where she was kneeling and patting snow. That answered the question of whether the kids were always paying attention or not.

"We get to have hot chocolate!" Drew added. "And popcorn."

Tom and Carson laughed. "I guess we're already going to that," Carson said, huddling against the cold that she still struggled, unsuccessfully, to get used to.

"Any chance you'd go with me?" he asked. His eyes were bright and hopeful. Tiny alarm bells started chiming in her head, warning her that she needed to slow down with him. She was leaving soon and getting attached to Tom Wyatt, as much as she enjoyed being with him, was going to cause a lot of pain when it ended. There was no other way around it. "Then I was thinking maybe we could walk around town and do a little Christmas shopping. Maybe stop for a hot toddy or something."

When she opened her mouth to voice her concerns, the only thing that came out was, "I'd really like that." The sound of a missile drawing near and then exploding was so loud in her mind she feared everyone around her had heard it too.

His smile warmed her, despite the frigid air and all the unknowns between them. "Good enough," he said and touched his finger to the side of her cheek. "See you tonight then."

Watching him turn and walk up the hill, Carson wasn't as shy as she should have been about admiring the way his butt looked in those jeans.

Once he was out of sight, she walked the few yards down the hill to help Lucy and Drew.

Lucy said, "He's really nice."

"Yeah, he is," Carson agreed, squatting down to help bank the side of the sled run.

"I think he likes you."

"Well sure he likes me. He's a nice man and we get along really well."

Lucy's eyebrow took on a severe arch and her resemblance to Nicole was uncanny. "I mean he *likes you* likes you."

Carson sat back on her heels and laughed. "And what do you know of *liking* liking someone?"

"I don't like anyone that way, but my friend Bryce looks at me like that and he said it's because he *likes me* likes me."

"Lucy, sweetheart, you're eight. You don't need to worry about people *liking* liking you. You know that right?"

"I know," she said. "I told Bryce that too, so we're good. But he still smiles at me a lot." With a shrug, she turned to her brother and said, "Wanna try to sled it now?"

Tom

I T WAS A STRANGE feeling to miss someone you'd only seen a few hours prior. But after not seeing Carson for a few days straight, the time between inviting her to the tree lighting and the time he walked over to pick her up felt like a whole other week had gone by.

The last time he'd gone to the town's tree lighting was the first and only Christmas he'd had with Heather at Whispering Hills. They'd moved out there permanently the previous summer and by the time the holiday season had rolled around, they were living with the underlying current of tension that ran through their life together as husband and wife, as well as small business owners.

In the intervening years, the giant evergreen in the middle of the park behind Main Street had been lit and then turned off without Tom ever having seen it happen.

He, Carson, and Drew took his truck into town while Nicole and Lucy had taken Nicole's car. Tom had never spent much time with kids but these two had started to warm him up to the idea that maybe kids weren't so bad. Making snow forts and maple candy with them had been surprisingly fun.

The entire downtown area had been transformed into a winter wonderland. Green garland wrapped with white lights had been strung along the storefronts on Main Street. Giant wreaths with bright red bows hung from every streetlight. Both ends of the road had been closed to traffic, allowing people to walk down the middle of the road and cross without worry to the other side.

The wrought iron fence around the town common had been strung with soft white lights. Banquet tables had been set up to dispense hot chocolate and hot apple cider and the local civic group sold popcorn bags and hot pretzels as a fundraiser for their organization. Since Hanukkah had ended earlier in the month, a huge menorah sat, each of its candles lit up, on the far side of the common, nearer to the road.

Despite the unseasonably cold air, the entire downtown area teemed with people, old and young, bundled up and seeming to enjoy the event. Hazelton High School's jazz band played a selection of seasonal music, helping to add to the festive feeling in the air. Groups of people milled around, talking and laughing as they waited for Santa to drive by in his horse-drawn wagon.

As the little group stood together, each with a cup of hot chocolate, and the kids with bags of popcorn, a feeling of comfort settled over Tom. He couldn't help but laugh as Drew attempted to eat his popcorn by shoving his face into the bag in order to keep from spilling his hot chocolate. Carson and Nicole attempted to keep him from spilling everything all at once, and that comfortable feeling spread into one of warmth, that deepened with each heartbeat.

Lucy shook her head at her brother's antics. "Would you please hold this?" she asked, handing Tom her hot chocolate. She proceeded to eat her popcorn with her fingers.

Hearing Carson and Nicole laugh together only made that warm feeling stronger. He'd known Nicole as his tenant for six months and barely even saw her smile. Something about Carson seemed to bring out the fun in everyone. Himself, begrudgingly, included. It was going to gut him when she left.

"Hello, everyone! Welcome to 'Holidays at Home' and thank you for coming out on such a chilly night," the Mayor said into her microphone. "I've been told that Santa Claus is taking time out of his busy schedule to make a quick visit to Hazelton." Some children jumped up and down, others made little excited squeaking noises. One of the parents in a group nearby lifted his little girl onto his shoulders, helping her see better.

Sleigh bells jangled in the distance and wagon wheels creaked along with the clomping of horse feet as the jolly man himself approached from the west end of the street.

Ben Bradshaw made a striking Santa Claus as he pulled the wagon to a stop and waved to the crowd, yelling out a festive, "Ho ho ho! Merry Christmas!" He'd been playing Santa for so long, an entire generation of children probably imagined his face as the one leaving gifts beneath their trees every twenty-fourth of December.

Ben waved and held his other hand over his belly, doing his best Santa laugh. "Hello girls and boys! Have you all been good this year?" Shouts of delight went up from the gathered crowd. "I knew you were all on the nice list this year," he said before calling out to the mayor, "I can't wait to see that tree when it's all lit up, Ms. Mayor!"

Mayor Sanchez gave a thumbs up and held up the microphone. "You heard him," she yelled. "Are you ready to light it?"

The whole crowd cheered, including Lucy and Drew.

"Ten!" the mayor shouted. She continued counting downward until she hit one. "Go!" everyone yelled and the DPW worker at the switch did his magic. The giant spruce glittered in bright primary colors with a big yellow star on top.

Everyone clapped and choruses of "ooohh" and "aahh" rippled through the common. With one last wave to the crowd, and a hearty "Merry Christmas!" Santa nudged the horses forward again and disappeared from view.

After a few minutes, one of Drew's friends came running up to the little group inviting him and Lucy to play tag with a bunch of other kids further down the field. "Stay where I can see you," Nicole called after them. "And make sure you listen for me if I call you!"

Lucy turned to say, "OK," then ran full tilt toward the other kids.

A tall figure cut his way through the crowd and once he got a bit closer, Tom realized it was Will. Assuming his friend was coming to see him, he was pleasantly surprised when Will's eyes found Nicole first. "Hey, guys," he said, standing beside Tom. "I thought I saw you all over here."

If he'd blinked, he would've missed the subtle smiles and furtive glances shared between sisters. But they were definitely there. At least he thought they were. Carson's and Nicole's faces showed absolutely no sign of anything, other than friendliness, as they picked up the conversation.

"Hi, Will," Carson said. "It's nice to see you again."

"I never miss this," he said, looking around. "It's nice to see that you managed to get this guy down here, though." He playfully smacked Tom on the arm and laughed.

"What do you mean?" Carson said. "It was his idea. *He* invited *me*."

Will's face split into a shit-eating grin. "Is that so?"

Tom knew he'd never hear the end of it when the women weren't around to hear Will bust his balls.

"Well, I won't get in the way of your evening. Just wanted to come over and say hi."

Tom was not an authority on women by any stretch of the imagination but there was no way he missed the look of disappointment on Nicole's face when Will mentioned he was leaving. It was fleeting but as real as the air they breathed.

"Yeah, I have to go check on my kids," Nicole said. "It was nice to see you again." She turned to find Lucy and Drew.

Will walked off in the opposite direction and Carson looked at Tom. "Please tell me you saw that, too," she said.

"Saw what?" Tom asked, unsure of anything he'd just witnessed.

"Obviously those two have something going on in their heads. Because I feel like if we weren't around, they totally would have spent the next hour lost in a world all their own."

Laughing, Tom said, "I don't know that I picked up all of that, but there sure seemed to be a little bit of tension in the air."

Carson clapped her mittened hands and squeaked, "Yay!" It was absolutely adorable. Pretty much like everything else she did. At least everything she did while she had clothes on.

The envy he'd felt around Will and Nicole the other day came rolling back, full force. Needing a bit of one-on-one time with Carson, he reached out and took hold of her hand. "Come on. Let's walk around and see what else is happening over there."

Carson

DURING HER TIME IN Hazelton, Carson had learned that it was tradition for the shop owners of the town to be open extended hours on the night of the tree lighting when most people would be milling around town and in a festive holiday mood.

Nicole had thought about opening up Happenstance but decided against it so she could spend the evening hanging out with her kids. In her absence, Carson had hung a sign on the door with little rip off tabs inviting people to come to the paint and sip at Whispering Hills the following Friday.

Slowly over the past week, new registrations trickled in, bringing their grand total to fifteen so far. At that rate, for the first time since it had been no more than an idea, she worried they might actually not have enough room if too many more signed up. Once she hung the sign, she ripped off a few tabs, thinking it would have a two-fold effect: First, it would look like other people were interested, thus encouraging others to take a tab. Second, it would limit the number of available tabs, hopefully keeping from having to turn people away.

As she and Tom walked hand-in-hand through town, she began to feel the press of time as if it were a weighted blanket that had been draped across her shoulders. Four weeks wasn't long enough.

The paint and sip was happening on Friday and a week after that was Christmas. She'd have one more week before the kids went back to school and she wasn't needed in Hazelton anymore. A soft melancholy settled in her heart, already missing the family she'd only gotten to know recently. And having to leave Tom would be hardest of all.

"Do they do things like this down in Savannah?" Tom asked.

"I'm not sure," she said. "For the past ten years, the big celebration for me was being in charge of the Hatch family's giant Christmas party."

"That sounds fun."

"Oh, it is. They're this super old family in Savannah and there are at least three generations in attendance every year. Sometimes four. And there are well over a hundred of them that show up for this party. Every. Single. Year."

She didn't realize her voice had betrayed her feelings until Tom asked, "It's fun but you don't really like it?"

Until she'd come back to Massachusetts, she would have said the Hatch party was the highlight of her year, despite not being part of the family. But feeling the warmth and connection with her own *actual* family brought the contrast into sharp focus.

"No," she said. "I like it just fine. They're really nice people and it's always a blast..."

"But?"

"I'm not sure I know how to explain it."

"Give it a try," he said, giving her hand a gentle squeeze.

"I love what I do very much but sometimes it's hard to watch everyone else celebrate. They're an amazingly generous family and I really do like them." She pondered her next words for a few seconds. "But they're not my family."

Tom nodded. "And it's hard being away from your family this time of year?"

"It is."

Gently pulling her to a stop, he said, "Have you ever thought of moving back home?"

"You sound like my sister," she said with a laugh. "This isn't my home anymore."

A group of children ran up the sidewalk toward them and she and Tom jumped out of the way of the horde. Jogging behind the kids, with a small girl on her hip, a harried looking woman kept yelling, "Slow down! Wait for us! Stop running!"

Carson and Tom fell into step again as Carson looked into the windows of each shop they passed. Strings of bright lights outlined the top of the front window, while artificial snow had been sprayed along the bottom of the window of the little touristy gift shop on the other side of the street. She grabbed his hand and pulled him toward the shop. "That looks like a fun place to find a few things for the kids," she said.

Browsing the shelves of books and toys at Greely's General Store, Carson enjoyed choosing things Lucy and Drew would like, not just because of their age and gender—the way she always chose their gifts in years past. This time she knew them as people and understood the things that would bring them joy.

"That's cute," Tom said when she held up a stuffed tyrannosaur she'd been thinking about for Drew. "He'll definitely like that."

"Yeah," she said, hugging the dinosaur tighter. "I have to admit, I usually do my shopping online. It's nice to get out and get a little exercise. Not to mention being able to touch things. There's something to be said for holding something in your hand."

A mischievous smile pulled at his lips. "Oh, yes," he said. "Touching things and holding them is definitely the way to go." His eyes laser focused on her and her entire body flamed in response.

Their dwindling time together weighed heavier on her shoulders. She would miss these flirty conversations with Tom, and she wondered if he'd miss them too.

Bringing Drew's dinosaur and a book on how to draw flowers she'd picked up for Lucy, Carson joined the line to the counter to pay for her gifts. Having Tom beside her, her body buzzed with awareness.

When it was her turn to pay, she reached into her wallet and fumbled to get her credit card. With a slight tremble she touched her card to the terminal. She waited to hear the beep, but the noise never sounded. Flipping the card around, she tried again. Aware of the line of people waiting behind her, her heart beat a little harder. Moving her card to a different spot on the terminal, she tried again, still with no response. Why was she suddenly unable to perform such a simple task?

Her fingers trembled and she laughed softly. "Sorry," she mumbled to the clerk. Suddenly, Tom's warm hand was holding hers and he led it over the small, blue square on the terminal—the only place she hadn't tapped the card. Two seconds later the machine beeped, and he released her hand. Relief poured through her. "Thank you," she said, and still fumbling, stuffed her card back into her wallet.

"See you later, Lou," Tom called out to the shop owner as they walked out the door. To the right of the door, on the glass wall that separated the outside world from the inside, hung a flyer that she instantly recognized but knew she hadn't hung there.

"Hey," she said, pointing to it as they passed through the door. "How'd that get there?"

"No idea," Tom said, a smile tugging at one side of his lips. An overwhelming jumble of emotions flooded her. Gratitude. Appreciation. Giddiness. Desire.

But underpinning all of it was that subtle preemptive sense of loss.

He took the bag from her hand then led the way through the gathering crowd.

"I can carry that," she said.

"I know." He made no move to return the bag.

"Chivalry and all that?" she asked with a quick peck on his cheek.

"Something like that."

They walked along in silence for a while, her arm linked through his, making their way up the street where the crowd was a bit thinner.

"I'm sorry," she said as they ambled along. "About overstepping at the winery last week."

Tom pulled up short. "What brought that back up? I haven't thought about that since the day it happened." He looked down at her. "You haven't been worrying about that all week, have you?"

"Maybe."

Rubbing a gloved thumb across her frozen cheek, he leaned down and brought his lips to hers. "There's nothing to apologize for," he said when he pulled back. "You didn't do, or say, anything wrong." He kissed her again and their cold lips warmed against each other. "I was wrong for the way I reacted."

"No, you weren't," Carson said. "You were one hundred percent right. I get excited about planning things and making things happen. I should have remembered that you told me you weren't interested in expanding your business any further than the distillery." She looked up into the warmth of his eyes. "How's that coming along, by the way?"

"It's good," he said, rubbing his hands down her arms. "But you're freezing, aren't you?"

She shrugged. "A little bit."

"Come on," he said, taking one of her hands and walking back toward the common and, presumably, back to Nicole and the kids.

"Do you know why I don't want to expand my business?" he asked after a few long moments of silence as they walked.

She shook her head.

"I told you I was married once, right?"

"Yeah."

He took a deep breath and blew it out, making a fluffy white cloud that dissipated as she watched. "When Heather and I moved out here and bought the vineyard, I had been under the impression that it was a mutually agreed upon change of pace for the both of us. I was so close to burning out in my job and I think I had some blinders on. I thought because she agreed to me buying the property that she was all-in on running it with me. I didn't realize she had no intention of staying out here."

"Tom, I'm so sorry that happened to you."

He shook his head. "Thanks," he said. "I appreciate that. We split up less than six months after I bought the place, and she went back to Boston. And for a long time I was angry."

"Of course."

"And I was closed off," he said.

"Rightfully so."

He looked over, the most genuine smile aimed directly at her. "You're sweet, do you know that?"

"So I've been told," she said, though she couldn't remember who, aside from her own parents, had ever said those words to her.

"The original plan was for me to do most of the behind-the-scenes work on the business and Heather was supposed to be the friendly face that stood between our customers and myself. Since she left it's been all me, all the time. And I'll tell you something—burnout is real, Carson. Having experienced it once, I have no desire to do it again. Especially not with something I love as much as I love Whispering Hills."

"And the distillery is going to stretch you, isn't it?" Carson asked.

He nodded slowly. "It will and it won't. I live for the physical side of my work."

Carson giggled inwardly because she knew how physically capable he was, in every way.

"I don't mind adding more work to my days. And I don't mind adding more product to my store. What I don't have, though, is more time in my day to do tours and wine tastings and all those other things. My life is busy enough as it is. There's no room for anything else."

No room for any*thing* else meant the same thing as no room for any*one* else. His life was full, and he'd just answered all her questions with that one statement. The thing happening between them was only temporary.

She swallowed around the disappointment and focused on the other thing she'd screwed up. "I am so sorry to have made that offer to Emma. When I see her again, I'll say something. I'll apologize and tell her I was out of line to offer something that wasn't mine to offer."

"Don't worry about it," he said as they neared the common. "We've only got a couple weeks left together and I don't want to spend it arguing over a non-issue like this."

A look passed over his face, a look that held some kind of meaning but Carson had no idea what. Maybe he didn't want her to talk to Emma. Or maybe she had done enough to get in his way over the past few weeks and it will be better for everyone, especially him, once she boarded that plane to Georgia.

Carson

W HILE THE KIDS FINISHED getting dressed and brushing their teeth, Carson hopped onto the registration page for the paint and sip. Relief, joy, excitement all rushed through her as she saw the current attendee count at an even twenty. It wasn't the thirty she'd been hoping for, but it was more than the fifteen they had the other day. With two more days to go, there was still time for a few more people to sign up.

Christmas was just over a week away, the paint and sip was only two days away, and Carson's friendship with Tom had more than passed the halfway mark. There were fewer days together ahead of them than they had behind them. Her belly pinched thinking about having to pack up her things and head back to Savannah.

"A RE YOU SERIOUS?" NICOLE asked as she pulled a turkey sandwich from her lunch bag. "You really have twenty people who've signed up... and paid... to do a paint and sip with me at Tom's winery? A week before Christmas?" She shook her head and let out a good-natured laugh. "Are you some kind of wizard, Cari?"

"No wizardry, I promise," Carson said, making a small X over her heart.

"No, you're right. It's not magic. It's just you being great at what you do and being an amazing sister on top of it." Nicole blinked back a few tears but then dropped her sandwich and moved to the front side of the counter to pull Carson into a hug. "Thank you."

"You don't have to thank me, Colie. You never have to thank me."

Nicole released her, wiped her cheeks, grabbed her sandwich from the counter. "Right," she said with a curt nod. "We're sisters. We take care of each other."

"Yes, we do." Carson's heart swelled with love for her sister and that dread at having to leave her in a couple weeks poked through, threatening to wreck their sweet moment.

The shorter her remaining time in Hazelton, the less Savannah felt like home. The comfort of the small town and the friends she'd made in such a short time pulled at her heart in a way it never had growing up. Back then she couldn't wait to leave her sleepy little hometown to live someplace big and exciting.

Lucy and Drew had gone into the small office to wait while Carson and Nicole talked, Lucy with her favorite book and Drew with his iPad. "How are things with Tom?" Nicole asked, keeping her voice low so the kids couldn't hear.

Memories of the last time she was with him warmed her instantly. "Pretty good," she said. "But still not a hundred percent sure if this was a good idea."

Nicole finished a bite of her sandwich. "Not even going to try the long-distance thing?"

"I can't see it working," she said. It was an idea that Carson had toyed with, but she could never think of a way to keep their fledgling romance going with such a distance between them. If he wasn't interested in trying to make things work with her in person, there was no way he'd have the time or patience to attempt something long distance.

Looking at her thoughtfully, Nicole tipped her head to the side. "You know there's an easy solution to this problem, don't you?"

"What's that?"

"It's the same one I had last week. You move back here. You get rid of your place in Georgia, and you come back home."

Home. There was that word again.

"Colie, this isn't my home. Not anymore."

Nicole's lips flattened into a straight line. "Do you seriously consider Savannah your home? Like, deep down in your heart of hearts, do you honestly believe that?"

"I have a job there. It's how I earn my living. That's not something a person gives up easily."

Plunking her elbow on the counter, Nicole rested her chin in her upturned hand and regarded Carson as if scanning her for the absolute truth that hid inside her. The truth that Carson was too afraid to say out loud.

The bell above the door jingled and Carson sucked in a deep breath of gratitude to be free of the gaze of her sister.

"Carson," Emma called. "Oh, I'm so glad you're here." The older woman shuffled through the store, being careful not to knock anything over with her big, puffy coat until she stood between the sisters. "Hi, Nicole. How are you this freezing cold afternoon?" She rubbed her hands together and her whole body shivered.

"I'm well, Emma, thank you," Nicole replied.

"One thing I just can't get used to living here these past forty years is the cold. Seems the older I get the less I enjoy it," Emma said to nobody in particular.

"Were you looking for me?" Carson said, drawing the older woman's attention again.

Emma's smiling face pulled a smile from Carson in return. "Yes, dear, I wanted to talk to you about your painting thing and I was hoping I didn't have to drive all the way out to Tom's place." Her smile transformed into a playful smirk. "Although, that's not really much of a hardship, is it?"

Nicole and Carson both laughed. "Not a hardship at all," Carson said. "That's for sure."

Emma waved her hand through the air, as if she was brushing away the tempting thought of making a pit stop at Whispering Hills. "But I just don't have the time for it today so I'm glad you're here."

"How can I help?" Carson said.

Plopping her large purple handbag on the counter, Emma unzipped it and started rooting through it until she found what she was looking for. "Here," she said, pulling some papers out of her bag, a look of triumph on her face. "I couldn't get the sign-up link to work. My husband kept telling me I typed it wrong, but whatever. Here's a check to cover me, Delores, her daughter, and her daughter-in-law." She looked at the check over the rim of her glasses then held it out for Carson to take. "That's the right amount, right?"

From behind the counter, Nicole let out a small gasp.

"Is this not OK?" Emma asked.

"Oh, no," Carson said. "It's totally fine. I think my sister is just a little excited to have more people at her big night."

"Absolutely," Nicole added. "I'm so happy this is coming together as well as it is and I'm so glad that all of you will be there."

Emma visibly relaxed. "Oh, good. Now I get to tell my husband he was wrong."

The women all laughed.

"I've never met Delores's daughter before," Nicole said. "Or her daughter-in-law."

Emma's hand flew to her heart, squishing the fluffy down of her coat. "You're going to love them," she said. "They are absolute dolls, both of them."

After a few more minutes of chatting about the paint night, Emma looked at her watch. "OK, girls, I'm afraid I've got to run. I need to pick up a few more last-minute Christmas gifts." She trundled back through the store and out into the cold.

Carson knew she should have mentioned something about not thinking before she offered Tom's business for her meetings, but everybody was in such high spirits, she didn't want to dampen the mood. Now that Emma was going to the paint and sip, Nicole could apologize there.

Beside her, Nicole's smile lit up the small space. "That's twenty-four, isn't it?" she asked.

"It is."

Nicole pumped her fist. "Yes!"

LUCY AND DREW FINISHED eating dinner first then retreated to the living room to watch *Elf* for at least the tenth time that week.

Carson and Nicole went back to their seats at the table as soon as the dishes were cleared and broke open the bottle of apple wine that Tom had given them.

With a touch of cinnamon, the sweet apple wine tasted more like apple pie in a glass. "My turn to ask questions," Carson whispered, her pajama-clad leg bent up beneath her as she leaned toward Nicole.

Nicole sipped from her own glass, regarded Carson over the rim. "OK..." she said, her tone wary. "What would you like to know?"

Carson scooted her chair closer to her sister. "I want to know everything there is to know about Will."

"Will?" Nicole echoed. "What about him?" She hadn't had enough wine for the pink hue in her cheeks to be anything other than a response to the mention of Tom's friend.

"I was hoping you'd tell me. He seemed pretty into you at the winery the other day. And at the tree lighting the other night." She leaned back in her chair. "And you've got to admit, he's not too difficult to look at."

Despite her attempted nonchalance, Nicole couldn't stop her giggle at Carson's observation and Carson's heart lightened at the hopeful sound.

"He is pretty cute, isn't he?" Nicole said in a hushed tone, presumably so the kids wouldn't hear her. But they were far too invested in the antics on the screen to pay any attention to the adults' conversation. "He's got a really nice body too." Her shoulders drooped.

"Is that a bad thing?" Carson had no idea how it could be.

"No," Nicole said with a shrug. "It's great for him, but look at me." She held her arms out to the side and stared down at her body. "I've had two kids, and it looks like I've eaten nothing but Christmas cookies every night for the last ten years."

Why the hell were women always so hard on themselves? Carson had never had children and she worked out regularly, yet how many times did she look at her own body and find it lacking, exactly the same way Nicole had just done? Something about hearing her amazingly kind, gentle, beautiful, loving sister disparage herself pissed her off instantly.

"Don't you dare," Carson said. "Don't you dare put yourself down like that. You are beautiful exactly the way you are. Your body is amazing, and it does amazing things." She lifted her gaze toward the living room where Lucy and Drew sat giggling hysterically. "It made those two incredible humans."

"But—"

"But nothing," Carson said, trying to keep her voice low. "Your value as a mom, as a woman, as a goddamn human being has nothing to do with what size pants you wear." The tips of her ears burned, and Nicole sat, staring at her wide-eyed. "You are stunning exactly the way you are. Right. Now." She jabbed her finger into the tabletop for emphasis. Then to lighten the mood, she tucked a few stray hairs behind Nicole's ear. "OK," she said. "I fixed that one last thing that wasn't quite right." Smiling, she said, "So, now I'm gonna need you to just go ahead and admit that you're a goddess."

Nicole snort-laughed and took another sip of wine. "Right," she said, raising her glass in a mock toast. "It's me, the goddess of single motherhood and loneliness."

"How about you are the most important person in their lives?" Carson said, indicating Lucy and Drew with the tilt of her chin. "But even without that, you are a-freaking-mazing, Nicole. And I'm telling you, even if it isn't Will that notices it, someone else is going to. With a gentle touch against her sister's cheek, she said, "I mean, how could they not?"

Nicole sniffed and wiped at her eyes and smiled a wobbly smile. "Do you really think he likes me?"

With a soft laugh, Carson said, "You didn't see the way he looked at you when you were all playing games at Tom's the other day."

"What? No he didn't. He was playing games with Drew and Lucy."

"Little sister, he couldn't keep his eyes off you. Every time your attention was elsewhere, his was fixed solely on you."

Nicole's smile grew. "And he was really great with my kids," she added softly. She raised her eyes to Carson's. "Wasn't he?"

Carson nodded. "Do you think you'll see him again?"

Nicole shrugged. "I mean, he said he's at Tom's kind of a lot. Maybe I should go over the next time I see his truck there."

With a distinct lightness in her chest, Carson said, "I think anything you do would be fine. Besides, I think he's planning to be there to help us get set up on Friday."

Nicole blinked and her lips curled into a smile as she raised her wine glass. Before she took a sip, she said, "He really is so freaking cute, isn't he?"

"Um... *yeah* he is." Carson took a sip of her wine, thought about Tom and how cute he was in his own right.

A peal of laughter rang out from the living room and Carson and Nicole laughed along with the kids even though they had no idea what they were laughing at.

"You know what would be fun?" Nicole said once they stopped laughing. "If you didn't have to go back to Savannah and you could just stay here, and we could all hang out together." She spun her glass in a slow circle between her fingers. "We could double date."

Carson's heart ached. Hanging out regularly with Tom and Nicole and Will sounded like a dream come true. But Tom had already made clear that what they had was a short-term thing. He wasn't looking to add anything else full-time to his life. And there was no way Carson would be willing, or able, to be anything less with him. Once she'd spent time in his orbit, learning his world, learning his body and his likes, there was no way in hell she could ever downgrade to just friends.

He had enough to worry about with a business to run, not to mention all the extra work the new distillery would be. As inviting as the fantasy sounded, it would have to stay just that—a fantasy.

"That would be fun," Carson finally said, swallowing a mouthful of wine to try to dull the ache in her heart.

Nicole sighed deeply, reached over and rested her hand on top of Carson's. "I really wish you didn't have to leave."

Tom

N OT TEN MINUTES INTO the workday Friday morning, a text came through from Will.

> Paint thing still on for tonight?

> Yep

> Got room for a couple more? Two of my SILs wanna go. Said it sounded fun.

Leave it to Will to be the social event manager for his sisters-in-law.

> Only two of them?

> Yeah. One has to work. Others have plans. See you tonight.

Sliding his phone into his back pocket, Tom stood and looked around the empty space in his store. With the wine racks moved to the perimeter and the extra room cleared out to make space for the plastic banquet tables, the wood floor seemed to expand for miles in every direction. Carson's idea for high-top tables flitted through his mind again.

So often after Heather left and it was just Tom alone in the store with his thoughts, the silence was like a friend to him, a therapist that listened to his thoughts without judgment and, most importantly, without expectation. This time, as he returned to sweeping the floor, the stillness and quiet that normally comforted him seemed instead to close in on him, sucking the air from the room.

What was it about Carson Everett that had him feeling both completely upended yet somehow completely grounded all at the same time? He wasn't sure if there was any one thing he could easily point to, or if it was simply Carson being Carson and Tom wanting nothing more than to be around her as much as he possibly could.

It scared him how quickly he had developed feelings for her. It wasn't supposed to be like that. He wondered, if he could go back a few weeks in time and tell her she couldn't use his store for her big event, would he do it? Would he save himself the potential heartache that awaited him when she eventually left?

Even *thinking about* disappointing Carson by telling her no left him unsettled. Sure, he would have avoided some unpleasant feelings, but he would have missed out on the fun they'd had together. And that wasn't even including the sex. Maybe he could simply enjoy the time they had left together and then once she left, he could avert his attention to the impending business expansion.

It was a solid plan.

Tom was lost in his thoughts until the bell over the front door jangled and Carson, Lucy, and Drew came bustling through with supplies for the paint and sip.

"Drew, you can put that box on the bar over near Mr. Tom," Carson said.

"What about this stuff?" Lucy said, three overstuffed shopping bags dangling from her tiny arms.

Carson's head whipped around in a semi-circle, searching the space. "You know what? Why don't we put everything up there for now and then we'll move it where it needs to go later." She caught Tom's eye. "Does that work for you?"

Tom leaned the broom against the bar and approached them. "Put stuff anywhere you want." He looked toward the door behind them. "Is there more stuff to come in?"

"Oh, yeah," Drew said, huffing out his words. "Lots and lots of stuff. But I could only carry this much."

With a laugh, Carson followed up on Drew's thought. "There's a bunch of stuff all stacked in Nicole's living room. But I don't want to take you away from your store. We can totally handle it, right kids?"

Lucy smiled brightly and nodded. "Of course."

Drew was another story. "I don't know, Auntie. That's a lot of stuff and my arms are kinda little."

"Why don't you hang out over here for me, then, and I'll go over and help carry the rest of your mom's supplies over," Tom said. "If any customers come in, you can just tell them I'll be right back. Sound like a plan?"

"Yeah, that's a good plan."

As overly dramatic as Drew had been, Tom realized quickly he was also right. Most of the supplies were fairly large things, like stand-up easels and folding metal chairs, that would have been difficult for him to help with.

Drew did a great job taking care of the store while the rest of them worked. After the dozenth trip across the street and back, Tom walked in to see the top of Drew's head from the other side of the bar with one arm up, dragging a cleaning cloth all along the surface.

"Whew," Drew said. "It was hard to reach it all, but it looks good now, doesn't it, Mr. Tom?"

Looking at the little puddles of water and streaky lines across the bar top, Tom smiled. "Dude, that's the best my bar has ever looked. When you turn eighteen, why don't you come back here, and I'll give you a job?"

Drew continued to 'clean,' and Lucy asked if she could sit down and rest for a little while and maybe read some of the book she brought with her.

Tom and Carson went back to Nicole's for the little bit that was left. It would have been the perfect time for Tom to share his thoughts with Carson without having a bunch of people around. But the words wouldn't come. The idea of asking her to give up her life down in the warm south, including her apartment and a job that she was obviously quite good at, to come back up to the cold and snowy north halted the words at the edge of his tongue.

How could he expect Carson, whom he'd known less than a month, to choose to stay in a place she didn't consider her home? He couldn't. So he didn't ask.

"Thank you for helping bring all this stuff over," Carson said as they finished gathering up a box of paint palettes and lightweight canvas aprons from Nicole's living room. "I'm so excited for tonight. It's going to be so much fun!"

Everything about Carson was fun and he had no doubt that the paint night would be every bit as successful as she hoped.

Rather than say anything in response, he simply took the canvas aprons from her hands and laid the box on the counter, then tipped her chin up and kissed her. Not just any old kiss, but the kind of deep, slow kiss that turns a person's insides to mush. It was the kind of kiss that he hoped showed her the things he couldn't otherwise get his mouth to say. It was a kiss filled with intention.

Surprised at first, she quickly leaned into the kiss, returning the passion he was trying to share with her with every sweep of her tongue or nibble of her teeth on his lip. He didn't want to let her go, but knew that he'd have to, if they didn't want to end up naked against the wall in Nicole's living room. The softness in his belly was quickly transforming into the desire to be skin-to-skin with her.

Her eyes fluttered open and she ran her tongue slowly over her puffy bottom lip.

"That was... umm... That was... I think the best kiss of my entire life," she whispered as she laid her head against his chest and wrapped her arms around his waist. He could have stayed like that forever.

A minute or so later, car tires crunched over the gravel outside. "Your sister's here. We should probably go make sure the kids are alright across the road."

Carson

Picking up the box, Tom followed Carson out the door.

"Colie, we're over here," she called. "Kids are running the winery."

After a quick hug, Nicole asked, "What still needs to be brought over?"

"Nothing. This is the last of it." Carson pointed to the box in Tom's arms and wished it was still herself being held there. "We didn't set anything up yet but it's all inside the store."

With her favorite playlist setting the mood, Carson, Nicole, Lucy, Drew, and Tom transformed the Whispering Hills Winery into a functioning, though temporary, art studio.

As a light snow fluttered through the soft porch light outside the door, the warm, soft-white glow inside the store would soon invite people in to get warm, drink some wine, eat some snacks, and otherwise simply enjoy the company of their friends and neighbors.

"Hungry?" Nicole asked. With an hour and a half before people started to arrive, she and the kids were running back to the house to have a quick dinner.

"No thanks," Carson said. "I had a late lunch. Go eat and I'll see you back here in a few." With less than two weeks left in Hazelton, Carson chose to stay at the winery and spend some more time with Tom.

"How many people did you end up getting for this?" he asked after Nicole and the kids slipped out the door.

Carson stood across the counter from him, and it felt much too far away. "Just this morning we reached twenty-four people who've paid. I can't believe how easily it all fell into place. Once we found the perfect place to host it, it was smooth sailing from there."

The number of times she'd woken up from a sound sleep over the past month fretting over the whole thing was something she actively ignored, along with the tenuous situation that would be her job when she returned to Savannah. The emails from Anderson hadn't stopped coming and she'd worked tirelessly to keep him appeased while she canvassed Hazelton to try to draw people in.

Maybe *tirelessly* wasn't the correct word, because she was more than tired. She was exhausted.

"Oh, good," he said.

She questioned him with a quick look.

"Will texted me and mentioned two of his sisters-in-law wanted to come tonight and I told him yes, but I never cleared it with either you or your sister and I was hoping you weren't sold out."

"Seriously? That's awesome! Adding those two, it will bring us up to twenty-six." She clapped her hands and did a little happy dance.

"Make that twenty-seven," Tom added. "Pretty sure Will wants to set up at a canvas too."

Carson couldn't have stopped the smile that bloomed on her face. "Is that so?" Even if the whole paint and sip thing had been a bust, the fact that Nicole and Will might—eventually—become an item would have made it entirely worth it. Seeing her sister happy meant everything to Carson.

With a gentle laugh, Tom shook his head. "I still can't believe you found that many people willing to leave their houses the week before Christmas to come hang around here."

"I told you I'd be able to do it," she said, standing up a little straighter and squaring her shoulders. Then she conceded, "But I think some of them might have signed up specifically to hang out inside here."

Tom's confused expression was adorable. He looked around the store. "Here? Why?"

"I do believe you're somewhat of an enigma to the people of this town. And I think, though I could be wrong, that the idea of coming up here for an evening like this was an invitation they couldn't pass up." His eyes narrowed as if he honestly had no idea the effect his scruffy face and devastating smile had on women and was baffled by what she just told him.

"If you say so." He shrugged then stretched out his hand. "Let me have your phone for a sec."

"OooKayy," she said, slowly pulling her phone from her pocket and holding it toward him. Before he took it, she pulled it away from his grasp. "Why do you want it?"

Playfully, he held her wrist with one hand, then took the phone from her with the other. He walked into the office and a few seconds later, "White Christmas" began playing throughout the interior of the store.

Looking up, she saw that a series of small black speakers had been installed at the top of the walls around the perimeter of the room. "Where did those come from?" she asked when he came back from the office, one of those devastating smiles on his face.

"Best Buy. I needed something to do to keep myself occupied when you were busy doing other things this week. You like?" He handed her phone back to her now that Bluetooth had connected it to the speakers.

"I love it!" Quickly she scrolled through her list and clicked on a new song; the sweet voices of "Carol of the Bells" took over. She queued up a perennial favorite, "Feliz Navidad," after it, and she smiled as the feeling of the day changed from slow and relaxed to upbeat and hopeful.

L UCY AND DREW PLAYED a board game behind the snack table while Nicole helped people get set up before the class started. The lights Tom had strung up the week before sparkled from their house across the street every time the door opened, and people began to fill up the space. From his post behind the wine table, Carson felt Tom's eyes on her as she helped explain the night to those who'd never done a paint and sip before.

Looking up she flashed him a quick smile and went back to her task. Several women made their way to his table to try the wines he had selected for the night. A young blond woman waited her turn to get a glass while Emma and Delores chatted with Tom. Once the young woman had his attention, she didn't seem to want to let it go.

She leaned over the table toward him, then flipped her hair over her shoulder and giggled at something he said.

"Which seats did you say were ours, honey?" Emma said to Carson, whose attention was still on the blond woman flirting with Tom. Admittedly, Carson didn't know him all that well, but she could tell the look of an uncomfortable face a mile away. He was struggling to be polite while the woman wore her interest like a flashing neon sign.

"Oh, right, sorry," she said, grinning and pointing to four open spaces. "We set aside that group of easels right over there for you and your guests," she said, remembering that Delores was bringing her daughter and her daughter-in-law.

Emma looked over at Tom then back to Carson, gave her a knowing smile and took a sip of wine before Delores pulled her over toward their seats.

"Am I late? We rushed over as soon as we could get here." With two women Carson hadn't met before standing beside him, Will stood in front of her as he took off his jacket. "Carson, this is my sister-in-law, Cammie, and my other sister-in-law, Hailey." Looking at the women, he smiled and said, "Sisters-in-law, this is Carson."

"Nice to meet you," Carson said, shaking each of their hands in turn. "I'm happy you could join us. Have you ever done one of these before?"

After Carson gave them the general idea of how it would work, she pointed toward two empty easels next to one another.

Will said to Carson, "Your sister said everyone that signed up was female, so I figured I might have a shot." He winked. "Can you put me next to a single lady?" Cammie and Hailey rolled their eyes, obviously used to their brother-in-law's antics and left to find seats near some other women they knew.

NICOLE WAS IN HER element as she led the gathered group through the creation of their paintings. Lucy, in her Santa pajamas, and Drew in his reindeer ones, had moved from playing games in the side room to watching movies on their iPad in Tom's office.

Carson cleaned up some of the empty glasses and discarded snack plates that had been left around the room. Tom wiped down his table then showed up by her side to help grab some napkins that had fallen to the floor.

"When did Will get here?" Tom whispered, so as not to interrupt Nicole's instructions.

"Right before we started. He said he was interested in meeting all the single ladies that showed up," she said with a laugh.

"*All* the single ladies? He's so full of crap. There's one single lady he's interested in." He turned and focused his gaze on Nicole, with Will painting on the canvas that was closest to her.

"Yes!" Carson said on a raised whisper. "I knew he liked my sister."

"Has since the first time he saw her over the summer." He shook his head. "I told myself I'd never say anything but if he honest-to-God showed up here for this thing tonight just to be near her? He must really have it bad for her."

She looked and saw the way Will watched every move Nicole made, similar to the way the other people in the room did, but with so much more intensity, and her heart squeezed in her chest. She bordered on tears seeing the way he looked at her. "He's definitely looking at her like he *likes her* likes her."

Then, suddenly, Carson was bordering on tears for an entirely different reason. She realized Tom looked at her the same way Will looked at Nicole. Isn't that what Lucy had noticed about him the other day in the yard? That Tom looked at her in a way that could even be understood by an eight-year-old?

Tom

H E HADN'T PLANNED ON spilling Will's secret, but it slipped out and there was no way to take it back. Nothing he could do about it now. Besides, Carson clearly figured it out just watching them together the few times they met. Maybe now, Will would finally make a move and ask the woman out instead of simply admiring her from a distance.

Standing at the back of the room allowed Tom to glimpse over the shoulders of the artists at work. It amazed him how different everyone's paintings looked, yet, they all looked strikingly similar to the snowman beneath the light post that he had picked out a month ago. He'd planned to give Will an earful of grief, then realized even his was pretty damn good.

Once everybody finished and started cleaning up their spaces, he expected them to start heading out the door. To his surprise, nobody left. Emma and her friends hung around together, laughing and munching snacks, each with a fresh sample of the chocolate port they'd waited in a long line to get refilled.

Groups of people gathered, some walking around and admiring all the paintings, some looking at the bottles of wine. More than a few picked some up, brought them to the bar to buy. Carson saw the line forming and jumped behind the bar to ring them up.

The upbeat music of Carson's playlist served as the perfect backdrop to what turned out to be quite a fun night. Having a store full of people wasn't a hassle. It wasn't intrusive. It was flat-out fun. Every now and then someone would laugh louder than the surrounding conversations and then every smile in the place grew in response.

The warmth and friendship he was witnessing was the exact thing he'd been hoping for when he bought the business. For the longest time, he assumed he'd just been looking for something that only existed in stories. Seeing it in person, with his own eyes, had him seeking out Carson, needing to see her, fully aware that she was the only reason it was happening.

"Can I buy a bottle to take home?" Becky Lawton was back. Apparently his *I'm not interested* body language wasn't successful when she'd approached him at the beginning of the night. "The cinnamon apple is my favorite. I'd love to see how you make it. Think you can give me a tour of the winery some time?"

Maybe in another lifetime, one where he'd never met Carson Everett, Becky would have caught his eye. It just wasn't happening in this lifetime.

Right as he was about to tell Becky he didn't offer winery tours, a warm arm rested across his shoulders and Carson's body was suddenly beside his.

"Thank you," she said to Becky. "I've been telling him for weeks he should be offering tours." Giving Tom a pointed look, she turned back to Becky. "I say we keep working on him and maybe next year we'll get him to add it to the calendar."

Becky was stunned. At least the way her mouth opened then closed and then opened again without any sound coming out made her look rather at a loss for words.

Ever the professional, Carson reached her free hand toward Becky. "Hi, I'm Carson. I'm so happy you could be here tonight. Did you have fun?"

Looking at Carson as if she wasn't sure how to answer, Becky awkwardly said, "Oh, yeah, it was great." Her eyes locked onto Carson's hand on his shoulder then snapped back to his face. "Maybe some other time for that tour," she said. "I don't think I have any free time coming up."

"Put your email address on the mailing list," Carson said. "You'll be among the first to know if I can get him to agree to adding tours." Grabbing a spare beverage napkin and a pen, she slid it across the table to Becky, who scribbled her name, her email, and her cell number on it before sliding it back over.

"Great!" Carson said. "We'll add you to the list."

Carson's dark green, fair isle sweater with the white snowflake pattern gave her the cutest festive flair, and all of a sudden Tom couldn't wait to take it off her. Something about the way her hand rested on and never left his back, that slightest touch of territoriality, of which Becky was well aware, had him turned on like a teenager in a stiff breeze.

Eventually they went their own ways, Carson folding up the empty wooden art easels while Tom refilled a few more cups and rang up a few more sales.

"What was that?" he said quietly, coming up beside her as she folded the next easel after he rang up his last customer.

"What was what?"

"Adding Becky to my mailing list?"

"What about it?"

"Carson, you know I don't have a mailing list."

"Well," she said moving to stack the easels against the far wall. "You have to start somewhere. You can't have a list of a hundred without starting with a list of one."

"You're never going to let me keep this business small, are you?" he teased.

"Come on, I'm only here for two more weeks. After that you can go back to being your regular mysterious self." With a smile that could light up the entire night sky, she turned around to go help Nicole.

As the store finally began to empty out, he carried the leftover opened bottles from the table to the counter, took a peek inside his office and saw Nicole's kids giggling over some cartoon they were watching.

Halfway through the night he had gone in and helped them switch from their little iPad to watching shows on his laptop while they snuggled up on the small couch eating popcorn and cookies and whatever else they were able to get their hands on.

Throughout the entirety of the night he'd sought out Carson, watched her engage with so many different people, some of whom Tom knew well, and others who were strangers. To Carson they were almost all strangers, yet the way she'd chatted and laughed with them all, one would think they'd known each other for years.

Emma Sheehan had brought a bunch of people with her, and they all appeared to have had a good time. As they began to gather their coats, Emma stood beside Carson, every now and then flicking a glance his way then leaning in and whispering something into her ear. It looked like Carson was trying her hardest not to laugh and he was dying to know what she was saying.

"Dude, this was a fucking blast," Will said, clapping him on the shoulder and breaking his attention away from Carson. "Now imagine if we get the distillery up and running and we can do this kind of thing again. But then we do a spirit tasting with the guys while the girls all do their painting."

"What are you talking about? *You* did the painting. You think only women paint?"

Will made a show of scanning the remaining crowd. "Aside from the little man in your office, find me another guy in the building."

"Fair enough," Tom said. "How'd you do tonight, anyway? Where's your masterpiece?"

Scrubbing a hand over his face, Will said, "Yeah, it's not much of a masterpiece but whatever. It's not really why I came here."

"No?" Tom asked, pretending to be shocked.

"Fuck off," Will said, looking around to see where Nicole was. He grinned. "I'm getting closer."

"That's awesome, dude."

Will's head pulled back, surprised to hear encouragement from Tom, maybe?

"I'm serious. It's awesome. And I'm pretty sure she thinks you're tolerable. So, maybe just ask her out?"

Tom continued to throw away trash and clean up around the places where he knew the painters had gone for the night. Will followed behind him, helping him work. "Don't you have to work tomorrow?" Tom asked. "You don't need to stay and clean up."

Will flicked a glance at Nicole, who was squatting down to talk with Lucy and Drew. They had emerged from his office and stood before her with sleepy eyes and big yawns. The three of them made a sweet scene.

"I don't mind," Will said and kept picking up paint brushes, stacking them in cups along the bar.

Emma came to find him before she and her guests headed out the door. "Thanks for doing this, Tom," she said. "What a wonderful time this was. I hope you do it again. And what a very sweet girl you have there." She looked at Carson then back at him. "Too bad she's leaving so soon." Emma took a couple steps toward the door and stopped. "Maybe you want to think about asking her to stay?" With a quick wave, she said, "Merry Christmas, Tom."

Tom stood, struck by the simplicity of Emma's words. As if it was just that easy to ask a woman to give up her life in another city to see where things between them *might* go. Sure, they'd slept together but they'd never talked about what would come next, if anything.

"Hey," Carson said, coming up beside him and wrapping an arm around his waist. "Would you be OK if I sent them home? Lucy and Drew are falling asleep on their feet. Nicole said she'd come back in the morning before you open to get the rest of her stuff out of here."

"Of course I don't mind. I'll probably stay here for a while and get as much done as I can tonight."

"I'll stay and help. They don't need me at home." She rubbed her hip against him. "And it could be fun to be alone with you here again," she whispered.

That sweater would be coming off soon. He swatted her ass playfully. "Go get them out of here."

Before she took the kids home, Nicole approached him, surprising him by throwing her arms around his neck and pulling him in for a hug. "Thank you so much for this," she said. "This was just awesome. And I promise I'll be back at first light to get everything out of here for you."

"I hate to admit it," he said. "But this was a lot of fun. And if you're interested in doing it again, we might be onto something here."

She clapped her hands and jumped up and down, and Tom smiled at the resemblance between the sisters.

"I'd like that," she said, then turned, picked up Drew and took Lucy by the hand. "Good night, Tom," she said over her shoulder. They made it about three steps before Nicole stopped and asked, "Do you have any plans for Christmas? Because if you're around, we'd love to have you over for dinner."

"Thank you," he said. "I'll think about it and let you know tomorrow, if that's OK."

Nicole and the kids disappeared out the door, Will grabbed his coat and, with a quick wave to Tom, followed them out. Tom had no idea if he was finally going to ask her out, or just be a gentleman and make sure she got across the road into her house safely.

Carson peeked out the window, turned the lock on the door, then spun and rested her back against it, letting out a huge sigh. "This was so much more fun than what I usually do." She pushed herself off the door and started walking around, picking up papers that had fallen. "Normally the events I plan are much more formal, nothing quite so laid back."

Her whole body was animated as she went from one task to another, this time gathering up the empty plastic wine glasses from the tables. "You have a lot of really nice friends and neighbors up here."

He couldn't resist the temptation to tease her. "Yeah, especially Becky."

She turned with a grin. "Oh, the blond lady who *likes you* likes you? She was nice. Are you going to ask her out? Bring her over for a private winery tour?"

He laughed, as each question was more absurd than the last. "No," he finally said. "To all of those things. There will be no private tours of anything for her."

Carson came over and wrapped her arms around him, sliding her hips against his. "Not even after I leave?" She pressed a kiss into his cheek, and he dropped his hands to her ass.

"Not even then."

It shouldn't have been so hard to ask about her plans, yet he couldn't bring himself to actually say the words. Instead, he said, "Let's get finished up here and we can go watch a movie at my house if you want to come over for a while. I'll even build a fire in the fireplace. If you're not too tired, that is."

Carson

WEARING A PAIR OF Tom's sweatpants and one of his T-shirts shouldn't have felt as sexy as it did. After throwing her hair into a loose bun and hopping in to take a quick shower, she had no clothes of her own to put on. Tom's pants sagged off her hips and the shirt hung more like a dress but when he looked at her wearing his clothes, she saw a flash of heat in his eyes that warmed her from ten feet away.

"You're adorable," he said as she cuddled up next to him on the couch. "I think you should only wear my clothes from now on."

"Ummm, I'm not sure that would go over too well when I go back to work, though."

Wrapping one arm around her, he pulled her closer and aimed the remote at the television. The fact that he didn't respond to her work comment wasn't lost on her. He seemed to be avoiding the topic that neither of them had wanted to talk about.

She pressed herself into his side and relaxed. "It feels so good to get off my feet," she said.

He looked down at her, patted his lap and said, "Put 'em up here."

"Don't have to ask me twice," she said, flipping her body so she lay on the couch beside him with her feet in his lap. When he pulled her first sock off, wrapped his warm hands around her foot, her eyes fluttered closed, and she moaned. His movements stilled for a moment before he went back to kneading his hands into the soles of her aching feet.

The noises that came out of her mouth were entirely accidental and she couldn't have stopped them if she tried. "Oh," she whispered as he pushed into the arch of her foot. "That feels heavenly." His fingers traveled up her feet and over her tired calves, massaging and rubbing and working her muscles into putty.

"Emma might be the sweetest person I've ever met," she said, thinking back over the fun night she had. "Seriously funny lady. And I can't quite tell if her crush on you is a joke, or if it's got a little bit of real in it."

"She's a riot," Tom said. "She hits on me every single time she comes into the shop. More than once I've been left with the feeling that she wasn't entirely kidding." He shrugged and huffed out a laugh. "Either way, she's not really what I want to talk about right now."

Peeking at him through slitted eyelids, she said, "What would you like to talk about then?"

Massaging fingers squeezed up her calf, moved up to her thighs. "Who says I want to *talk* about anything?" His hands moved further up her hips until his fingers hooked onto the waist of her pants. Lifting her hips, she allowed him to pull the sweatpants down and off her feet. Sucking in a breath, he said, "Carson. You're not wearing any underwear."

"Very observant of you. Did they teach you that in knight school?" He was so easy to be around. Even lying half naked on his couch she was comfortable enough to be making jokes.

His house was cozy and warm, just the way his personality became the more time she spent around him. Gone was the unchivalrous jerk she met in the front yard when she'd first arrived, and in his place was a kind man and an attentive and highly skilled lover.

It was far too soon to say she loved him, but she undoubtedly had a serious case of the *likes* for him.

"Hmmm... knight school was so long ago. Let me think..." As his hands teased the insides of her thighs, he leaned over her, their body heat mingling. "They definitely taught me to make sure my damsel was entirely comfortable with the things I was doing and also that she was entirely naked when I do them."

Heat spiked through her body, and the flush of desire pulsed up into her neck and face and down between her legs.

"I am quite comfortable, so that makes you one for two," Carson said as she raised her arms above her head so Tom could pull the T-shirt off. When he exposed the rest of her naked body, he stopped to let his eyes roam over her before his hands followed suit. "Now you're two for two," she said. He leaned over to take her nipple into his mouth.

Letting him take his time to savor her wasn't easy. She'd been looking forward to spending the night with him all day and going slow with anything had never been her strong suit. While his mouth tasted, his fingers explored. She warmed all over in response to his touch. Moaning and whimpering, her body moved of its own volition, hips rocking, legs falling open.

When he leaned down to kiss her, he lay, fully clothed, on top of her, crushed his mouth down and captured her moan. The roughness of his hands as he ran them down her sides and her hips ignited deeper feelings and needs that she'd been ignoring for far too long. She wanted to hold onto that feeling, make it last as long as she possibly could. She wanted to hold onto Tom for as long as she could, too.

Nobody she'd dated in Savannah had ever made her feel the way Tom Wyatt had in only three short weeks. Even losing Patrick, the one man she might have called the 'one that got away,' now seemed to be more blessing than curse. As she reveled in Tom's attention, the weight of his body pressed her into the warm, blanket-covered, leather couch cushions. The heat given off by the crackling fire warmed her bare skin and the flickering flames bathed the room in enchanted, dancing light.

She couldn't wait to see him naked, to have his skin directly on hers, to look into his eyes as he entered her. His fingers twirled into her hair, tilted her head back so he could kiss down her chin to her neck, then down further to her breasts again. Unable to hold back, she started groping for the edges of his shirt, pulled it up and over his head, enjoying the feel of his chest against hers.

"Will you kiss me again?" she asked, wrapping her arms around his solid back and holding him close.

Without a word he obliged, slipping his tongue into her mouth, swallowing down every moan and every whimper she couldn't hold back as he rocked his jean-clad hips between her bare legs. The friction of the fabric against such delicate skin bordered on torture as she waited, feeling his hands slide lower between their bodies to unbutton his fly, then let down his zipper.

"Give me one second," he said pulling off her. "I need to be inside you, and these have to go," he said, pushing his jeans down over his hips and kicking them off his feet.

He was only away from her body for a few seconds while he took off his pants, grabbed a condom from the table and rolled it on. It was still a few seconds too long. When he kneeled one leg onto the couch beside her, she wrapped her legs around him and dragged him back down. "That's much better," she said.

A look of utter peace and contentment passed over his features as he angled himself to enter her. Spreading her legs wider, she let him slide in, seating himself deep while she closed her eyes and stroked her fingertips over his back and shoulders.

They rocked together in gentle rhythm at first. Carson twined her legs around his calves, using his body to push against as they moved together. The background noise of the unwatched movie on the television and the heat from the fireplace wound into her senses, becoming part of the details that were etching onto her heart. She curled her body up to snuggle her nose against his neck, breathing in his warm scent.

His hands worked up beneath her shoulders until they cradled her head, bringing his body down tighter onto hers. "Does this feel OK?" he asked.

With a breathy moan, she rocked her hips and tightened around him. "God, yes," she whispered.

Hooking his hands under her shoulders, he used his position of leverage to increase his tempo and his pressure as he drove into her. What started out as a gentler, easier experience suddenly blazed with passion and heat and intensity as she tried to keep up with his pace, loving the strength and power he wielded over her.

Her fingers curled against his back and her eyes slammed as the first inkling of impending release took root in her brain and her belly. What felt like a dark purple lightning bolt abruptly split her in two as the orgasm ripped through her, and she clung, shaking and shuddering, to his body to keep herself from breaking into pieces.

"Oh, my God," he mumbled into her ear as he thrust into her. She felt his entire body squeeze tightly as he let go with a loud groan, then he went still as he waited out the ride of his own orgasm. Collapsing in a sweaty heap on top of her, he started to pepper her face with kisses. She grabbed onto his cheeks and returned them, kissing every available inch of his face she could reach.

"**A**RE YOU AWAKE?" SHE said into the quiet darkness. Her eyes quickly adjusted to the moonlight pouring through the window-wall in Tom's bedroom. His eyes barely opened.

"Yep."

"OK."

Carson propped herself on one arm, looking at the solid form of him in the bed beside her. Fear and lust and need and desire and longing all tumbled through her and she couldn't think of another way to get out of the way of the avalanche in her own heart. Or at least slow it down so it didn't hurt so much when it hit.

"Something you wanted?" he said, his voice thick with sleep.

Rather than answering him with words, she moved closer, slid one leg across his body and climbed up. She draped her naked body over him and nestled her hips into his. She nuzzled his neck, leaving a trail of kisses everywhere her lips landed. "Is this OK with you?" she whispered against his warm skin.

His strong hands slid up her thighs, stroked along her backside then continued up the sides of her body until he reached her face. Cradling her cheeks in his hands he raised her head to look him in the eye. The intensity she found in his gaze touched that raw nerve of imminent loss and she had to close her eyes against it.

"Open your eyes, Carson." His voice was gentle.

She needed this to not feel so final. They still had two weeks together but something in her bones told her to prepare to let him go. Returning her focus to him, she took a deep breath to steady her nerves.

"This is more than OK with me," he said. "As long as it's what you want." His tone of voice had her wondering if he was feeling the same separation she was, the one she was fighting so hard to resist.

She nodded and sat up a little straighter, feeling him between her legs, knowing she only had to angle her body slightly and he could be inside her in the time it took her to inhale a breath.

"You know I don't wear a condom to bed, right?" he teased, reaching up to brush her hair over her shoulders.

"I get the shot and I'm clean," she whispered.

"I'm clean too."

Lifting her hips, she positioned herself to slide down onto him. She made eye contact with him, needing to feel that connection, that sense of being needed and wanted. As she settled her hips onto his he breathed out a contented sigh.

"You feel incredible, Carson." He rested his hands on her thighs, traced lines over her belly and her chest, then held onto her hips.

Her movements were slow and deliberate. There was no way she would hurry what was happening. From the way she swayed her hips to the way she curled her fingers into his chest hair, everything she did was meant to draw out the pleasure they took in each other.

Tom's eyes closed and his hands held tighter to her hips, his body moving in slow rhythm with hers. Everything felt right. She was aware of every place their bodies touched, her connection to him deepening even as their time together waned. If she thought any more about it, she would cry and that was the last thing she wanted to happen while they were making love.

The silvery moonlight heightened the sense of intimacy they shared, and Carson needed to feel something other than the subtle sadness she couldn't shake. Sitting up straighter, she began to move her hips, eventually grinding herself against him until the sparks of orgasm began going off in her fingers and her toes, causing that coiling spring to tighten in her stomach.

Letting go of all her thoughts and feelings and simply letting herself be in the moment, her toes curled, and she tightened around him as she rode him right to the edge of the cliff and then threw herself off with a scream of release. She collapsed against him, her body shuddering, as she waited for the aftershocks to roll through her.

He gave her time to come down from her high before he flipped her over onto her back and picked right up where they'd left off. The way he held her, his arms beneath her shoulders, her body pinned to the bed beneath him, Carson needed to throw her arms around him. She held him close until he thrust into her with a guttural groan one last time. His hips stilled as his chest heaved and he raised himself off her, looking down with a smile that could melt the icecaps.

Bending his arms, he lowered his chest to hers and whispered against her cheek, "Was that what you had in mind? Because I don't think I've ever had a better wake up in my entire life."

"Thanks," she said. "I just kinda needed that."

"Carson, that was my absolute pleasure." He lifted himself up and flopped onto the bed beside her. "Like, seriously, anytime you want to do that again you just let me know."

Tom knocked off fairly quickly, but Carson only dozed on and off through the rest of the night, her mind reeling and her heart breaking. By breakfast the next morning, she knew that what they had couldn't last. There was no way to maintain chemistry like that over texts and phone calls. And then what? She would come up to visit Nicole and the kids once a year and they would finally get to see each other in person?

It couldn't happen. Eventually he'd get tired of waiting and move on and find someone who didn't live ten states away. Or worse, he'd let his work be his life and he'd never let anyone into his little circle, and he'd spend the rest of his life alone.

Tom

THE NEXT MORNING AS Tom and Carson shuffled bottles of wine from one rack to another, he couldn't shake the feeling that something had changed between them. Some kind of shift that he didn't notice as it happened, but that couldn't be ignored now that it had settled around them. It hadn't been there when they went to bed, but it was certainly there during their quiet coffee and breakfast.

She had started stacking boxes of Nicole's supplies by the door and he attempted to help. Putting his hand on her back to get her attention, she stiffened beneath his fingers. Something had definitely changed. "Is everything all right?" he asked, stepping back from her.

He'd been feeling the approach of the New Year and Carson's subsequent departure, and he wondered if she'd been feeling it too. It sure seemed like she needed distance between them and was doing what she needed to do to protect herself.

"Of course," she said. "Just packing stuff up." Without another word she returned to her task.

Tom walked into the office to turn the thermostat up a few degrees to at least remove the environmental chill from the air. When he came back out, Carson wasn't where she'd been only a few seconds before. Soft footsteps drew him to the side room that had been emptied for the paint and sip. He found her standing, arms folded across her chest, staring down the length of the open space.

"What's going on?" he asked quietly, breaking the silence.

Startled, she turned, her face cheerless. She breathed out a small sigh. "There's just so much potential here." Stepping to the middle of the room, she pointed to the wall at the back. "Can't you just imagine a dartboard right there? And a stack of board games on a low shelf over there," she said, pointing in the opposite direction.

Spinning around she looked into the store proper. "Look at all that space." She took a few steps forward. "You could put a high-top table right there." Her excitement grew as she paced the floor. "And you could put another one there. God, you could fit six of them in this space alone. Not to mention the eight or so stools you could fit along the bar."

Her eyes suddenly burned with a bright passion, and he understood how she was so good at her job. Similar to himself, it seemed the love of what she did flowed through her as naturally as breathing.

"You could do all kinds of events here. We could even sell cheese and crackers or something small like that. Just to make sure people had food in their bellies."

We?

Tom tucked that one little word away. One small word that she didn't even seem to notice. Had it been a throwaway word? A word she let slip, or had it been a word that betrayed her true feelings?

Tom followed her as she continued her planning trip around his store, not knowing what meaning, if any, that small word carried.

"You have so much space along the outside of the building. You could even put up one of those big canvas tents and have events out there in the nice weather."

The more excited she became, the deeper his confusion grew. Everything she said and everything that happened the night before led him to believe she was going to Savannah in less than two weeks' time. Her ticket was bought and paid for. She was leaving on the third to go back to a job and an apartment and a whole life down there that didn't include him. Why was she doing all of this now?

"Stop," he said.

She stopped. Then quickly turned to look at him. "What? What's the matter?"

Why did she have to be so beautiful? Why did she have to look at him with those expectant eyes? What exactly did she want from him? What was he supposed to say to her?

"The matter is all of this." He held his hands out to encompass the entirety of the store. "All of those plans and ideas and changes you're throwing out at me. But you seem to forget, no matter how many times I say it, that I'm a one-man show here." His intention was not to be mean or make her feel bad, but he had to get her to understand.

"I know that those things would be great. I know how much fun it would be to run that kind of place. But I can't do it, Carson. I'm only one person." He scrubbed a hand through his hair and blew out a hard breath. "I'll have the distillery up and running soon enough and now you want me to over stretch myself until I burn out again. But I can't fucking do it. I won't do it."

Her eyes flew open wider than he'd ever seen them as she took a couple faltering steps backward. Away from him.

The front door opened, and Nicole and Will pushed through, laughing over some shared joke that Tom hadn't heard.

Carson shook her head. A minuscule movement that wiped away the look of being struck and left Tom feeling like a giant ass. Though, what other choice did he have? Didn't she know she was destroying him with every word she spoke? Every one of his dreams for Whispering Hills—for his life—being thrown around like confetti, all while knowing they would never happen. Could never happen.

Nicole's laughter died away. "Is everything OK, you guys?" she asked, looking from Carson to Tom and then back to Carson. Protectively, she stepped in between them, blocking Carson with her own body as if she was in some sort of danger. Neither of them knew it was him that was in danger. It was Tom that needed someone to keep him from falling apart when Carson boarded that plane next week.

"You OK?" Nicole asked her.

"What do you mean? I'm fine, Colie." Carson's voice was unnaturally bright.

Nicole shot him a look over her shoulder that bordered between confusion and 'what the fuck did you do to my sister?'

Carson stepped out from behind Nicole as Will approached. "I told you," Carson said. "There's nothing wrong. Tom and I were just talking about some thoughts I had for the store. Nothing serious." She waved away Nicole's concerns like she was swatting away a nuisance fly. "Come on. Let's get this place cleaned up. We've only got an hour before the store opens."

The women walked away to keep cleaning up. Will looked him dead in the eye and said, "Well that was a line of bullshit if I've ever heard one. What the hell is happening here, brother?"

Carson

W ITH THEIR PARENTS STILL away visiting Aunt Peggy it would only be Carson, Nicole, and the kids celebrating Christmas together. Tom had declined Nicole's invitation when she asked again after they cleaned up Whispering Hills. He'd told them he was already committed to going to one of Will's brother's houses for the holiday. The news briefly appeared to be a shock to Will, who was gracious enough to cover for Tom. "Oh, yeah. Grayson is super interested in hearing all about the distillery and that's the only time we'll all be able to get together," Will had said. It wasn't a great lie, but Tom obviously appreciated it.

Time had been steamrolling toward her but having him decline their offer to join them for Christmas meant the clock had finally run out. He'd had enough of her. Whatever it was they had started together had reached its conclusion.

"I don't know," Carson said as she and Nicole sat down that night to wrap some more presents once the kids were asleep. An instrumental Christmas played quietly in the background. "Everything just let so final."

"What do you mean? What felt final?" Nicole asked. "Is it the fight you had or is it because he's going to Will's for Christmas and not coming here?"

"It's all of that, but it really started the other night." She tried to put into words exactly what had been happening in her heart and her brain when she woke Tom up to have sex in the middle of the night. "It was like I needed to do it as a way to say goodbye. And I guess maybe I was hoping he understood that and... I don't know... asked me not to go?"

Nicole frowned. "Admittedly I'm no expert on relationships but I can speak to communication, or more to the point, the lack of communication and how terrible that is. I'm not saying that Ian and I would still be together if we talked more but I'm not saying that we wouldn't be either. What I do know is that every time we didn't talk about the things bothering us, it was just one step closer to the end of our marriage."

Carson ripped off a piece of tape, placing it on the neat seam of the Ninja Turtles wrapping paper covering Drew's new pajamas. "You can't expect me to just come right out and tell him I don't want to leave, Nicole. You haven't heard him tell me over and over again that he's not interested in expanding his store. He told me he's got no room for anything else in his life. Which means he's not interested in me staying here to help him do any of it. It was a short-term thing between us and that's all it was."

"Why can't you just tell him and see what he says?"

"If I just come right out and tell him and he's not interested in seeing where this goes... then what?" She stacked the gift with the others then grabbed a boxed night set of a bathrobe and sleep mask for Lucy. She measured the paper to wrap it as she talked. "If he tells me no, it will destroy everything we've had over the past month. And then I get on a plane, depressed as hell, and try to go back to my old life as if nothing ever happened."

She shook her head. "I can't do it. It's better to leave things the way they are. We both still like each other and can look back on what we had and be happy for it." The scissors sliced through the paper with a satisfying whoosh.

"You think living in denial is a good thing?" Nicole asked, stacking the wrapped box of LEGO with Lucy's other gifts.

"It's better than living with a broken heart."

Nicole was quiet for a moment, thoughtful. When she spoke, her voice was barely above a whisper. "No, Carson, it's not."

Carson stilled her movements and focused on her sister, giving her the space to share whatever was weighing on her.

"Do you remember all the commotion you caused when you found out about Ian cheating on me? How Mom and Dad were beside themselves and everyone was running around trying to figure out how to help me now that I was obviously going to be kicking him out of the house?"

"I remember." It started when Carson had seen a photo of Ian and some woman in a bikini in a mutual friend's social post. That photo had been the beginning of the end for Ian and Nicole's marriage. *Why didn't you tell me you were going on vacation?* Carson had texted Nicole when she'd seen it. *Just saw a pic of Ian on the beach. Who are you guys with?*

After that, it had been a constant stream of phone calls and text messages about alternate living situations for Nicole and the kids, as well as connections to lawyers that could get her everything she was entitled to. Therapists were contacted, visitation schedules worked out. They worked hard as a team to make sure Nicole, Lucy, and Drew were cared for during such a tumultuous time in their lives.

"It wasn't news to me, Cari. Ian had been cheating on me for close to a year as far as I could figure," she whispered.

Carson's hand dropped to the table, the scissors clattering on the tabletop.

"Ian and I were a disaster together but at least the kids had a stable home and..." Her voice trailed away.

"Why didn't you tell me any of this?" Carson asked, reaching across to hold Nicole's hand.

Nicole looked up through watery eyes. "For one thing, I was totally embarrassed." She huffed out a humorless laugh. "I knew the woman he was having an affair with, and she could wear a bikini on the beach." She looked down at her body. "I'd had a baby six months before the affair started. I wasn't wearing a bikini anytime soon."

A rush of emotion swirled through Carson's heart. Humiliation on her sister's behalf. Unadulterated fury at what an asshole Ian turned out to be. Guilt at her own failure at being able to maintain a relationship with her own sister and not knowing what had been happening in her life.

"Nicole, I am so sorry. For everything," she said, scooting her chair closer and wrapping one arm around her sister's shoulders, leaning her head against Nicole's. "I promise if Ian ever comes back around here, I will do everything in my power to let him know what I truly think of him, way deep down in my soul."

Nicole laughed, the sound a little less sad than before. "As much as I would love to see that, please don't. I don't want my kids to see that."

"Fine," Carson said. "But I can pull him in for a hug and maybe hold a little too tightly while I cut off the circulation to his brain."

"That's not very Christmas-y of you, big sister."

"I thought it sounded like a good plan."

"You know what I think sounds like a good plan? Going across the street and telling Tom that you really like him—"

Carson pushed back in her chair. "Nicole..."

"I'm serious, Carson. Living with your heart in a million pieces? It's not the way to go. Nothing good will come of that." She hesitated then added, "Did you know how angry I was with you when you sent me that message about Ian?" Quietly, she said, "I blamed you for wrecking my marriage."

"Me?"

"Relax," Nicole said, picking up the next gift to wrap. "I know it wasn't you. It was Ian and his inability to realize the amazing life he already had. And his inability to keep his dick in his pants. But when you brought it out into the light, I was mad at you. And then you know what happened?"

"You secretly wished for me to drive over him with my car and bury him in the woods, like any good sister would do?"

Nicole laughed out loud, a good, solid laugh that meant it sounded like a good idea to her too.

"No, psycho." Nicole bumped shoulders with Carson. "Sure, I moved home with Mom and Dad for a little while so I could get back on my feet and get my kids the help they needed. But then I opened my own store in a town that I've come to really love. I've got this great house where I can raise my kids. And I've reconnected with you."

"Let's not forget that you also have a new admirer who looks like he wants to eat you for dinner every time he looks at you."

Nicole sighed wistfully. "That sounds good to me..."

Carson burst out laughing then slapped a hand over her mouth, so she didn't wake up the kids.

They sat together giggling like the girls they used to be until Nicole said, "That's enough wrapping for tonight. Let's bust open that bottle of chocolate port and watch *Christmas in Connecticut*.

Carson had already changed into her pajamas, so while she waited for Nicole to change and come back to the living room, she opened her laptop and replied to Anderson's latest email. *I'll be on a plane to Savannah on January 3. Ready to work on the 5th.* She peeked down the hall and saw Nicole coming out of the bathroom and going into her bedroom to change. Quickly, she sent off another email to the client she'd be meeting with as soon as she got back into town. *Can't wait to get started planning your daughter's wedding. It's going to be amazing.*

She should have been ecstatic at the upcoming events on her calendar, but she couldn't get her heart out of Whispering Hills and into Southern Dreams.

When Nicole came out and threw the DVD into the player, Carson was hit with a great idea. She grabbed a notebook from her bag, and sketched and made notes as she sipped her wine and tried to pay attention to the silly love story on the screen. Her pencil flew over the page, ideas pouring out as fast as she could get them down.

Tom

H E HADN'T MEANT TO put Will on the spot the way he had. Thankfully he rolled with it and didn't call Tom on his bull-shit excuse for declining Nicole's invitation. With Christmas only a day away, Tom already found himself missing Carson much more than he thought possible.

It was just a feeling, he told himself. A feeling that would pass. He'd known the woman less than a month; there was no way she'd worked herself so deeply into his heart. Only, that's exactly what she'd done. Gone from a roof-crawling pain in the ass to the woman who invaded his dreams, both sleeping and waking, every second of the day.

Turning down the invitation to dinner was the only way to get himself back on track. She'd be leaving soon, and it wouldn't do him any good to spend more time with her. He needed to get back to work, back to planning the future of his business. As soon as the ground thawed, the distillery would start construction and he would have no shortage of tasks to keep himself busy. Hopefully by the time that happened, he'd be over his infatuation with Carson Everett.

That's all it was, he reasoned to himself. It couldn't be anything more than that. It was a crush and that was all. Except he'd never had a crush like that.

She was physically nowhere near him, yet she was everywhere he looked. Sitting at his kitchen table drinking coffee. Walking through his house wearing his baggy clothes. Lying naked on his living room couch. There wasn't a single place he could go and not see her.

Needing a neutral space, he hopped into his truck, ignoring his memories of their time together there, and took off to the only place he could think of going. Twenty-five minutes later, he sat at one of the tall tables in Donny Weaver's tasting room.

The Loom, a clever play on Donny's last name, was everything he had wanted for Whispering Hills when he and Heather bought the place. The vibe was a little different. Where Whispering Hills could take advantage of its rustic New England architecture, The Loom had been opened in an old industrial building with brick walls, cement floors, and exposed ductwork in the ceilings. But everything else was exactly what Tom had envisioned; tables full of people, bright, festive decorations, a live musician set up in the corner playing requests from the crowd.

Instead of giving him a respite from thoughts of Carson, his brain spiraled into thoughts of what could have been if he'd only had the courage to do what Emma Sheehan had suggested. Why couldn't he just ask her to stay? Why couldn't he tell her that she could have free reign of the store if only she wouldn't go back to Savannah?

Because he knew the pain of being rejected by someone you love. He knew the heartache of watching the woman you love pack her things and drive away without so much as a backward glance. That's why Emma's idea couldn't work. Carson had a life. She had a job. She had an apartment.

Hell, she told him straight away that Hazelton was boring. She'd looked at him like he'd lost his mind when he told her he gave up life in Boston to buy a winery in the mountains. There was no way she'd stay. Or worse, she'd humor him, stay for a while, and then hightail it out of town.

"Tom!" Donny Weaver approached his table with a bottle in his hand and after a quick hug, he put the maple whiskey on the table between them. "How the hell are you? Haven't seen you in months. What's been going on up there in the hills?" He pulled out the chair opposite Tom and plunked himself into it.

"Working. Paying bills." *Waiting for my heart to implode inside my chest.* "You know how it is."

Donny nodded knowingly. "That I do, my friend." He slapped one hand onto the table. "Hey, so, Will tells me you guys are getting into the distillery side of things."

"Yeah, we're gonna give it a go. I got the approval from the state a couple days ago."

"That's fantastic, man. I think you're really gonna love it." He looked around the room. "Turned this place around a hundred and eighty degrees. I'm looking at upping production significantly in the next year or two." His smile barely fit his face. "And if you need help getting started or just want to come by and hang around and see how we do shit, just give me a shout. Come on by any time at all." Donny opened the bottle and filled the empty glass in front of Tom.

"Thanks, man. I appreciate that." He took a sip of the whiskey, still impressed by its taste and smoothness. "Damn, this is good, Donny."

Somehow Donny's smile grew bigger. "Thanks, man. It's sort of my pride and joy."

"I can see why," Tom said. "It's absolutely amazing." He took another sip and Donny hopped up from his chair. "Enjoy that and make sure you come back. I'll spill all the secrets I have so far." He leaned closer to Tom, pointed to the shot glass and said with a laugh, "Except how I make this."

Being away from the house, and away from Carson, helped for a little while but the longer he sat at Donny's place, the deeper his envy grew. Watching Donny and his wife laugh and joke and flirt with each other behind the bar was bittersweet. It was great to see his friend so happy and successful. And it sucked that Tom had been so close to having the same thing himself but was unable to make it happen.

He paid his tab, grabbed a bottle of Donny's single malt vanilla whiskey and headed back to Whispering Hills.

If he couldn't get Carson out of his head by willpower alone, perhaps a vanilla-flavored helper could do the trick.

I T WAS FIVE O'CLOCK on Christmas Eve when Tom flipped Whispering Hills' sign from *Open* to *Closed*, locked the deadbolts, and headed back to his empty house. He'd told Carson he had planned to go to Will's brother's place, but she knew it was a lie and was kind enough not to point it out, allowing him to spend the holiday the way he deserved. Alone.

The lights on Nicole's place brightened the top of the street, the small Christmas tree visible through the window from where he stood on his side of the road. He imagined the warmth and fun being shared inside the small ranch house and looked up at his own large log home with all the fireplaces and realized it would have none of the warmth a house like Nicole's could provide. The irony wasn't lost on him.

With a sigh he trudged up the small hill, stomped his boots at the door and shut himself inside to wait for the holiday to pass by.

A hot shower and a plate of reheated Chinese takeout did little to lift his spirits, so he made himself comfortable by clicking on the television for some background noise, pouring a shot of Donny Weaver's vanilla whiskey and settling in to do some reading. Picking up *Sustainability in the Distilled Spirits Industry* from the table beside him, he opened at the bookmark and tried to give it another go.

A loud knock sounded from the front door. He closed the book and stood, thankful to have an excuse to stop reading. He hadn't absorbed a single word of what he read anyhow. "Coming!"

Before he could lay a hand on the doorknob, the door opened and Will stepped through, taking off his coat and tossing it onto one of the hooks beside him. "Merry Christmas, you stupid bastard," Will said as he closed the door behind him.

With a laugh, Tom said, "Stupid bastard? Me?" He turned to go back to the living room, Will following in his wake. "And Merry Christmas to you, too."

Tom poured Will a shot, refilled his own glass. "What are you doing here?" Tom asked. "Don't you have a brother, or ten, to visit?" He tossed his shot back in one gulp and the trail of fire that burned all the way down warmed him from the inside.

"Yeah, I'll get there. But I don't have to go see all of them. They're all nice enough to meet at my parents' place. Saves everyone a ton of driving, you know?" Will tipped his glass and took a sip. "Damn, that's good."

Tom nodded, still unsure why Will was in his house on Christmas Eve, then sat on the couch. "Like I said, what are you doing here?"

With his characteristic grin, Will flopped onto the chair and threw one leg over the other, finished his whiskey in a quick gulp and held the shot glass on the arm of the chair. "Long version—I told my mother you were avoiding a woman by telling her you were doing Christmas with us. My sister-in-law said you really should come and have dinner with us, and I said no, you shouldn't. Then my mother told me if I didn't get my ass over here to pick you up and bring you back to the house, she'd give my slice of pecan pie to my nieces' dog."

He tilted his head in Tom's direction. "Nobody screws with my pecan pie, my friend. Not even you. So, here I am. Now grab your coat and let's get the hell out of here." He pushed off the arms of the chair as he stood.

Tom could picture the scene at Will's mother's house as if he'd been there to see it himself and it pulled a reluctant smile from him. "What's the short version?"

"Huh?"

"You said that was the long version. So, what was the short version?" Tom asked.

Will sighed. "The short version is 'what the hell are you doing?'"

"I'm not doing anything."

"And that's what I mean," Will said as he started pushing Tom toward the door. "You have something good started with Carson and you're letting it slip right through your dumbass fingers." He waited while Tom buttoned up his heavy flannel and they walked through the door into the chilly Christmas Eve air.

Looking across at Nicole's house again, the pull to go over and at least talk to Carson tugged at him. But he knew better. He knew she was leaving, that she wanted to leave, and that his best plan would be to have dinner with Will's family and consider it a gift.

"I'm not letting her slip away," Tom said as they closed the distance from the porch to the truck. "I'm giving her exactly what she wanted. A friend to hang out with for a few weeks and then the freedom to leave and live the rest of her life now that those weeks are over. Simple as that." He hopped up into the passenger seat and pulled the door closed.

Instead of being a smartass, Will turned the key in the ignition, looked at Tom as he backed down the driveway, and said, "Is that what you want? To get on with life the way it always is?"

Tom didn't answer.

"Because from where I'm sitting, that's total bullshit, and you know it." Will headed the truck down the street, slowing briefly as they drove past Nicole's place, both men trying to get a peek at the women that had captured their interest.

"It's not bullshit," Tom said. "It's the way she wants it to be."

"Right, but I asked if that's the way *you* want it to be."

"Of course that's not what I want," Tom said, his words laced with anger.

"Have you told her what you want?"

"No."

"The fuck? Why not? She may be a great person with a lot of things going for her but I'm willing to bet she's not a fucking mind reader, brother. If you want her, you've got to tell her," Will said.

The truck rumbled down the dark, winding road, the pale moon reflecting off the blanket of snow stretching in every direction.

Tom wouldn't admit it, but Will had struck a nerve. "Don't give me that shit," he said. "How long did it take you to even talk to Nicole, let alone ask her out?"

Tom's voice had grown louder, though Will's was completely even when he said, "That's not the same thing at all."

"How the hell do you figure that?"

Will cast him a sidelong glance. "Well, for starters, when I was just diggin' on her, there was no expectation of anything—on her part or mine. You, on the other hand, have been having sex with Carson for the past what? Two? Three weeks?"

"Three," Tom mumbled.

"Three weeks you've been having sex with her," Will echoed. "And don't go giving me any of the 'no strings attached' bullshit either. You really like her, and she really likes you. And that, you stupid ass, is where the expectation comes in."

"What am I supposed to do, Will?" Tom's frustration was nearing a boiling point. "What the actual hell am I supposed to do? How do I know what her expectations are?"

"Ask her."

"What?"

"You heard me. If you want to know, you have to open your mouth. And. Ask. Her."

"There's no way she's going to stay even if I do ask her. She's got a job and a whole life down in Savannah," Tom said.

"Jesus Christ, Tom. Will you just fucking ask her?"

"I can't," Tom said, his anger withering. In its place, fear twisted like a snake around his heart.

"Why not?"

Tom hung his head, breathed out a heavy sigh. "Dude, I couldn't even get my own wife to stay here with me. You think someone like Carson is going to do what my wife, who was supposed to be my life partner, wasn't willing to do?"

Will didn't respond right away. He pulled the truck to a stop in front of his mother's old farmhouse with the big front porch, and cars lining the street on either side of the driveway.

"I don't know what she is or isn't willing to do, Tom. But I do know two things that you don't seem to be taking into account."

"Yeah, what's that?"

"First, and most importantly, Carson is not Heather."

"No, she's not. You're right about that. What else?"

"You won't know until you ask her."

Carson

CHRISTMAS DAY WITH NICOLE and the kids was exactly as fun as Carson allowed it to be. When she focused on the kids unwrapping their gifts, her heart couldn't have been happier. When she glanced out the window toward Tom's house, the crack in her heart threatened to break wide open and swallow her alive.

More than once she wiped tears from her eyes and she had to narrow her focus to what was immediately in front of her: cooking dinner with Nicole; snuggling up with Lucy and Drew to watch *Frosty the Snowman*; talking on the phone with her parents and wishing Aunt Peggy a Merry Christmas.

As long as she could keep her mind on track, she was fine. By the time she crawled under the covers on Christmas night, the first tears fell as she pulled the extra blanket up by her chin, and the last ones fell as her mind eventually drifted off into a welcomed sleep.

The week between Christmas and New Years were the last days she had to spend with Lucy and Drew while Nicole went back to work.

Nicole had taken the twenty-sixth off to be with the family but being a small business owner meant she had to go back the next day.

"Do you want us to work on taking the tree down?" Carson asked as Nicole packed her bag to head out on the twenty-seventh.

She stopped with her laptop halfway in her backpack. "What? No way! We leave our tree up until New Year's Day. Do you take yours down earlier than that?"

With a shrug, Carson said, "Don't usually do a tree so... not a decision I have to make."

Nicole wrapped her arms around Carson. "I really wish you'd stay here. I hate that you're going back there all by yourself."

WHEN NEW YEAR'S EVE finally rolled around, Carson wondered how much more she could handle. Cars had been pulling up to and leaving the winery for the past few days. Tom left his house at the same time each morning to make sure the store was open for customers, then left the same time each night after closing. She'd seen his truck drive by the house several times without so much as slowing down to see if she was even looking for him, which, of course, she was.

Her body was in a state of withdrawal from him, her heart broken and longing.

As much as she loved being with Nicole and the kids, she needed to be away from Hazelton, away from Whispering Hills, away from Tom Wyatt. The notes she'd sketched watching *Christmas in Connecticut* with Nicole sat in an envelope, untouched, on the top of her bureau. All week she'd looked at them, willing herself to finally have the courage to go after what she wanted but unable to pick up the envelope and walk it across the road.

"Please, please, please come with us," Nicole asked for what felt like the hundredth time that day. "It's a big New Year's Eve party and you're going to miss it sitting here wallowing in sorrow over a guy. I don't want that for you, Cari. Please come with us."

Mountain Tap Brewery, the restaurant she had originally eyed as a potential host for their paint and sip night was having their grand re-opening/New Year's Eve party. Earlier in the day, Carson had given some thought to going out with Nicole and the kids, but when she found out Will would be taking them, she changed her mind. She liked Will enough and she was happy that Nicole had found him, but she didn't have any interest in being the sad-puppy third wheel.

Once the house was quiet, she planned to spend the evening washing her laundry and packing her things for her return trip to Savannah. Even in her mind she couldn't call it going home.

"I'll be fine, Colie." Carson hugged her sister. "Besides, I'm not going to be sitting around wallowing. I'm going to be doing lots of laundry and packing and probably watching a nice rom com on Netflix. I will not be sad because I will be too busy to be sad. And besides, I'm completely over my crush on Tom Wyatt so I'm not sad, anyway."

"You are the worst liar on earth," Nicole said with a small, half smile. "But I can't make you go somewhere you don't want to go."

The lights of Will's truck shone through the front window, lighting up Nicole's face as he pulled into the driveway. The look of pure excitement and eagerness Carson saw there warmed her heart. She loved Nicole so much and she loved seeing her happy. Even if the relationship was very new and they had no idea where it would go, seeing that look in Nicole's eye was worth everything Carson had gone through.

Silently, she gave herself credit for bringing them together. Had she not needed Tom's store to host the event, the two would-be love birds may never have met.

A few seconds later, Will's knock sounded on the front door and Lucy and Drew sprinted from the kitchen table to be the ones to open the door for him, practically knocking Nicole and Carson over in their attempt to do so. It was such a sweet moment, she almost cried again, only these would have been happy tears.

"Have fun, you guys," Carson said, ushering the little crowd out the front door with a wave.

Dressed in her favorite comfy pajama pants, sweatshirt, and fuzzy snowman socks, Carson went back to her room to gather up her dirty clothes and toss them into an empty laundry basket. With the basket tucked under her arm, she headed toward the door when her vision caught on the envelope and stopped her in her tracks.

All at once she was transported back to the day that Patrick told her he and the woman from the wedding really hit it off and he couldn't go on seeing Carson anymore. *"I know you want to keep things casual, Carson, but I'm ready to move on to something more permanent. You can understand that, right?"* Patrick had said to her. And then he ended it between them by saying, *"I hope you eventually find that someone that makes you see permanent as a good thing."*

Patrick's words played through her mind as the envelope sat, unopened and ungiven, on her bureau. What would she do with it? Her first thought was to bring it to the kitchen and toss it in the trash, effectively removing it, and Tom Wyatt, from her life. She reached her free hand toward it, hovered over it, unable to pick it up.

The small bedroom walls closed in around her as her heart began a frantic pounding in her chest. Fresh air. She needed to breathe fresh, cold air into her lungs. And into her mind.

Dropping the basket to the floor, she hurried down the hallway, turned and rushed out the front door. Sweat broke out along her hairline and down her back, despite the frigid night air. As her heart pounded, she plopped down onto the steps and worked to pull in a deep breath.

Inhale...

Exhale...

Inhale...

Exhale...

After a few minutes of deep breaths her body started to go back to normal.

Her plane would be leaving in less than three days. Did she truly want to leave things so strained between her and Tom? It was going to be difficult enough leaving Nicole and the kids, did she honestly want the heartache of a broken friendship, as quick and hot as it was, weighing her down when she went back to her old life?

But more importantly, was she willing to let Tom slip away because she didn't have the courage to tell him what she wanted. To have faith enough to put her heart out there and see where it would lead her if she'd be brave enough to follow.

A shiver tore through her as the cold from the brick steps seeped through her pajama pants directly into her bones. Rising, she lifted her head and looked up at the beautiful log house at the top of the road, the windows dark, and no signs that anyone was home.

Two minutes later, after a quick trip back into the house to bundle up in her warm winter coat and a ski hat, she began the short walk to Tom's house.

Tom

BEFORE SHE'D COME TO stay on the hill, Tom used to sit on the front porch all the time, no matter the season. He hadn't done it much since he'd met Carson. Probably because he'd spent so much of his off time with her, and she was always so cold he couldn't bring himself to ask her to sit outside and freeze with him. But something about the cold night air called him outside.

More than that, it was calling him to walk outside and continue until he reached Carson's front door. What he did after that was up to him.

Stepping onto the front porch, the cold air from his deep inhale burned his lungs but he blew it out and pulled in another one. It reminded him he was alive, his heart still beating, still pumping and keeping him warm against the winter's chill.

The light spilling out of Caron's place caught his eye and he looked up in time to see her, dressed in a long, puffy coat and a ski hat with cheek flaps, closing the door in her wake. She descended the steps and walked toward him, breathing out puffy little white clouds as she neared.

With the small gift bag in hand, he walked down the steps. Their eyes met and held each other's gaze as they neared one another.

"Hey," she said when they stood toe-to-toe in the middle of the road.

"Hey."

She scrunched her shoulders as she shoved her hands deeper into her pockets, protecting herself from the cold. Shifting her weight from one foot to the other, she said, "Happy New Year."

"Thank you," he said. "Happy New Year to you." He tipped his chin in the direction of her house. "Those guys couldn't convince you to join their New Year's plans?"

"Nah, I've got too much stuff to get done." She was quiet for an extra beat. "Lots of laundry and packing to do."

The statement hung in the air between them, and Tom wasn't sure the right thing to do. He wanted more than anything to take Will's advice and just ask her if she would stay with him, but he couldn't get the words to form. He nodded.

"I... um... I have something for you," she said, reaching into her pocket and pulling out a long white envelope. "It's nothing major and I hope you don't take any of it the wrong way, but I had some thoughts the other night and I needed to write them down." After handing him the envelope, she added, "It's really no big deal. I just didn't want to leave without giving it to you."

The woman in front of him made his heart and his belly do weird things. He wanted to pull her into his arms and kiss her until she couldn't see straight. At the same time, he wanted to shove the envelope back into her hand and send her away where she couldn't create such havoc in his steady, predictable life. He wanted both those things in equal measure.

Holding up the envelope, he looked at his name in her neat but flowy script by the pale light of the moon. "What is it?" he asked.

Smiling, she said, "It's a gift, silly. Open it." She shoved her hands back into her pockets for warmth.

Pulling a few folded sheets of paper from the envelope, his curiosity got the best of him, and he struggled to make sense of what he was seeing. An overhead layout of his property had been sketched on a piece of notebook paper, with little notes all over it. Inside the store, she'd drawn circles labeled 'high top,' and placed squares along the bar, indicating the stools she thought he needed. All the wine racks had been accounted for and had been set up in an X pattern, with small areas of seating in the corner spaces they made. Outside the building she'd drawn a new shed out back and labeled it 'distillery.' On the far side of the building was a new rectangle shape that said, 'event tent.'

Even after he'd been an ass to her when she'd made these suggestions in the store, she'd written them all down for him. She knew he was only one person and couldn't do all the things she'd suggested on his own. But she still believed he had the potential to run the kind of business that people would love to visit and spend their money. A place like Donny Weaver's.

"What do you think?" she whispered. "You're not mad at me, are you?" Her words were soft as she said, "I know you can't do it all on your own and a lot of this you can't do anytime soon, but if you found the right people to work with you and work for you, this is a totally doable thing. You already have such a special place here. Imagine how many more people could see it and enjoy it if you made the space to let them in."

Carson's eyes had taken on a glassy sheen, and he wanted nothing more than to reach out and touch her face, to take away the look of uncertainty and doubt that lingered there.

"Thank you for this, Carson. This is... this is really thoughtful of you." He thumbed through the rest of the pages which laid out a rough timeline of when things could happen, what he'd need to implement each change, as well as the number of people he may need to bring on to make these changes last.

It was time to lay it all on the line. It was time to tell her how he felt and see what she had to say.

"As it happens, I have a little something for you, too."

Carson

"HERE," HE SAID, HANDING her a small, but unexpectedly heavy, gift bag. "This is actually for Lucy and Drew. I meant to give it to them for Christmas, but I haven't seen them. Do you mind bringing to them?"

"Of course," she said, then peeked inside. It was a bottle of pure maple syrup and a bundle of wooden lollipop sticks tied with a red ribbon. Carson's throat was suddenly too thick to speak. "It's perfect," she whispered. "They'll love it."

Tom was still for a few seconds, then reached into his back pocket and pulled out an envelope like the one she had given him. He handed it to her. "I was going to wrap it, but it seemed like a weird thing to do, wrapping an envelope."

Flipping it over she saw a snowman gift tag. *To: Carson, From: Tom*

"The snowman reminded me of the one from the paint night, so I chose that tag."

It was sweet to know the thought that he put into small, seemingly unimportant things, and Carson's heart ached at the thought of having to leave with nothing but memories.

"What is it?" she asked.

One side of his mouth quirked up. "It's a gift, silly. Just open it."

After tearing the envelope open, she withdrew several sheets of paper that looked shockingly similar to the ones she had given him only moments before. The biggest difference being that, as opposed to her hand drawn version sketched out during a free moment, these were professionally drawn up plans of Tom's store and another one of the property as a whole.

The map that showed the whole property had been drawn up with several new outbuildings, including one large one at the side of the property with the word 'distillery' written across it. A second one had been labeled, 'barn,' and a third, 'event/gathering tent—semi-permanent.'

It took an extra few seconds to focus on the page with the store blueprint on it because looking through watery eyes made everything blurry. She wiped away the gathering tears and looked at the paper. The layout included tables, shown as large circles with four little squares attached to each one, scattered around the store. More racks had been added to hold the liquor from the new distillery, the extra room had been labeled 'indoor small function space,' and included some furniture and bookshelves. Even the barstools had been included along the currently empty bar.

"I don't understand," she said through her constricted throat. "You had these plans drawn up anyway?" Raising her eyes to meet his, she said, "Even though you have no intention of going through with any of it? I'm a little confused, Tom." She took half a step back. "And why did you give this to me? What does any of it have to do with me?" She was confused to the point of overwhelm. The multitude of emotions swirling like a blizzard through her mind made it impossible to make any sense of the situation.

Tom took a deep breath. "What do you think of Will?"

Her confusion only deepened. Hesitantly, she said, "He seems like a really nice guy."

"He's the best friend I have since I moved out here," Tom said. "You know how I told you I was going to his brother's place for Christmas?"

She nodded, more confused than ever.

"That was a lie. I just couldn't bring myself to do Christmas with you and your family. But Will came and picked me up and brought me to his parents' place anyway so I wasn't alone."

"OK." That news wasn't shocking to her, and she couldn't help but wonder, still, what any of it had to do with her.

He stepped closer, closing the distance she had put between them, then reached out and put his hands on her arms. Holding her gaze, he spoke, his words deliberate. "Will and I talked on the ride to his parents' house. Mostly about you."

"Oh," she said, an ember of hope flickering to life amidst the confusion. "What about me?"

A small smile played at his lips. "Mostly about expectations."

She hurried to say, "Tom, I don't have any expectations of you. I understand this was just a short-term vacation fling. I get it. You don't owe me anything."

Smiling down at her, he said, "That's not exactly true. I do owe you something, Carson. I owe you the truth." He dipped his chin toward the papers in her hand. "Take a look at that and tell me what you see."

"I see all my thoughts and ideas put onto paper."

"Yeah," he said. "That's true. But look closer. Behind the bar."

Carson lifted the paper and noticed something that had eluded her before. A single letter written behind the bar, with no illustration or any other indication of what it meant. "It's a letter C," she said. "I don't know what that means."

Tom leaned down and kissed her softly. Her heart squeezed, reminding her that those were lips she could kiss forever.

"Having all of those people in my store for your painting night was exhausting, Carson."

She opened her mouth to interrupt, but he stopped her with a quick look. Instead she waited for him to finish his thought.

"It was exhausting and exhilarating at the same time. Seeing my neighbors and my friends, not to mention a bunch of people I'd never met before, hanging around together in my space was... It was a gift you gave me. It was a glimpse into what Whispering Hills could be... if, like you said, I just let people in."

Carson swallowed down the tears that threatened to fall.

"All those changes you want me to make?" Tom said. "Those all hinge on one thing." He tapped the paper with the letter C on it, that she still didn't understand.

"What is that?" she asked.

"It's you," he said. "C for Carson."

Seeing his face made thinking clearly all but impossible. She closed her eyes to focus her thoughts and get a better handle on what was happening.

"It takes a ton of energy to be around all those people, energy that I don't naturally have," he said. "But being there with you, watching you be amazing and keep everything under control and running so perfectly? That was nothing short of miraculous to me. You want to know the best part?"

She nodded.

"Going home and being able to bring you with me. Laying on the couch with you, talking with you, touching your skin, kissing your entire body, making love to you in front of the fireplace... everything about that night. It was literally the energy that refueled my tank.

"Getting the distillery up and running is going to be a ton of work," he said. "I'll have Will to help, of course, but even with his help, doing things like setting up and running events and giving tours and everything else will just be too much for me to do on my own."

Carson's confusion had given way to another rush of emotion. But she needed to understand exactly what he was saying.

"Are you offering me a job?" she asked.

A half smile tugged up one side of his mouth. "Sort of."

"What, exactly, are you offering me, Tom?"

He was quiet for an extra heartbeat before he looked her directly in the eyes. "Me, Carson. I'm offering me. And everything that goes along with being with me. I can't lie to you. The past few weeks with you have been nothing short of life changing for me."

"For me too," she whispered as she squeezed his hands.

He squeezed back. "I was hoping you might consider staying up here. In Hazelton. Even if you wanted to stay with Nicole. I'm not trying to push you into anything." He blew out a breath. "I guess what I'm saying is that over the past week without you, I've realized that I don't like being without you. I finally feel like I need someone in my life, and I haven't felt that way in a long, long time."

"I could always look up Becky's number for you if you're just lonely," she teased.

His eyes snapped to hers. "Don't you dare. Friends don't do each other dirty like that."

"Is that what you want, Tom? To be my friend?" Could her heart handle his answer if it was simply, yes?

"Of course I want to be your friend, Carson. But I want a hell of a lot more than that. I want to be yours. Full stop."

"Oh," she said, overwhelmed with the truth of what he just told her.

He wanted her to be the one behind his bar. He wanted her to be part of his long-range plans. He wanted her to stay in Hazelton. He wanted her to be his, and him to be hers. In short, he wanted her.

Tom huffed out a breath. "I know you have a job down in Savannah and your whole life is down there and what I'm asking is pretty huge, so don't feel like you need to give me an answer right now. And to reiterate, you don't *owe me* anything. Don't feel bad if you choose to go back to Georgia. I will absolutely understand and, even though I will be sad to see you go, I will wish you nothing but success and happiness when you do."

His expression was earnest, and she believed he would wish her every happiness.

But where was she most likely to find that happiness? Would it be in a city where she had a job and an apartment, but no real friends to speak of? In Georgia, she was surrounded by people with these big, sprawling families while she had no blood relatives within a four-state radius. In Hazelton, she had a sister, a niece and nephew, and parents nearby.

"I... um... I like what I do very much," she said.

"I totally understand," Tom said, obviously working to keep his expression neutral.

"No, you don't." Squaring her shoulders, she said, "I love what I do but not where I do it. And I really don't like the company I work for."

Tom's eyes widened a touch.

"So, yes, I love it, but I can do it anywhere. I can start my own agency if I want to." Isn't that what Melody Hatch had told her? That she would be amazing at owning her own agency? Maybe it was time to put that theory to the test.

"Savannah holds nothing for me," she added. "I go to work, I do my job, and I go home. Aside from pride in a job well done, there's nothing emotional about what I do." She let her eyes slide down to her feet. "I'm actually pretty lonely there most of the time."

"What are you saying, Carson?" Tom stepped even closer.

"I'm saying I love the way I feel when I'm here. I love being around my family. I love being at Whispering Hills. More than anything, I love being around you. And those are feelings I really want to keep."

She took a deep breath. "I'm also saying that I'm tired of being scared to go after the things I want. I'm tired of watching other people get their Happily Ever Afters because I'm too afraid to step out and take a chance on something." She sniffed and wiped her eyes. "And I guess I'm saying that I want to take a chance on us. I want to see what we could be. Together."

Tom reached down and took hold of her hands, squeezed them before bringing his fingers up to gently cradle her cheeks. Leaning in, he placed his lips on hers, his breath warm as she parted her lips and let him kiss her good and hard. When he finally released her, he wrapped his arms around her, pulled her against his chest.

"Carson," he whispered into the top of her hair.

"Hmm?"

"Do you think it's possible to fall in love with someone after only a few weeks?"

She didn't hesitate for one second. Hugging him tighter, she said, "I know it is."

He hugged her back. "Merry Christmas, Carson."

"Happy New Year, Tom."

Tom

ONE YEAR LATER

IT WAS COMING UP on a full year. One year since they stood in the middle of the road on a pitch-black New Year's Eve, surrounded by a sleeping vineyard and a sky bursting with stars. One year since he asked her to stay with him in Hazelton. One year since, to his utter astonishment, she'd said yes.

Once Carson had canceled her lease, quit her job, and moved her life back up to Massachusetts, she'd spent the first few months living with Nicole. But by late spring, they'd decided to try living together in Tom's house. Within days, it went from being *his house* to being *their home*.

From little touches like vases of flowers and colorful throw blankets, to big things like shelves of her books living alongside his in the library, to her array of body washes and shampoos and lotions in the bathroom, her presence was felt in every room. And Tom wondered how he lived so long without her.

Now, as the second annual "Happenstance Paint and Sip at Whispering Hills" was drawing to a close, Tom looked around, somehow found himself even more grateful for the life he lived.

Between Carson and Nicole, the store had been transformed into a Christmas wonderland. White lights hung in loops along the walls, the giant tree in the corner kept watch over the excited crowd. All his old decorations had finally been retired and replaced, with the exception of the ceramic angels that sat on the shelf over the window. Carson had insisted they stay.

Coming up beside him, she looped her arm around his waist. "Isn't this amazing?" she said. "Look at all these people. I still can't believe we managed to fit them all in here."

They'd had to move all the high-top tables and chairs into one of the sheds out back to make room for all the easels. Even the big wood table at the front of the store had been moved, repurposed as the snack table in the side room because so many people had signed up for the event. Carson's parents had both showed up. Even Tom's sister and her kids came to paint. It was truly a family affair and he'd never seen Carson shine so brightly.

Over the past year, Tom had become addicted to her. Her laugh, her smile, her easy-going and fun-loving nature. She was his extrovert, and he was her introvert. They complemented each other and fit one another in every way.

They'd worked to mesh her ideas into the business and together they'd started something special. The distillery building was completed by early summer, and they had it up and running within weeks. Carson had spent hours reading up on the processes of winemaking and distilling so she could ask questions and make suggestions as they came up with the verbiage for their new tours and tasting room.

Once people had learned about the tasting room, it didn't take long before Whispering Hills' email newsletter list went from one person to upwards of one hundred people, with more signing up every day. The maple whiskey he and Will distilled and aged in the small oak barrels didn't come out quite as smooth as Donny Weaver's, though it was still damn good in its own right. And it gave them something to shoot for when they made their next batch.

Will sat with Lucy and Drew behind the snack table. When they weren't helping people with plates and napkins and snack choices, the three of them had a quiet but animated game of UNO happening. Every time Tom glanced over, Will had an overflowing handful of cards, Lucy had less than ten, and Drew wore a smile that never seemed to fade.

It wouldn't surprise him if Will proposed to Nicole within the next few months.

"You're amazing," he said, wrapping his arm around Carson's shoulder and leaning to kiss the top of her head. "But now that we've called this the second annual event, that means it has to happen every year. Think you can handle that?"

She snuggled closer to his side. "I was made for this," she said.

"Nah," he said. "I think it's pretty clear you were made for *me*. But this—" He looked out at the assembled crowd, laughing and talking and eating cookies and untying their aprons. "This is where you get to shine." He rested his cheek on the top of her head. "I love you so much. I hope you always know that."

Tilting her head to look up at him, she said, "I always know it because I always feel it—" she touched a hand over her heart, "right here. And I hope you always feel how much I love you." She moved her hand to rest over his heart. "Right here."

When Tom moved to Hazelton and opened Whispering Hills, he had envisioned exactly the scene before him. What he hadn't envisioned was all of the heartache and growth it would take to get there. With Carson standing by his side, every second had been worth it.

Carson

THE SECOND PAINT NIGHT was every bit as successful as the first one, maybe even more so. They'd had to clear more room because so many people had signed up and she worried that they may have to turn people away next year if that kept up. The winery was only so big and could only hold about forty people.

In similar fashion to the previous year, friends and family members hung around once the painting instruction had finished. Rows of potted poinsettias painted on canvas stared back at her as she stood with her arm securely around Tom.

"This is so fun," she said. "Everyone is having such a good time, nobody's leaving."

Her parents approached the wine table and had their tasting glasses refilled. "I've got to tell you, this was a lot of fun," her dad said. "We had to be with Aunt Peggy last year, but even so, I'm sorry we missed this."

"Did you see mine, Cari?" her mother asked. "Who knew I could paint?" She turned to Tom. "And, Tom, thank you so much for letting the girls use your store like this." Looking around the room, she added, "It's so beautiful in here. It's just perfect for this kind of thing."

"No need to thank me," Tom said. "All I do is pour the wine. Your amazing daughters do the real work."

While Tom and her parents chatted, Carson excused herself to go check in with Nicole. "You were fantastic," she said. "Those poinsettias look so great. I think next year I'm setting up an easel."

Nicole's eyes found and then focused on Will and the kids chatting with several of Emma's book club friends who'd approached the snack table. Lucy was smiling and laughing, and Drew helped them choose snacks while Will stood off to the side, his head thrown back in laughter.

"He's really something, Colie," Carson said.

"He is, isn't he?"

"Yeah, you definitely got a good one there."

Nicole's eyes tracked from Will and the kids to somewhere behind Carson. She smiled and took a step backward. "Excuse me, everyone," Nicole called out. Carson figured it was getting late and she needed to get the kids home to bed, so she readied herself to start cleaning up. "Everybody," Nicole called out again. "Can I just have your attention for like two minutes?"

Once the din of conversation dropped to a murmur, Nicole grabbed a nearby chair and climbed up. "Thank you," she said. "First of all, I really want to thank you all for being here. Even though we've only done it twice, spending this night painting with you is quickly turning into my favorite Christmas tradition." Ripples of agreement spread across the room and Nicole waited for them to stop before she went on. "Another of my new favorite traditions is spending Christmas with my sister, Carson."

Emma had come to stand nearby and gave Carson's shoulders a little squeeze.

Gentle footsteps sounded behind her, and Carson turned to see Tom approaching, his hands behind his back. She assumed he was coming to stand beside her and was shocked when he continued right by, walking sideways so she couldn't get a peek at his hands.

Tom stopped next to Nicole, while Will approached from the other side and helped her down from the chair. Nicole reached up and gave Tom a quick hug, whispered something into his ear which made him smile, then stepped away.

Whatever he'd been carrying, Will had taken from his hand and put down on the chair Nicole recently vacated but Carson still couldn't get her eyes on what it was.

"Thanks for coming, everyone," Tom said to the crowd. "I was hoping I could monopolize your evening for just a few more minutes." He looked around the room then focused solely on Carson, her heartbeat suddenly hammering in her ears. "Carson," Tom's voice as was steady and even as ever. "I had originally planned to do this once everyone had gone and it was just the two of us. But the more I thought about it, the more I knew that wouldn't have been the right thing to do."

Her fingers trembled and her vision began to blur. Suddenly her parents were beside her and Nicole beamed at her from her place beside Will across the room. Time slowed down as Tom reached behind to the chair and brought back a bottle. He took a few steps toward her, holding it out. Frantically she wiped at the tears so she could see what he was showing her.

"I don't know how many of you have ever heard this story," Tom said to the crowd. "But the first time Carson and I met face to face was when she got stuck on the roof of her sister's house across the street.

She had it in her head that Lucy and Drew needed to be sure that Santa would know where to find them now that they were living in a new home."

Carson swallowed, trying to keep the tears from falling.

"But as you all know, Mother Nature can be fickle in New England and this lovely woman found herself stranded on that roof with no way to get down. Her cell phone figured it out, though. And left Carson behind to fend for herself."

Ripples of soft laughter rose around her, and she laughed through the tears with them.

"From that day to this, you have shown me time and again the kind heart you have for others and the undimmable joy that lights up everything you do." He carried the bottle closer so she could see it through her tears.

"It's called Rooftop Rescue," she said, leading a round of hearty laughter. Then she looked closer and saw the label. It was an illustrated rendition of Tom holding the ladder while Carson climbed down, strings of Christmas lights strewn around the roof. At the bottom right of the panel, Nicole had signed her name.

The floodgates opened and Carson couldn't hold back the tears that fell. Her mother pressed a napkin into her hand.

"The thing is," Tom continued once the laughter stopped. "It's called Rooftop Rescue but, in the end, it was you who saved me, Carson. You helped me see that inviting people into my life was the way out of the dark space I'd made for myself. You reminded me that there was a whole life waiting for me if I would only have the courage to reach out and ask for what I need.

"Carson." His voice had taken on a slight tremor. "I asked you to stay with me almost one year ago. God only knows why you said yes—"

"Because I love you, that's why!"

"And do I ever love you," he said. "So, right now, in front of our friends and our families—" he reached into his pocket as he lowered to one knee before her, "I'm going to ask you to stay with me again. But this time, forever." His gaze held her motionless. "Carson Everett, you are already everything else to me. Will you please—" Reaching out he took hold of her left hand. She spread her fingers as he slipped on the emerald studded gold band. "Accept this ring and agree to be my best friend, my lover, my wife?"

Dropping to her knees to be at his level, she threw her arms around his neck, kissing his cheeks then his mouth, knowing there was no other answer. "Oh my God, yes," she said against his scruffy bearded cheek.

From behind Tom, Will called out, "She said yes!" and the entire room erupted in applause and shouts and pats on the back.

It all drowned into silence as she kissed the man of her dreams, their tongues meeting, their hands running through each other's hair, their hearts beating to the same steady rhythm.

"Merry Christmas, Tom," she finally said.

"Happy New Year, Carson."

I HOPE YOU ENJOYED Tom and Carson's story. If you did, please consider leaving a review at any or all of the usual places. For indie authors, reviews are our bread and butter!

And, if you sign up for my twice-monthly newsletter, Whispers and Works in Progress, you have access to all of my bonus content, including a sweet story about Will and Nicole. It was written for everyone who wondered what happened after they left the paint and sip night.

Scan the QR code below to sign up for free today!

BOOKS BY E.A. BRADY

Berkshire Romance Series

One Week at the Faraway Inn
Picture Me Yours
Christmas at Whispering Hills

Built to Last Series

Stitches and Sparks
Barstools and Beginnings
Coffee and Kisses

Stand Alone Books

Keep Me Warm: A Christmas Novella
Print Readers – links can be found at home.eabradyauthor.com

About the Author

Despite spending my first few years in New York, I consider myself
a New Englander, through and through. My stories are set in fiction-

alized versions of several of my favorite New England locations and my characters are "real" people who are trying their hardest to make it through to their very own happily ever after.

When I'm not working on new stories, I spend my time working on my Muay Thai round kicks and trying to perfect my left hook. I live in a 130-year-old (haunted?) house with my husband, two amazing kids, and two spoiled tabby cats. I wouldn't have it any other way.